PJ Grondin

The Footlocker

PD House Books

PD House Holdings, LLC
910 S Meadow Drive
Sandusky, Ohio   44870

www.pjgrondin.com

pjgron@pjgrondin.com

Library of Congress Control Number: 2025910676

ISBN: 979-8-9988666-0-9

Dedication

This book is dedicated to the men and women of the Greatest Generation. Faced with the burden of stopping a madman hell-bent on taking over the world, they left comfortable lives, families – wives, children, parents, aunts, and uncles – homes, jobs, and more. They joined the military and learned new skills in support of the war effort. Hundreds of thousands of these patriots never returned. The sacrifice they made to their country, and those made by their families have never been, and can never be, repaid in full.

Acknowledgements

My father was one of those who took up the call and faced an uncertain future when he joined the Army Air Corps. He was a Navigator for the 303rd Bomber Group, 359th Squadron. He never spoke of the war or the five missions in which he participated, except for one story that he wrote about his first mission. That story, titled "A Terrifying Experience" by Nicholas A. Grondin is printed at the end of this novel. I used a fictionalized version of the story within the body of this novel. Dad passed away in June, 1994. He was 74.

Thanks to all the business owners in Sandusky, Ohio and the surrounding area for graciously allowing me to use their business names in this work. I encourage everyone who reads their names to patronize these businesses.

My sincere thanks to Bonnie Lukcso for her proofreading and editing skills in reviewing this novel. I am forever grateful.

Also, a sincere thank you to members of the Writer's Circle of Port Clinton Ohio. Your feedback after hearing excerpts of the story helped fine tune the final version of *The Footlocker*.

The
Footlocker

Prologue

1945 - Wednesday, April 4
1:17 p.m.

The deafening explosion produced shock waves that rocked the mighty B-17C bomber. Mickey Navigator Joseph Traver believed the aircraft might shake into a thousand pieces. A second explosion, only a heartbeat after the first, sent a piece of hot metal through the bottom of the plane, passing between his legs, burning the skin on his left inner thigh, mere inches from his groin. He screamed in pain, interrupting his communication with the pilot of the *Mean Streak*, the lead aircraft for the 303rd Bomber Group's mission number 351. He looked down between his legs where the metal had torn through his flight suit and grazed his leg. The wound bled, but the hot metal had not cut deep enough to hit major arteries or cause serious physical harm. It would undoubtedly leave a nasty scar. He looked up at the offending piece of shrapnel, embedded in the overhead of the plane's fuselage. Seconds earlier, he had been leaning over the plot map of their primary target. Had he not leaned back to pull his flight jacket tighter around his neck to fight off the chill from the freezing temperatures, the metal fragment would likely have struck him in the head. The thought sent chills through his body worse than the cold air within the craft's interior.

"You alright, Nav?"

Second Lieutenant Harrison Grobe, the pilot of the lead bomber in the mission, calmly called over the interplane headset, hoping everyone in his crew remained unharmed from the anti-aircraft barrage.

Grobe piloted twenty-three previous missions over Germany. He believed that he and his men were safe from harm. The level of defensive anti-aircraft fire at this late stage of the war had dwindled to a fraction of what the pilot had seen only months ago.

"I'm good, Cap. My leg got nipped is all. I'm fine."

Traver gritted his teeth, the pain causing genuine discomfort, but not to the point of affecting his ability to concentrate on the task at hand. This was Traver's first combat mission since completing training stateside. His hopes that the war would be over by the time he shipped overseas to Molesworth Air Base in England were dashed when he stepped off the transport aircraft from the United States and reported for duty. He had looked around at the dreary weather conditions, feeling the penetrating cold bolstered by a wet fog.

Having little time to find a bunk with an open locker, he received orders to report to Grobe. Within hours of touching down in England, he was back in the air, directing the thirty-nine aircraft of the 303rd bomber group. The crew of the Mean Streak greeted him warmly and informed him that he landed in good hands with their experienced pilot and crew. He quickly learned the meaning of teamwork as the crew worked together as a cohesive unit.

He informed Grobe, "We're twenty minutes to target. Ground visibility is good. Expect to see target within eight to ten minutes. We won't need to divert to our second alternate. We're right on track, no course corrections needed."

"Copy, Nav."

With the roar of the engines from his plane as well as the others in the squadron in his ears, Traver focused on the mission, ignoring the burn of his inner thigh. He closed his eyes, thinking of the payload of bombs that his and thirty-eight other planes prepared to drop on a factory in Unterluss, Germany. The factory, the secondary target of the mission, became the number one target when storm clouds formed over the Fassberg airfield. He rotated his head and neck as tension built from his lower back up his spine. The freezing temperature in the cabin of the aircraft increased his discomfort.

Looking forward past the bombardier, Traver saw the outskirts of the city. He closed his eyes, took a deep, calming breath, and said a prayer for the souls of those who would die in the next ten minutes, wondering if God would forgive him and his crewmates. He knew the air strikes to be a necessary course of action to defeat the German war machine which already claimed countless lives. After completing his prayer and making the sign of the cross, he took another deep breath and brought his attention back to the maps on the navigator's desk. He eyed the buildings on the ground as they approached the target area. The familiar outline of the factory just east of the city came into view.

He spoke into the microphone on his headset, "Nav to Pilot, target in view. Bombs away in approximately three minutes."

Grobe's reply came in loud and clear, "Bombs away in approximately three minutes, copy. Bombardier, do you concur?"

"I concur, Captain."

"Bombardier, you are free to release payload when target is acquired."

"Release payload when target acquired. Copy, Captain."

Traver heard his pilot relay the information to the other pilots, knowing that the individual navigators on the other aircraft would confirm the information. The anti-aircraft gunfire intensified for the next sixty seconds with multiple explosions causing shockwaves that shook the massive bomber. Almost as soon as the intensity picked up, the explosions stopped. They had a clear run to their target.

***

The combined total of bombs dropped from all thirty-nine aircraft included over three hundred 500-pound general purpose bombs and one hundred fifty 500-pound M17 incendiary bombs. With the successful mission completed, the squadron headed back to Molesworth Air Base. Except for minor damage, all aircraft reported fit for their next mission. A brief inspection would occur once the squadron landed safely, but the process of refueling and reloading the aircraft with a fresh load of bombs would begin immediately.

With over two hours remaining on the return trip and no hostile aircraft expected, Joseph Traver settled into as comfortable a position as possible. He reached into his flight suit jacket inner pocket and retrieved two letters: one from his wife, Ada May Traver. The second from Ingrid Engel. Both letters weighed on his mind from the moment he read each one for the first time.

Traver married Ada May Lapoint on Friday, April 9, 1943, days before his departure to join the Army Air Corps. He joined the Army and volunteered for Navigator's school, hoping to avoid being drafted into the infantry. His initial test scores easily qualified him for a shot at more advanced positions than toting a rifle all over Europe. Once commissioned as a Second Lieutenant, Traver attended Preflight Navigation School then Advanced Navigation School at Selman Field, Monroe, Louisiana. He finished top in his class and transferred to Bomb and Navigation School at Langley Airfield in Virginia. He hoped to take a short leave and visit his family, but his superiors denied his request. Every available man shipped off to Molesworth to staff the bombers now laying waste to the German war machine.

His wife, Ada May, sent letters roughly every month, which he answered in kind. Their storybook romance had been on track for a lifetime of love and devotion, having been high school sweethearts from their senior year through Joseph's first year in college. Their friends seemed to think they were inseparable.

During Joseph's second year at Fenn College in Cleveland, he met a young lady, a foreign student, from near Bergen, Germany: beautiful, shy, and brilliant Ingrid Engel. She stood out among the other students for many reasons, but her accent caused a stir. Her classmates avoided her. Most simply turned their backs on her when they heard her speak.

Others mumbled insults under their breaths and a few became openly hostile.

But Joseph Traver approached her and greeted her with compassion and empathy. He tended to be shy when in a crowd, awkward in social situations. He saw her reluctance to interact with American students and understood why. Word of the war in Europe and around the world reached the United States, which remained reluctant to take sides. The tenor of the conflict became known. Calls for the U.S. to join the fight to defeat Germany grew louder. Many of Traver's friends had already joined the Army or the Navy, and others were contemplating the move, trying to avoid the draft which had been initiated late in 1940. Like many others, Traver had hoped to remain on the sidelines.

As he spent more time at school, word of his relationship with Ingrid, though it remained just a friendship, made its way back to Ada May. She was heartsick thinking that her Joseph spent time with another woman, especially a German girl. Their relationship became strained. The end came quickly as their dates turned into arguments, all about *the Nazi girl*. Joe tried to justify the relationship, but Ada May did not believe him and she broke off their engagement.

The sudden and emotional separation left a void in Joe's heart which Ingrid quickly and willingly filled. Her warmth and support for the man who befriended her warmed his heart. Ada May had been the only woman he ever loved. The new experience of being with Ingrid lifted his spirits. Though Ada May remained on his mind, Ingrid now monopolized his attention.

They talked at length about her home in Bergen, Germany, a lively, lovely city in northern Germany south of Hamburg. She spoke of the beautiful countryside and her parents. She grew up in a loving, supportive family. They hoped that she might find a nice young German boy and marry and give them grandchildren. But when Adolf Hitler's Nazi party rose to power, her father grew anxious for his family's safety. He hoped to finance her education and send her to

America. With the timing of her trip to America accelerated because of Hitler's aggressive military actions, she made the trip across the ocean on a merchant ship. She prayed that her parents would follow her, but she lost contact with them both after arriving in New York. Her mother's last letter advised her to remain in America and they would contact her once the war ended.

After a long night studying and talking, Ingrid and Joe shared a bottle of wine and brie cheese. Talk turned to light touches then to passion. For Joe, there was no turning back.

After six weeks, a period where Joe and Ingrid spent all their free time together, Joe heard from Ada May. She said that she needed to talk with him, that she missed him. The pleading tone in her message grabbed his attention.

The next morning at Palizzi's Diner in downtown Sandusky, Ohio, Ada May and Joe sat in a booth across from each other in silence. They ordered coffee and toast.

Finally, Ada May looked up at Joe. With tears welling in her eyes, she said, "I'm pregnant."

Joe's heart sank. His jaw dropped open. He had just joined the Army, scheduled to leave for training the following week. He planned to ask Ingrid to marry him later that day. Ada May's revelation changed everything.

The groans of the engines came back to him. He looked at the letter from his wife, Ada May Lapoint Traver. Then he looked at the letter from Ingrid Engel. He took a deep breath, hung his head, and sighed. He held the picture of Mark and Maryanne Traver, already fourteen months old. This cursed war kept him from hearing their first words, seeing their first steps and being with them on their first birthday. He longed to see them in the flesh.

Seeing Ada May was a different story.

The war appeared to be winding down. He prayed it would end soon.

He wondered if he would ever see Ingrid again.

Chapter 1

2009 - Wednesday, May 6
2:15 p.m.

Mark Traver angled his rented Chevy Silverado into the driveway of the familiar two-story home at 626 Jay Street in Sandusky, Ohio; his childhood home. He disconnected the call to his wife informing her that he arrived in Ohio, safely, after the long flight. Taken aback by the general decay of the house and the neighborhood since he left his hometown in May of 1966, he shuddered as memories flooded his mind. Except for the hideous peeling, flaking, and fading paint over most of the asphalt shingle exterior, not too much had changed. Overgrown shrubs covered the lower half of the front and side windows and the lawn long ago surrendered to a fresh growth of dandelions and other assorted weeds.

The truck came to rest after rolling over the uneven, cracked drive. In all, the property needed a serious overhaul, as did most of the homes in the neighborhood, except two or three whose owners worked diligently to keep ahead of the forces of time and blight that attacked the aging housing stock of the city. He planned to tell the real estate agent to sell the property as-is, to avoid sinking any time and money into a project for which he had no interest. He doubted that his two sisters would object.

When Mark learned of his father, Joseph Traver's, death yesterday morning, he booked the first flight out of Sanford-Orlando International airport to Cleveland Hopkins. Stepping into the crisp, spring air, he shivered, realizing that he did not bring even a light coat to fight off the chill. He forgot how cool the temperatures could get this time of year, especially compared to the heat and humidity of Maitland, Florida, his residence now for over four decades.

After renting the pickup truck, he made the hour-long drive to Sandusky, marveling at the thin, new growth of leaves on the trees along State Route 2. The flight and drive offered plenty of time to think of the finality of death. He could no longer call his father just to talk about the past, the elder Traver's grandchildren, and hopes for the future, none of which he ever did. That opportunity, which he considered many times, was gone forever.

Mark and his father, Joseph Traver, never enjoyed that kind of close, father-son relationship, and Mark never understood why. The atmosphere around the Traver residence seemed dark and cloudy, the mood never happy even on those days when parents should be celebrating their children's milestones and accomplishments. Mark and his sister, Maryanne, being fraternal twins, shared the same birthdate – January 14, 1944. But even on that date during the birthday "celebrations," a foul mood hovered, their mother and father barely speaking. Mark, Maryanne, and their younger sibling, Caroline, never spoke of the gloom that seemed to drain the joy from their home. When young, they believed it to be normal. But as they grew older and visited the homes of their friends, where conversation and laughter filled the air, they understood that their homelife was not the norm, but an outlier among families in the neighborhood.

Mark could hardly wait to enroll in college and live in a dorm away from home. After his sophomore year, he met Denise Collins on a double date with a close friend. Mark and Denise immediately made a connection and fell in love. They married in a secret ceremony devoid of family members, only inviting their closest friends to the casual affair. After they both received their bachelor's degrees, they announced that they were man and wife to their families. Denise's parents were shocked, pleading with the young couple to have a formal ceremony to share with their families. Mark's parents appeared indifferent, though his mother's pained expression never left his mind. Over time, Denise's parents accepted the secret marriage, the subject even laughed about as time passed. The rushed, secret marriage seemed to work for them having been happily married after two children, two grandchildren and the passing of forty-three years.

When Mark's sister, Maryanne was a high school junior, she became infatuated with senior Richard Campbell. They both attended Sandusky High School on the outskirts of town. His plans to attend college evaporated when his father died in a freak accident at a local manufacturing plant. He took a job at the New Departure ball-bearing plant and quickly moved up in the company, switching from line work to quality control, then to a management position. Someone in the very infantile computer industry took notice of his rapid rise in the company, along with the skillset he possessed, and offered him a job at an up-and-coming computer firm in Redmond, Washington. The couple moved west, which pleased Maryanne, allowing her an excuse to get away from her parents. From that day forward, she never traveled east of the Mississippi River.

Four years after Mark and Maryanne moved away from home with their respective spouses, Caroline decided that she could no longer tolerate the dark mood that consumed the Traver household. Caroline moved to Bowling Green, Ohio in September of 1970 to attend college. She lived in a dormitory until she met Steve Eastman in a philosophy class. After her second semester, she moved in with him. They never married. She reasoned that, if marriage caused so much heartache, she wanted nothing to do with organized religion or any of its rules.

The last Mark had heard, though it had been many years ago, they remained happily unmarried with three children and seven grandchildren.

The day after Thanksgiving, 1970, two months after their last child moved out of their Jay Street home, Ada May Traver took a .38 revolver and killed herself. According to her husband, Joseph, she did not say a word to him about her intentions. She just walked down to the basement, opened her husband's gun cabinet, picked up the gun and ended her life. She died in the room once used to store coal before the new gas heater had been installed. A very tidy woman who always kept the home in pristine condition, Joseph had commented to the priest that she probably wanted to keep the mess isolated so cleanup would be easy.

And just like that, Joseph Traver became a widower.

Joseph lived in the house for the rest of his life. His grown children never visited to attend their mother's funeral, for any holidays, or to introduce their children to their grandpa. Mark sent pictures of infants after their births and school pictures as they grew, but the elder Traver never laid eyes on even one of his grandchildren in the flesh. Mark's son and daughter lived in central Florida most of their youth. They traveled on family vacations all over the country. They even visited Sandusky and spent the day at the world-famous amusement park. But Mark did not offer to introduce his children to their grandfather, the chasm between father and son so deep. No feelings of hatred or malice existed. They lived like strangers in a shared house, hardly speaking or interacting in any way. It was not just Mark and his father. Every member of the Traver family remained isolated, as much as humanly possible, from the others.

Mark had not spoken with either sister in years. Now, his position as executor would force him to make the calls. He bore no animosity towards either of them. They moved on with their lives, going their separate ways. They built lives of their own with their spouses, children, and grandchildren. Having never been close, the lack of communication seemed natural, even if such a relationship appeared abnormal to their friends and others who observed the Traver family dynamic. In conversation, when asked how his sisters were, Mark simply answered that he believed they were happy, but he really did not know. That response invariably drew an awkward silence or odd looks from those making the inquiry.

What made the Traver family situation more peculiar was that the Travers, parents and siblings, interacted with anyone outside the family as normally as the next person. They made friends easily, participated in school activities such as sports, cheerleading, band, choir, and pep club. Caroline even ran for, and won, a seat on student council. Up until her death, Ada May attended monthly meetings with a book club and participated in the church choir. Joseph hunted and attended a weekly poker game for as long as Mark could remember. Outwardly normal, but at home, grossly abnormal.

***

Mark stepped out of the truck and stared at the house, wondering what made his homelife such a dreary experience. While living at home, with great effort, he trudged through the morning until he could run out the front door. He remembered the feeling of crossing the threshold, running to the corner of Jay and Monroe Streets, meeting his friends to head to Barker Elementary School. In later years he rode to school with a friend's older brother until he grew old enough to find work and buy his own car. He never rode the school bus. His sisters received rides from their friends and never even asked to ride in their brother's car.

Shaking his head to clear the memories, he plodded up the four steps. He found the house keys right where his father's attorney told him they would be: in the mailbox to the right of the front door. The gloom he felt as a boy growing up in the house seemed to emanate from the other side of the locked door. He took a deep breath, turned the key, twisted the knob, pushed the door open, and stepped inside the vestibule.

To his relief, none of the old feelings engulfed him, as if the gloom of the past escaped by his opening the front door. Just a feeling of emptiness remained.

Mark took a deep breath and looked from the vestibule into the living room. He frowned, seeing that everything looked identical to the last time he stood in this spot. The only difference appeared to be that everything had aged. The paint, the carpet, the furniture, the light switches, the light fixtures, the banister along the stairs leading to the second floor; nothing had been upgraded in over forty years.

He stepped into the living room and glanced around, taking in his childhood home, nearly choking on the stale air. The early afternoon sun pierced the threadbare curtains showing the dust particles floating in the air, apparently kicked up from the moment he entered the residence. Dread again filled his entire being as the task at hand gripped him. Most of the furnishings would go straight to the landfill, though he would make those decisions with the auctioneer.

He crossed the room and opened the nearest window, hoping to recycle the dank interior with fresh, crisp, spring air. He opened a second window on the other side of the house to get some air flowing to help the process.

He moved quickly through the house, giving a fleeting glance at the few pictures on the walls. The family photos were old and faded, the color leached from behind the glass frames. The kitchen showed little signs of use, except the full trashcan. Styrofoam containers marred with ketchup, mustard, mayonnaise, and cheese poked up over the edge of the container.

Mark headed up the stairs to the second floor. He took a cursory look in each of the four bedrooms and their associated closets. The rooms that had been his and his sisters' each had a twin bed with no sheets or blankets. They appeared not to have been touched in years. The closets contained nothing but empty hangers.

The mattress on the queen-sized bed in the master bedroom looked ancient with a severe depression in the center, being decades overdue for replacement. The threadbare sheets and blanket sat heaped in a pile at the foot of the bed. Mark wondered how his father endured this existence for so many years. He shook his head and moved towards the attic door.

The steps creaked with each step. A moldy scent emanated from the cooler air as Mark stepped onto the plain pinewood floor in the attic. Cob webs festooned the area along the rafters where the frame of the house's roof met the attic floor. Mark looked around at the nearly empty space. Several boxes that had obviously not been touched for ages sat along the far end of the open space near a tiny window. The only other object in the attic – a blue footlocker with words stenciled in white – 2nd Lieutenant Joseph Traver.

Chapter 2

Mark frowned, having no memory of ever seeing the footlocker. Then he realized that he had never been in his childhood home's attic before. His father kept the door locked, telling his children that they were not allowed in the attic, that there was nothing up there for them to see. Mark recalled that this directive had piqued his interest, but he feared what his father might do to him if he defied those orders. That fear overrode any desire to see what adventure might lie behind the locked door.

Mark stepped towards the footlocker, reading his father's stenciled name and rank clearly visible through the accumulated dust and cob webs. He knew that his father had been in the military, but did not know what he did, what time-period he served, and where he was stationed. Even the rank of second lieutenant meant nothing to him, having never served in any branch of the service himself.

During the Vietnam War, he avoided the draft by sheer luck due to his high draft number. By the later years of the conflict, his age placed him beyond the desired age group for induction. Two of his close friends with low numbers both joined the Navy to avoid service in the Army. They survived the Vietnam war with many tales of adventure during ports of call.

Mark stood over the footlocker, admiring the workmanship that had gone into manufacturing the trunk. The dark exterior remained intact through the years with no visible scratches or tears. All the hardware, from the latches, hinges, and the hasp, though tarnished by the passing years, looked to be in perfect working order. The footlocker was closed, the latches snapped into place, and the hasp secured. He wondered if he needed a key or if the hasp would simply open. Mark moved closer and squatted down on his haunches to get a closer look. He placed his hands on the latches…

The ringtone of his cell phone startled him. Standing, he took a deep breath and looked at the number on the screen. He recognized the caller and answered.

"Hey Allen."

Allen Westridge, Joseph Traver's attorney and friend, called Mark very early the previous morning advising him of his father's death. He mentioned that he would call today to make sure Mark made the trip north safely. He also instructed Mark on the location of the house keys. He remarked that there were quite a few details to cover, but that they would talk when Mark settled into his hotel room.

The older man's gruff voice sounded weak. Mark could tell that he had been a smoker, a fact that the attorney confirmed, having apologized for the persistent cough during the previous day's phone conversation. He even joked about being surprised at outliving Mark's father.

"Mark, you have my sincere condolences."

"Thank you, Allen."

A brief silence followed, Mark wondering if the old man expected to hear more. When the silence dragged out, Allen said in a raspy voice, "You know, your dad and I go way back. He and I were classmates in high school and we joined the Army Air Corps at the same time. Did your dad ever tell you any war stories?"

"No, sir, he didn't. He never once spoke about his time in service."

The attorney chuckled quietly, as though he did not have the energy for a belly laugh. He breathed deeply then said, "Well, I could tell you a few stories, but we have serious matters to tend to first. Can you meet me at my home office in the next day or so? I'm actually retired, but I still do work for a few of my clients. It keeps me busy, but like your father, they seem to be dying off. I'm down to a half dozen or so, last I checked." He paused to take a deep breath. "I better look the obits over from this morning before I make that claim." After a pause when

Mark did not respond, he said, "That's just a little dark lawyer humor. Anyway, I'm open all day tomorrow if you want to stop by."

Mark replied that he could be there first thing in the morning and that Allen should name the time. They set a meeting for 9:30 a.m. The lawyer gave Mark the address and instructions for entering his home when he arrived.

"Oh, and Mark, two more things." Another deep breath took several seconds. "First, I called your sisters after I called you to let them know of your father's passing. They both said that you would be handling the estate. I don't know how they knew this without talking with you first, unless this had been prearranged."

Mark briefly thought about his sisters and their assumption that, as the executor, he would handle everything. That they assumed he would handle everything irked him, though it did not surprise him.

Mark disregarded the lawyer's last statement and asked, "You said there were two things?"

"Yes. In the kitchen drawer to the left of the sink, you'll find a set of keys. There is a key for the detached garage, another for the cellar, which you can access through the garage, another to his gun cabinet, and keys for his car. There are a few other keys that I could not identify, and your dad has a safety deposit box at Citizens Bank, downtown. We can talk more about that when you come in. I have a document which explains a few things but let's leave all that until tomorrow."

Mark acknowledged the old attorney's remarks and disconnected the call.

With the meeting set, Mark took a deep breath and turned his attention back to the footlocker. He again sat down on his haunches, rotated his head and neck to ease some of the tension, then flipped the latches open. He pulled on the hasp, but it would not budge. He frowned, then thought that it must be locked. He looked around for the key, then realized he had to make the trek down to the kitchen and grab the set of keys that Allen had described. After standing and taking a deep breath, he looked around the attic before heading for the stairs. It looked as if no one had been there for decades.

Once in the kitchen, Mark opened the drawer to the left of the sink and found the keys under a stack of threadbare dishtowels. Most of the keys had labels identifying which door they unlocked. Mark noticed the wavey handwriting as if written by an elderly person. *Allen Westridge.* He performed a short inventory and, as the attorney said, the doors for the home, garage, and cellar were labeled. Of the dozen or so keys, only one had an unusual shape. He reasoned that it must be for the footlocker's hasp.

As he left the kitchen, heading for the second-floor steps, his cell phone sounded again. He looked at the number. It took a moment, then recognized his sister, Maryanne's number. Dropping the keys into his pocket, he answered the call.

"Hi, Maryanne."

"Hi, Mark. Just checking to see if you'd left Florida yet."

"Yeah. I caught a flight right away. I'm actually at the house now."

Mark looked around the living room as he spoke, picturing his sister sitting in an old chair, doing her homework, while their younger sister played with a doll.

After a long pause, Maryanne said, "I'm sorry to leave all the work to you. I know it won't be easy. Is there a lot of clean-up to do?"

"Don't worry about it. I plan to hire an auction house to sell off anything of value." *Which isn't much.* "Then I'll get a realtor to sell the house as-is. No sense spending a lot of money trying to spruce the place up."

"Is it as bad as I imagine?"

"Depends on what you imagine. Dad didn't replace a single piece of furniture in the entire house." Without specifically saying so, he intimated that the house was as gloomy as it had been when they both lived at home. "I'm meeting with Allen Westridge tomorrow morning. I'll let you know what he says and when everything's done. I'm not really sure how they do this in Ohio."

"Me either." A long silence followed, their awkward

relationship not changing with the passing of time. "Mark, whatever you decide, you don't have to check with me to see if it's okay. I'm sure Caroline feels the same way."

Mark took a deep breath. "I will call you both after my meeting tomorrow, just to let you know how this is supposed to happen. Thanks for the call, Maryanne."

Without another word, his twin sister disconnected the call.

Mark dropped his cell phone into his pants pocket and heard the jingle of the keys. He held the keys out and looked them over again then headed up to the attic, a bit anxious at what he might find in the footlocker. He had no idea what secrets his father guarded over the years.

Once again crouched in front of the trunk, he took the odd-shaped key and inserted it into the hasp. It fit perfectly. He turned the key clockwise and heard the mechanism click. The hasp disengaged. He pulled the hasp towards him and upward then lifted the lid.

A tray approximately four inches deep sat on top of a lower compartment. His father's military uniform hat sat in the right part of the tray on top of numerous papers. On the left sat a stack of pictures. He drew in a quick, sharp breath. A picture of Joseph Traver in his uniform, likely his official picture upon completing his initial training, stared back at him. Mark believed he could have been looking at a mirror image of himself at that age.

He leafed through a few other pictures. Some were of his mother and father, arm in arm, likely before they were married. Ada May Traver looked so young and happy. Her face beamed so much that he could not reconcile the photo with the woman he knew as his mother. He never remembered her smiling when he lived at home and he never saw her again after the day he moved out of this house and away from Sandusky. He turned the picture over. A handwritten notation dated the picture July 27, 1942, a full year and a half before he and his sister were born.

Mark continued looking through the old photographs, noting the dates on the back. Every picture showed a happy couple or a happy young woman just blooming into womanhood. The date on the last picture in the stack – February 9, 1943. The smile on his mother's face had been replaced with a sadness that he could feel emanating from the black and white picture.

Tired from jet lag and anxiety, Mark closed the footlocker and headed downstairs. He took one last look around the living room, taking in the enormity of the task at hand. He noticed a four-foot tall by three-foot wide bookcase overflowing with books. He noted one author in particular: J. T. Skipjack, who wrote historical fiction, one of his favorite authors. He smiled then headed out the front door.

He checked into his hotel room, turned on the television, and put his clothes in the dresser. He believed that he would be in Sandusky for at least one week, maybe longer. He pulled out his cell phone, looked at the time – just after 7:00 p.m. – and called his wife.

She answered in a soothing voice, "Hi, Darling. How was the trip?"

"Long. The drive from the airport was relaxing. The house looks like it should be in a museum. Everything is old."

"Didn't your dad replace the furniture at least?"

"Not a thing. Except for aging badly, it looks identical to the last time we were there."

Denise Traver winced. She told Mark before he left their Maitland, Florida, home this would take a toll on him. She said that his sisters should help and make the job go faster. He knew that was not likely to happen.

"I can come up and help."

"No, Sweetheart. I'll handle it." He took a deep breath. "I'm whipped. I'm meeting with Dad's attorney in the morning. I'll give you a quick call after."

"Okay. Love you."

"Love you, too."

Mark fell back on the bed and fell into a restless sleep. Exploding bombs and air-raid sirens filled his dreams. He jerked awake to a sitting position, breathing deep and covered in sweat.

Chapter 3

Mark shaved and showered in preparation for his meeting with his father's elderly attorney, Allen Westridge. The entire time since waking, he wondered about the dreams from earlier this morning; what, if anything, did they mean? The urge to reschedule this morning's meeting nearly overwhelmed him. He thought about heading back to his childhood home to continue looking through the footlocker. But his mounting curiosity took a backseat to listening to his father's legal counsel. Wrapping up the estate had to take precedence over what novelties might lie in an old trunk.

Thankful that he remembered to bring sunglasses as the sunlight angled in from the southeast, he drove across town to Wayne Street. Mark remembered the stately homes from years gone by. Many of the elegant homes of Sandusky's inner city had been relegated to rental properties, the heirs of the city's wealthy families subdividing the buildings into one and two bedroom, or studio apartments. Allen Westridge's home and office stood between two such buildings. As Mark pulled the rental truck into the driveway of 820 Wayne Street, he noted the well-manicured lawn and hedges of the stylish home. A new coat of paint kept the wood trim and siding of the home in perfect condition. A sign, about two feet square, proudly hung from a post next to the steps leading to the front porch; *Allen Westridge, Attorney at Law*. Mark smiled, thinking here was a man proud of his work and his chosen profession.

He walked up the steps to the front porch. An elderly gentleman with a stooped posture waved him in through the glass front door. The exaggerated bend in the man's back shortened his height to just over five feet. Mark pulled the door open and walked in.

Allen Westridge appeared every bit as old as his voice had indicated, the signs of the lawyer's advanced age were obvious. Pale skin hung loosely about his face, leaving the impression that he had been a fit man in his younger years but lost some weight due to fleeing muscle mass. Bright, gray eyes surrounded by dark circles gave Mark the initial impression that the man sported bruises from being punched, but he quickly realized that dark blotches ringed his neck as well. He could not stand up straight or it was just easier to remain hunched over from the middle of his back to his head.

"Mr. Westridge?"

"Mark, let's forego with the formalities. Call me Allen or Al."

"Alright, Allen."

"Did you have any trouble finding your way here? People tell me Sandusky can be a difficult place to navigate."

"No, sir. I lived here until I turned twenty or so. I remember my way around fairly well." He paused, then said, "You have a lovely place. You've managed to keep it up beautifully."

"Thank you. I used to do the work myself, but now I'm lucky if I can open a can of paint without pulling a muscle. I contract out all the upkeep. I fear when I die, my son will do what everyone else does around here and chop it up into low rent housing." He coughed for several seconds, then said, "Ahh, but you didn't come here to listen to the ramblings of an old man. You have some work ahead of you. Let's go sit in my office."

Mark followed Westridge as he slowly shuffled down a dark hall and turned into a room ringed in dark wood bookshelves. Mark did not know his wood types well, but he assumed the wood to be walnut. Thousands of books adorned the shelves, from old law books to modern day novels – an impressive collection.

In the middle of the room sat a massive, dark-wood desk, the wood matching that of the bookshelves. Two identical chairs made of the same type of wood as the desk sat facing the front of the desk while a massive, padded chair sat behind. Westridge slowly maneuvered his frail body into the comfy chair and motioned for Mark to be seated in either guest chair. A single manilla folder had been placed in the center of the desk.

The old man coughed once into the sleeve of his cardigan sweater, then looked at Mark. "Thank you for making the trip so promptly. This should be a relatively simple process. It may take some time to complete, but in addition to a will, your father had a revocable living trust, which makes this process much easier. I spoke with your sisters, letting them know of your father's passing."

"Thank you, Allen."

"But you have to get the will and trust and send copies to your sisters."

Mark looked questioningly at the lawyer.

"Your father's original will, the trust, and other documents are in a safety deposit box at Citizens Bank." He opened the manilla folder and handed Mark a small red envelope. Inside were two simple keys. "The keys are numbered and the number of the safety deposit box is on one of the forms in this folder. It is also penned on the outside of the envelope with the keys. If you have any questions when you review the documents, call me." He paused then coughed into his sleeve again. "Sorry about that. I took the liberty of ordering the death certificate and a few extra certified copies. You'll need to file the original with the probate court. There is an instruction page in here," he tapped the stack of papers, "on how to do it."

Mark's jaw hung open slightly. He seemed bewildered at what to do first.

Westridge said, "Relax, Mark. The steps are listed here in a check sheet. If you have questions, I'm here to help. My number is on the inside of the folder. And all this legal advice is free to you and your sisters. Your father paid me well before he died."

Mark's shoulders sagged in relief, just knowing that Westridge would be available for any questions he might have.

"As I said, when you get the will and trust, you need to make three copies of each and maybe one extra copy. Mail your sisters one copy of each document. You file the original will and a copy of the death certificate with the probate court. I believe your father had a life insurance policy. Mail a copy of the death certificate to the life insurance company."

Westridge paused, then coughed hard into his sleeve. He continued to cough for nearly ten seconds, his face turning a bright red. When he finished, he smiled at Mark and said, "Maybe you should take this folder and review it on your own. I might not be able to help much longer."

Mark's jaw dropped a bit. He did not know what to say.

"Just kidding, Mark. More dark lawyer humor. Anyway, you can go ahead and contact a realtor to list the house. Contact an auction house to sell off any assets like furniture, household goods, anything you don't wish to keep. The trust allows you to dispose of those things. I think your dad had a few gold coins, things of that nature, probably in that safe deposit box. If you need my help to contact a reputable broker, call me."

"Thanks," Mark replied.

"Before I let you go. I wanted to tell you that your father really was a good man. He confided in me that he had not had much contact with you or your sisters for many years. He told me it was his fault, that home life was not a pleasant experience for you and your two sisters."

Mark shifted his body in the hardwood seat and nodded his head slightly, not wanting to start a discussion about his homelife. He believed it was not anyone's business but his.

Westridge continued, "He was a navigator on a B-17C – the flying fortress, they called it. We were all a bunch of scared kids, but your dad helped us keep it together in the face of real danger."

Mark did not know how to respond to this revelation. He only saw the gloomy, moody side of his father.

"We were all jealous of your father, too. He'd get two or three letters every week or so from some women back home. We ribbed the hell out of him when he'd go off to read his mail. Asked him to read them to us. He'd just smile and walk away. Then something changed. The last couple of months, he seemed

… I don't know … anxious, worried. One day he announced that he was the father of twins; you and your sister. A year later, we were set to go home and he still wasn't his old self. Maybe he worried about the flight home, that he survived the bombing missions, but would die in a crash on his way stateside. I never did find out." Westridge paused, took a deep, wheezy breath, then said, "But we made it. When I set up my practice, he came to me and we did the will. After a few decades when trusts became all the rage, we wrote that up."

Mark sat quietly, stunned and clueless, hearing facts about his father for the first time.

Westridge continued, "We used to hunt deer up in Michigan. It was fun. Hunted for a few hours then drank and played cards half the night. Until the accident. Then the trips stopped."

"The accident?"

The lawyer's eyes seemed to glaze over. "Yes. A good friend of ours died on the last trip. Lyle O'Conner was his name. Accident, they determined. Shot in the chest."

"That's horrible."

"Yes, but your dad was cleared of any wrongdoing. You would have been about ten or eleven years old, if I recall."

The last statement shocked Mark. He had never heard a single word about a hunting accident. He realized that he knew little of his father's life. He began to wonder if moving away from home and distancing his own family from his parents had been such a good idea.

Mark shook his head and asked, "Is there anything else I should know before we wrap up?"

Westridge handed the folder over to Mark and said, "No. I think this will get you started. Remember, my number is written on the inside of the folder. If you have any questions, call me. It is a pleasure to meet you, Mark. Your father would be proud of the man you've become."

"Thanks, Allen. I can show myself out."

They shook hands, Mark trying to not squeeze too hard, realizing the frailty of the old man. He forced a slight smile, turned, and walked out of the home office.

Once back in the truck, Mark headed to Columbus Avenue, then turned onto Campbell Street, heading south towards Berardi's Family Restaurant. After the meeting, he wanted time to review the contents of the folder. He needed a good cup of coffee and brunch to help concentrate on the task at hand. He briefly thought about going back to the house on Jay Street, but decided he needed to stay away from the footlocker. He did not want to get sidetracked.

After brunch and reviewing the documents and forms in the folder, Mark looked at the time. It was well after 1:00 p.m. Allen recommended a few real estate firms in town, but suggested that one, in particular, might be his best choice. He decided to follow the lawyer's recommendation - *Home Again Realty. Clayton Biggs, your hometown realtor.* He dialed the number.

"Home Again Realty, your hometown realtor. How may I direct your call?"

"Hi. I'm trying to reach Clayton Biggs."

"May I tell him who is calling?

"Yes. Mark Traver."

"Oh yes, Mr. Traver. He's expecting your call. I'll put you right through."

After a few seconds, the phone clicked and a baritone voiced man said, "Mr. Traver, this is Clayton Biggs. I'm so sorry to learn of your father's passing."

"Thank you. I guess you know why I'm calling."

"Yes, sir, I do. I'm sorry we have to conduct business under these circumstances, but it is part of life, I guess. Would you like for me to tour your father's home so we can get a good valuation of the property?"

Mark did not hesitate. Clayton Biggs seemed personable and confident. If he wanted a quick sale of the property, this man seemed as good as any.

Clayton also offered, "If you want to get a second opinion, you are free to do so until we sign an agreement granting our company the rights to represent you. I wouldn't be offended at all. It is part of doing business, but I can assure you that we will provide prompt and professional services to you and your family."

Mark took a deep breath. "That sounds great. When can we meet at the house?"

"I'm open tomorrow morning. Would 10:00 a.m. work for you?"

"That works fine, Clayton. See you then."

After the call with the realtor, Mark called the auction house and the funeral home listed in the folder. He arranged for the auctioneer to meet on Monday, May 11. He directed the funeral home to work with Firelands Medical Center and take possession of Joseph Traver's body.

Progress.

Chapter 4

Still sitting at the diner over four hours after first arriving, Mark felt the tension creep up his back and neck. He knew he should move soon or the owners might ask him to leave. He purchased a piece of pie and more coffee so they might tolerate him for a little longer. He looked around. Only one other table had patrons, but dinner time for retired folks neared. A few cars parked outside the window in handicap spots, and several cars turned into the parking lot. He looked at his watch – 3:45 p.m. Too late to head to the bank and look through the safe deposit box. He decided to head back to Jay Street and look through the contents of the footlocker which had been on his mind all day. Comments by Allen Westridge caused him to think back on his father and their relationship, or lack of one.

As he closed the folder, his high school aged waitress came over and, with a broad smile, asked, "Would you like anything else, like, maybe a perch sandwich to go?"

He thought for a moment then returned her smile with one of his own and replied, "Sure, that sounds great."

"Fries, chips, or anything else on the side?"

"How about a side salad with blue cheese dressing. Can the dressing be in a container on the side?"

"Sure thing." Her smile beamed. She added his new order on her pad, topped off his coffee cup, turned, and headed for the waitress station.

He leaned forward and opened the folder again, reviewing the forms that he had filled out. He wondered if he would escape Sandusky anytime soon. There seemed to be a mountain of tasks to complete. He sat back in his chair, trying to relax and thought *One step at a time.*

Just as he polished off the last sip of coffee, his waitress returned with his to-go order and the bill. With another bright-white smile, she thanked him for coming in and left. Mark settled the bill, leaving a generous tip.

On the way back to Jay Street, he stopped at Dick's Carryout for a six pack of beer. As he stepped up to the counter to pay, the clerk, a woman in her mid-forties with wavy, rust brown hair to her shoulders looked at him with a questioning expression on her face. She asked, "Are you Mark Traver?"

Surprised, he replied, "Yes." He paused, then asked, "How did you know?"

The woman smiled then replied, "I'm Peggy Whipple. The resemblance to your father is hard to miss. My husband and I live on Jay Street down the street from your dad. I just heard about his passing from Mrs. Holtzmiller. She lives next door to your dad's house, on the left. I'm so sorry about your dad."

Mark nodded and quietly said, "Thank you. I appreciate that. I remember Mrs. Holtzmiller. She used to give us cups of Seven Up when we were just little kids playing around the neighborhood. Told us to not tell Mom and Dad. You must have known my dad if you recognized me."

She smiled, "I did some cleaning for him in his later years. Have you been in the house yet? I thought I saw a truck there yesterday."

"Yeah. I just got in yesterday afternoon. You said your name is Peggy?"

"Yeah. Peggy Whipple. I haven't been in the house for over six months now. He told me cleaning the place was a lost cause. He'd been kind of down the last year. I think he started losing his will to live." She paused, then said, "Your dad was a nice old man. He paid me well and treated me so nice. I used to go there to clean and we'd end up talking for hours. I told him that I should be working but I think he just appreciated having someone to talk with."

Mark smiled, but his smile had a sad, guilty backdrop. Peggy Whipple, twenty years his junior, knew his father better than he did. She probably spoke to his dad more than he had his entire life. How had he let that happen?

He said, "Thank you for taking care of my father and for being so kind to him. He had no family in the area, so it was nice of you to help him."

"Well, he did have a woman visitor from time to time. I could tell when she visited him. He always seemed to perk up afterwards. She drove him somewhere, sometimes for the whole day. I don't know where. Whoever she is, it put a little lift in his mood."

Mark gave Peggy an inquisitive look, as if he wondered about this mystery woman. He thought about what other surprises he might uncover.

He picked up his beer, thanked Peggy and turned to leave. He slowly turned back around and said, "If you see my truck at the house, if you want to stop by and talk about Dad, just drop in. I didn't know Dad that well. I know how that makes me look, but I'd like to hear more about him if you think of anything of interest."

Peggy smiled. "I might just do that."

***

Back in the attic on Jay Street, with limited light from the single bare bulb above the footlocker, Mark again went through the stack of pictures. There were well over one hundred photos, the sizes ranging from three by five inches up to eight by ten. Most were black and white. Even the color photos had faded, losing most of their color to time.

An envelope on top of the stack contained pictures of his children and their cousins. As he looked through the pictures, he noticed that none of the pictures of the children was beyond their high school years. His own children were now in their forties. For over twenty years, Joseph Traver saw no pictures of his grandchildren. He never met them in person. A sadness poured over Mark as the realization hit him; he and his sisters deprived his father the pleasure of knowing his family.

He wiped his watering eyes and continued to look

through the stack of pictures. Those just below the few family pictures were photos of men in uniform posing in two rows; the back row standing, the front row kneeling. The shots were taken in front of a large aircraft. These appeared to be pictures of the bomber crews. Mark looked closely at the young men. They looked happy in the photos. The men in the back row of each photo wore billed hats, while those stooping down in the front row wore some sort of cap with ear flaps. Mark reasoned that the men were of different ranks, those in the back being officers, those in front, enlisted men. There were seven such pictures. Mark flipped the first picture over. The name and rank of each crew member was written on the back. A date and a mission number were also written below the crew names. Mark saw his father's name, then flipped the picture over and looked at the man he immediately recognized. His father wore a smile, something he never saw on his face while he lived at home.

Mark noted that none of the photos listed identical names on them. Many of the names repeated from one photo to the next, but appeared to change by at least two or three out of the eight members for each crew.

The next series of photos showed an aerial view of bombs exploding and burning on the ground, evidence that the missions had been a success. The black and white photos depicted different targets. A couple shots were of large buildings while others appeared to show runways or railways; transportation hubs. Mark imagined the carnage, the massive loss of life, that these bombs must have caused. He wondered what a psychological toll this knowledge must have taken on the men who dropped these weapons on the populace below. Thinking back on history lessons from high school, he knew that Hitler had to be stopped or the war would have continued and millions more would have suffered and died. The world was indeed on fire during those horrible years. He shivered at the realization that his father took part in stopping the madman.

Mark shook his head to clear away the gloomy thoughts and refocused on the footlocker. Everything he viewed was in the top tray, a vast space under the tray yet to be explored. He lifted the tray and set it aside on the floor. He glanced back into the trunk. Small, cardboard boxes of varying sizes were neatly stacked on the right side. On the left side, one larger box took up most of the space.

He removed a small box and lifted the flaps exposing a half dozen medals individually wrapped in plastic. Mark did not know what the medals represented. He lifted one, surprised by its weight. He took them out of the box, one-by-one and laid them on top of the pictures in the tray on the floor. The medals looked brand new, as if they had just been purchased at a department store. Mark knew these could not have been purchased; they were earned. A heavy feeling came over him as he began to feel the gravity of what his father endured during the war. His curiosity ramped up, wondering what else he would find out about a man he barely knew. A twinge of guilt nicked at his brain.

His cell phone rang, breaking him out of his fog. He looked at the screen - his son's name displayed on the screen. He answered and said, "Hi, Elliot."

"Hey, Dad. Are you at Grandpa's?"

"Yeah. I'm in the attic right now. I'm glad you called. I have dinner downstairs."

"It sounds like you need a break, which is why I called. Can you use a hand? I don't have any classes this weekend. I'm supposed to monitor a test Saturday, but I can have another staff member stand-in for that. I can be there day after tomorrow and work with you through Sunday."

Mark's son, Elliot, was a Professor of Economics at the Ohio State University, just a two-hour drive from Sandusky.

Mark paused before answering, not sure what the realtor and the auctioneer would do yet. He might not be able to do much of anything until next week.

"Why don't you hold off coming for now. I have meetings set up for early next week. After that, I'll know better what we'll need to do with your grandpa's stuff."

"Okay, alright. But if you need me, just call. If you need anything, Dad, I'm here."

"Thanks, Elliot."

"By the way, are Aunt Maryanne and Aunt Caroline coming in to help? I would think they would at least offer."

"Probably not. I spoke with Maryanne and she doesn't plan to make the trip here. I'll call them later today and give them an update. I spoke with your grandpa's lawyer this morning. He informed them about your grandpa's death. They told him that they were leaving the estate work up to me. So, I'm not expecting much from them."

His voice sounding a bit angry, Elliot said, "That sucks, Dad. They should be there."

"Don't take this the wrong way, son, but you shouldn't judge your aunts for not being here. Maybe you and I can have a beer sometime and we can talk about life with your grandparents. But that's a topic for another time."

"If you say so. Listen – and I mean this – if you need anything at all, you call me. Anything."

"That means a lot to me, son. And I will."
Mark could barely hold himself together, choking out the last words, trying to sound normal. The call disconnected and Mark's eyes watered, realizing the vast difference of growing up in one Traver household to another.

Chapter 5

After the call from his son, Mark headed down to the kitchen and pulled the perch sandwich and salad from Berardi's, and a beer from his father's ancient Frigidaire. As he ate his dinner, he reviewed the papers in the manilla folder. He concluded he could do no more with the forms. With the probate checklist all but memorized and the courts closed, he felt the tension in his neck and back slowly loosen. Then he thought back to the pictures, the medals, the call from his son, and the surprise conversation with Peggy Whipple at the carry out store. He felt the urge to head back into the attic and again sort through the various curiosities left by his father.

When he received word from Allen Westridge about his father's death, he made flight, rental car, and hotel arrangements for the trip, then he sat with his wife Denise. He told her that he expected to be in Sandusky possibly as long as a week, but no longer than ten days. The more he looked at the tasks that lay ahead, he began to wonder if he had underestimated the scope of laying his father to rest and setting the wheels in motion to settle his estate.

Beyond the anxiety associated with the tasks at hand, a sadness crept into his mind. Just a few brief conversations with people that knew his father made him wonder what he missed by not engaging with his dad over the years. He reasoned that he may have deprived his father of a relationship that might have benefited them both. Worse, he denied his father the opportunity to meet his grandchildren, and they to meet him. Did his sisters follow his lead in isolating their father, keeping him away from the only family he knew?

But it could not have been all his fault that his parents barely spoke with one another in a civil tone. They hardly spoke at all. Mark noticed when they looked at each other, they could not hold eye contact for long. At the dinner table, the conversation revolved around manners and either mother or father telling the kids to keep their mouths closed when they chewed their food. When in their teens, they sought invitations to eat dinner at friends' houses. The children never invited their friends over for dinner or for any other reason. When Mark and Maryanne turned sixteen and could drive, they both held jobs and spent as much time away from the house as possible.

As the twins approached their twenties, Caroline reached her teens. Not as introverted as her older siblings, she asked her parents why they never spoke. She had been to friend's houses and recognized the total disparity in atmosphere from her own home to her friend's. One time at dinner, shortly before Mark planned to move out on his own, Caroline asked her mother point blank, "Why don't you and dad talk?" She looked from one parent to the other, expecting some sort of answer. When her parents looked at each other, the dark mood took a downward turn. Her mother stood and left the dining room, crying as she ran up the stairs to the second floor and closed the bedroom door.

Caroline, unsatisfied that she received no response, turned to her father and asked, "What happened to you two?" Their father looked at his daughter for a moment. Without another word he finished his dinner, walked out of the house, started the car, and left.

Caroline turned to her siblings and said, "You can't leave me here alone! When you leave, one of you has to take me with you! I can't stand living here!"

Maryanne reached over and placed her hand on her younger sister's arm and, in a sympathetic voice, said, "We won't leave you here alone."

But they did.

Mark shook his head as he looked around the dining room where the family shared their meals. He could count on one hand over the twenty-plus years at home where a family member smiled. He drew in a deep breath, thinking that this house sucked the life out of everyone who entered, except maybe Peggy Whipple. She seemed to have fond memories of talking with his dad. He looked down at the Styrofoam box that held his dinner and thought *Mom would have never let us eat from a box like this.* Tears again formed in his eyes at the dreadful childhood he and his sisters experienced. *I've got to finish up here and get home to Florida. This is killing me.*

He finished his sandwich and beer, stood, grabbed another cold beer from the refrigerator, headed up the steps to the second floor, then on to the attic. The footlocker seemed to have a gravitational force, pulling Mark to further explore his father's, and their family's history. He sat down and looked at the objects that he already found, wondering if what remained was just the worthless trinkets of a man collected over the years. He pulled another box from the interior of the trunk and opened the cardboard flaps.

Mark looked down at two stacks of letters, one held together by twine, the other by pink ribbon. At first glance, he calculated that there must be somewhere between forty and sixty letters in all, the stack bound by twine thicker by about an inch. In each bundle, the last envelopes sported a blue and red border indicating that they had been sent by airmail. The envelopes had turned a dingy yellow over the years. He lifted the larger bundle and noted the addresses. The top letter was to his mother at an address he did not recognize in Sandusky. His father sent the letter from 5400 Operations Road, Selman Field, Monroe, Louisiana.

He picked up the second bundle bound in the pink ribbon. These letters were from his mother to his father at the same addresses. He took a deep breath, wondering what to do next. Should he untie the binders that held the envelopes together and read the very private thoughts of his parents, or should he place the stacks aside and tell his sisters about what he found? He looked at the postmark on the top envelope; April 19, 1943, the year before he and his twin sister were born. He looked at the first letter from his father postmarked May 11, 1943. Apparently, the mail back then was slower, or his father could not respond quickly. *Maybe a combination of both.* He set the letters aside for a moment and looked in the trunk below where he removed the box of letters. Several larger envelopes, about twelve inches by eight inches sat on the very bottom of the trunk. By their appearance, discolored with torn edges, they had been handled frequently over the years. He reached for the envelopes and pulled them from the trunk. The flap used to seal the envelope had been completely torn off. He reached inside and pulled several five by seven inch black and white photographs; one of a boy, the other a girl. He turned the pictures over. A name and date had been penciled in - Maryanne Traver, January 14, 1944. On the other – Mark Traver, January 17, 1944.

Mark frowned. He and his twin sister were born on January 14, 1944. He wondered at the difference in dates. Maybe the pictures were taken on different dates for some reason. Could there have been a medical reason for the date difference? He shrugged and placed the pictures back in the folder, then paused. He again removed the pictures and compared his and his sister's images. His sister's face appeared cheeky with a little pug nose; the picture with his baby face less chubby with a narrower nose. After a long look, he again placed the photos back in the folder and placed them in the stack of items on the floor next to the trunk.

He looked in the footlocker once again, but his attention came back to the two bundles of letters. He picked up the bundle from his mother to his father and slowly untied the pink ribbon. He felt like a voyeur, peeking into the private lives of people he did not know. He hesitated, then took the top letter in his hand. He lifted the letter from the envelope and carefully unfolded the stationary, impressed by his mother's perfect penmanship.

He began reading:

My Dear Joseph,

I hope your trip to Louisianna...

Mark's phone's ringtone sounded, causing him to jerk in surprise. He looked at the time on the display; 6:58 p.m. He did not recognize the local number, but he answered after the fourth ring.

"Mark Traver."

"Mr. Traver, this is Dylan Hart. I'm the director at Hart Funeral Home. Sorry for the late call."

Mark relaxed. He called the funeral home earlier to set up a meeting, but had to leave a message because no one answered. "Yes, Mr. Hart. That's alright. I'm just going through my father's things. I take it you got my message."

"Yes, Mr. Traver. I'm sorry for your loss. Losing a parent is difficult."

Mark thought *Not as difficult as you think.* He said, "Please call me Mark. May I call you Dylan?"

"Certainly, Mark. Do you have time to come in tomorrow to talk about arrangements for your father's interment?"

"Yes. I have some appointments coming up. Let me think. I have to make sure I've got my dates straight. What time would you like me to come in?"

"Could you come in at 2:00 p.m.?"

"I believe I can. Let me write this down. If I can't make it, or I have to reschedule, I'll call you."

"Wonderful. Mark, I know this can be overwhelming, but I wanted to let you know that your father has a prepaid funeral policy with us. We have the original document. Your father should have kept a copy with his papers somewhere. If you can't find it before tomorrow, don't worry. We'll provide you with a fresh copy."

Mark thought for a second then asked, "Where will my dad be interred?"

"A niche at Calvary Cemetery. Are you familiar with the facility?"

Mark did not know where his mother had been buried so he asked, "Will my dad be interred alongside my mother?"

A long silence ensued where Mark could hear paper being shuffled. Finally, Dylan Hart said, "I'm sorry, but I do not know where your mother is interred. But it says right here in your dad's instructions that he be cremated and placed in a niche at Calvary. Your father's nameplate is already affixed to the niche. We just have to add the date of his death."

This news rendered Mark speechless. The more he learned, the more questions arose in his mind about his father and mother and their odd family life. He should have been relieved by putting another hurdle behind him, but an uneasy feeling began to build in his chest. His gut told him that the next week might be more difficult than he assumed.

He ended the call, bewildered by what he just learned. He went back to the letter but his mind raced and he could not concentrate. He finished his beer, closed up the house, and headed for the hotel room to try and get some rest. He needed to clear his mind and call his sisters just to let them know where he stood with funeral arrangements. He wondered if he should mention this new twist, not that they would be interested.

Chapter 6

Mark sat at the computer table in his hotel room near the intersection of U.S. 250 and Ohio State Route 2. A hot shower helped cleanse his body, but not his mind. Still grappling with the newest twist in the growing oddities surrounding his father and mother, his sisters, and his peculiar homelife, he wondered what he might learn next. He thought back to the chance encounter with Peggy Whipple at Dick's Carryout, how she recognized him simply by his resemblance to his late father. Sandusky, a small town back in the 1950s when he and Maryanne were pre-teens, had not changed much in over fifty years. Everyone seemed to be related to each other by some close or distant familial connection. Everyone knew something about everyone's business. Being away from his hometown placed him out of the gossip loop and at a disadvantage to his father's friends and acquaintances.

The next order of business before he called it a day: call his sisters and give them an update on where he stood with their father's estate. The process might go quickly, but he did not know what roadblocks he might encounter along the way. But he felt obligated, as the executor, to give them as much, or as little information as they desired. At this moment, it would not be significant.

His tension level again ticked up a notch, his mind still racing, trying to sort out pertinent facts from his own perceptions. Maybe his sisters pondered the same questions as he did. Maybe they knew something about their parents that he did not. The only way to find out? Make the calls. He looked at the clock; 9:42 p.m. A call to Maryanne in Washington State meant that his sister should be finishing dinner. He hoped that he would catch her when she had time to talk, even though he did not know where the conversation might go. If the past is any indicator, it might be a short call.

His youngest sister, Caroline, lived in West Salem, Oregon, the same time zone as Maryanne. At least he would not be calling right before bedtime. Both women lived close to the west coast, but the distance between Redmond, Washington and West Salem, Oregon was nearly four hours by car. He wondered if his sisters ever visited one another or if a chasm existed between them as it did between him and the two of them. He shook his head again, wondering where their family unit fell apart, or if family ever really meant anything to each of them in the first place.

With his phone in hand, he opened the phone app to recent calls. He found Maryanne's number from the time she called him late yesterday. He hit dial and listened as the rings sounded. On the fourth ring, Maryanne answered, "Hi Mark."

"Hi Maryanne. I hope I'm not interrupting dinner or …"

"We're just cleaning up now. So, your timing's good."

Mark paused, hoping she might say something to offer him a good lead in to telling her what little information he needed to relate. When the silence dragged on, he said, "I told you I'd call with an update, but there isn't much to tell you. Allen gave me a checklist of things for probate court and I can't do much until tomorrow morning."

"Mark, you don't have to call every day. I spoke with Caroline and she feels the same way. Just let us know when everything's pretty much settled."

Maryanne's remark in such a flat tone pulled at his heart. He wondered how she could be so cold to him. He understood that she remained bitter about her upbringing because he felt the same way. But why direct her annoyance towards him? He replied, "What if I find something extraordinary?"

She took a deep breath that conveyed her irritation. He wondered if she put extra emphasis on the volume of her inhale so that Mark surely would hear it. She said, "Listen, Caroline and I both don't want anything to do with Dad's estate. We're not expecting anything, we don't need or want anything. If we could sign off that our share of whatever is left after probate goes to some charity, we would. Please, just deal with it. Call me when it's over and done with."

Mark started to reply when he heard silence. He looked at his cell's screen. She had disconnected the call. Mark looked at the phone, astonished. Should he even bother to call Caroline? He meant to ask Maryanne if she remembered the footlocker, but that would have to wait for another time. In no mood to call her back after her reaction, he lifted his beer bottle to take a drink, but it was empty. *The story of my life*. He strode to the in-room refrigerator and took out another beer, popped the top and took a long drink. Shaking his head as he smacked his lips, he thought it might be a good idea to wait to call Caroline. He sat back down at the desk and rubbed his tired, itchy eyes.

His phone's ringtone sounded. He looked at the display – Caroline saved him the trouble of a call.

"Hi Caroline.

"Mark. I understand that Maryanne cut you off a few minutes ago."

"You could say that."

"We talked after the attorney called us. We both agree that we really don't care about the estate."

A question came to Mark as he listened to his younger sibling. "Caroline, do you and Maryanne talk much or get together out west?"

This drew a brief, somewhat bitter-sounding laugh. "Mark, Maryanne and I haven't spoken in decades. She called me yesterday to talk about the estate."

"So, you two aren't close?"

Caroline's voice sounded incredulous, "Are you kidding? I hated Maryanne – and you, Mark. You both left me to fend for myself in that god-awful house. I hated you for leaving first. Maryanne cursed you for months until she could get out herself. I begged her to take me with her, but she refused."

A tense silence lasted for what seemed like an eternity.

Mark finally said, "I don't know what to say. I'm sorry doesn't seem to come close to covering it."

"Mark, I'm happy. I have Steven, my husband. Technically, we never married, but that doesn't matter. I have my kids and my grandkids. They are my family. I adore them. How I survived that house with my sanity, I'll never know. But I did."

Mark's throat choked up hearing his sister's anxiety. Hurt that his sister believed that he played a part in making her life hell, he tried to think of something to say. But no words could repair decades of pain.

He finally said, "Caroline, I am truly and deeply sorry for any pain that I caused you. We can't turn back time. I wish I could do something to make this right."

"There is, Mark. Let Dad be dead, let me live my life with my family. Leave me out of this. I want nothing to do with Dad or his estate. I never understood why our family couldn't be – I don't know – civil? No, that's not the right word. I'm not sure there is a right word. We were like strangers living in the same building. Never mind. This is pointless."

Mark's pain at his sister's words intensified with each moment. It struck him that he and his sisters felt the same about their homelife. Instead of coming together to support each other, they remained in their own shell, trying to protect themselves from the cloud of gloom that occupied every cubic foot of the house. *But we were just kids.* Very early on, they had no idea what a happy household looked and felt like. As they experienced the home life of their friends, they realized that something was off in their home. But the three siblings never got together to compare experiences and confront their parents about their feelings. Something kept them from broaching the subject. Fear of reprisal? Fear of an argument? Fear that their father or their mother might leave? Looking back, anything would have been an improvement over the status quo.

"Caroline, if I caused any of your misery all those years, I am truly sorry. I felt the same way you did back then. I wanted out of there. When Denise and I married and we moved away, it felt like the weight of the world had been lifted from my shoulders. I should have thought about you and Maryanne being left there."

"Hell, Mark. You did what you thought you needed to do for you and Denise. I don't blame you now. But you and Maryanne, you're both part of a past that I'd just as soon forget. Do you understand? Dad's death; hopefully it's the final chapter in part of my life that I hope I never think about again. I pray to God that my kids never experience the total lack of love that we experienced in that house."

He knew what she meant. He felt the sudden need to talk with his wife, Denise, and tell her just how much he loved her. He was not sure if Caroline wanted to say anything else, so he said, "If you want, I won't call you again. I'll just send you the final package with any inheritance you have coming. I don't know what it will be, but …"

"Listen, Mark, I apologize for being so blunt. None of this is your fault, or Maryanne's fault, or mine. I have a sense that something happened between Mom and Dad and they just let it eat them alive, and we were collateral damage, so to speak."

That reminded Mark. He asked, "Before you hang up, do you remember Dad having a footlocker up in the attic?"

Caroline hesitated before answering, "Yes, but I was afraid to go up there, that there might be dead bodies or something. Why do you ask?"

"I wanted to tell you and Maryanne this, but she hung up before I could say anything. As I looked through the house, I found Dad's footlocker from his military days. I'm sorting through it. There are letters to and from Mom and Dad. I plan to read them. I hope you and Maryanne don't mind."

"Do what you want. I already told you how I feel. I'm pretty sure Maryanne would agree. And, Mark, I'm sorry for dropping all this on you. I said some horrible things about my feelings towards you. I realized some time ago that it wasn't your fault."

"Thanks, Caroline. I'll let you know when I'm done."

The phone went silent. He wondered briefly if he should call Maryanne back and ask about the footlocker, but knew she would not remember it and would not appreciate another call.

Instead, he called his wife, Denise, and poured his heart out. Denise previously heard her husband's stories about his home life, but Mark always held back about the truly dark mood around the home. When they dated, she experienced the feeling first hand. Even with limited exposure, she told Mark that she hated going to his parent's house. After an hour, he told her that he needed to get to bed, that tomorrow would be a big day. He told her how much he loved her and how she saved his life so many years ago, and he meant it with all his heart. Reluctantly, they said their goodnights.

Mark changed into his night pants and crawled into bed. He literally counted sheep, but sleep eluded him once again. He looked at the bright red numbers on the hotel clock on the night stand and counted off the hours as they passed.

Chapter 7

Despite getting very little sleep, Mark awoke at 6:10 a.m. without the benefit of an alarm. He stripped off his night pants and headed for the shower. His agenda for the day included calling Allen Westridge to keep him apprised of where he stood with his father's estate. He surmised that Allen would want to know about the appointments he made with the realtor, auctioneer, and appraiser. The realtor should arrive at the house at 10:00 a.m. He expected that this meeting and walk-through would take about an hour. His next task involved going to the bank to inventory his father's safety deposit box. With several hours to burn before the bank opened, he left the hotel, and drove to Berardi's Family Kitchen.

While sitting in his truck in the parking lot, he hit the call button on his phone for Allen Westridge. After four rings, the elderly man answered, "Mark. Good morning to you."

"Good morning, Allen."

In a gravelly voice he said, "At my age, any morning where I make it out of bed is a good morning. Now, what can I do for you?"

"I just wanted to let you know that I have meetings scheduled with a realtor, an auctioneer, an appraiser, and the funeral director at Hart Funeral Services. I hope to get all these things finished as soon as possible. I also ordered several copies of Dad's death certificates."

The lawyer's frail voice replied, "You've been a busy man. That's good." Mark heard Allen cough. After several seconds, he came back on the line and asked, "When did you plan to go to the courthouse?"

"I thought I'd wait until first thing Monday morning. I have a busy day already."

"That's fine. When you get to the office at the courthouse, tell them I sent you. I think a couple of the ladies there knew your father, and they definitely know me. You can drop my name if you think it will help you get better service. I'm not sure it will, but you never know."

"And I'm going to the bank this afternoon and see what I can find in Dad's safety deposit box."

"I'm pretty sure you're going to find his will, his trust documents, and a number of things related to his financial plan. You may find some other things of interest. He mentioned to me that he owned a few gold coins, some stock certificates … who knows what else. You can clear the box out now or you can keep anything of value in that box. It's paid for through the end of this year and you can't get a refund if you clear it out. No sense not using it, at least while you're in town."

The conversation stalled. Mark told Allen that he would call back if he had any questions about the process. When the call disconnected, Mark headed inside the restaurant. Seated immediately, he ordered a black coffee and a loaded omelet. He did not have the folder with him, so he spent the time waiting on his breakfast looking at the other patrons in the rustic diner, many of whom gave him a curious look back. A voice that he recognized said, "Hi, Mark."

He turned to see Peggy Whipple standing next to his table. A man about her age stood close at her side.

Mark stood and said, "Hi, Peggy." To the man he said, "Hi."

"Mark, this is my husband, Randy."

Smiling, the men shook hands.

Randy said, "Sorry about your dad. He was a good man."

Mark looked at Randy for a moment then asked, "How did you know my dad?"

"My dad and your dad were friends. They used to meet at the VFW down the street here." He nodded his head towards the east.

Mark remembered driving past the VFW building yesterday when on his way to the grocery store. It had not changed a bit from when he was a child. Decades ago, he went into the bar with his dad. He expected that the bar, stools, even the pictures on the walls of planes, tanks, and military bases remained the same. He wondered if they even changed the pictures of the president to the man in the White House today.

Randy continued, "They had a lot in common, from what my dad told me. He said your dad was a navigator on the B-17 flying fortress. My dad was a gunner. They were never on the same plane, but they flew the same missions a couple times. I guess they swapped stories at the bar. Dad died about twenty-four years ago. He smoked and got lung cancer. I remember your dad took it hard."

"I'm sorry. That's a tough way to go."

Randy's face said as much. After a brief silence, Mark's breakfast arrived, the waitress arranging the plate of food just so. She said, "Sorry to interrupt, but is there anything else you need right now?"

Mark shook his head and smiled and thanked his waitress. She returned his smile then retreated to the kitchen.

Peggy said, "We better let you get to your breakfast. I'm sure you have a busy day."

"Nice meeting you, Mark. Maybe Peggy and I could drop by sometime before you finish up at your dad's place."

"I'd like that. Nice to meet you, too."

As Peggy and Randy walked to their table, Mark sat and took a deep breath, taking in the wonderful aroma of a good breakfast.

***

After breakfast, Mark headed back to the house on Jay Street. As he waited for the realtor to arrive, he walked to the detached, two-car garage and unlocked the door. A car covered in a light-gray, dusty tarp sat in the middle of the garage. Intrigued, Mark walked to the front driver's side of the car and lifted the tarp to see what was hidden underneath. He could hardly believe his eyes - a light blue, early 1960's era Ford Mustang. He continued to pull back the protective tarp. The hard-top vintage car appeared to be in mint condition. His father must have put a coat of wax on the exterior recently.

Mark knew a little bit about old cars. This car commanded a good market value.

He began to wonder again about the man he never really knew. Did his father have an interest in restoring cars? Is that the way he filled the void of not having a relationship with his children and grandchildren? He walked around the beautiful Mustang and marveled at the craftsmanship of the restoration. It literally looked brand new, as if off the showroom floor. He opened the driver's door and leaned in. The odometer read 17,224. Were these original miles? Had the odometer been changed? Did his dad own any other cars?

He heard a car door shut and looked at his watch – 10:00 a.m. Leaving the garage without covering the car, he walked along the driveway towards the white sedan that pulled in behind his truck.

Clayton Biggs stood over six feet tall and walked with a slight, but noticeable limp. He wore sunglasses even though the day sported dark clouds, threatening rain. His dark skin contrasted with his bright white smile. In a deep, confident voice as he closed the distance between them, he said, "You must be Mark Traver."

"I am. Clayton Biggs?"

"One and the same. I'm sorry to be smiling on such a sad occasion but you look so much like your father."

Mark nodded. "You're the second person to say that. He must have been a handsome man." He smiled at his little joke.

Clayton Biggs let out a belly laugh, his smile brightening even more.

"You have your dad's sense of humor, too."

The men shook hands. Mark had no idea how to process all the information about his father. Were they talking about the same man with whom Mark spent his younger years? It did not compute with what he knew of his father so many years ago. What had he missed? Or what changed?

Mark said, "Let's head inside and we can talk a little business. Maybe you can tell me how you got to know my father."

"It would be my pleasure. I'm a little slow so don't mind me if I can't keep up."

"I noticed the limp. What's wrong?"

"Well, I had a little accident back in the early seventies. I stepped in the wrong place and a …"

Clayton lifted his pant leg and showed Mark the prosthetic ankle. He lifted his foot out of the black athletic shoe and exposed the mechanical foot.

"What happened?"

"Let's go have a seat and I'll tell you all about it. Then we can get down to business."

Mark and Clayton sat at the dining room table. Mark offered his guest a drink. Both men decided a glass of water would be best while they conducted business.

Clayton started out, "After I was drafted into the Army in 1969, I shipped over to Vietnam. I saw some action, but somehow escaped any harm … that is, until …"

Clayton spent the next fifteen minutes describing the most horrific depiction of battle in war that he had ever heard. The majority of Clayton's platoon, caught in the crossfire between North Vietnamese regular troops and Viet Cong, had been killed. At the call for retreat, he scrambled and ran for his life. He stepped on a boobie trap made from bamboo shoots. The sharpened bamboo sliced through his foot in multiple places, but he kept running. He made it out alive, but by the time he received treatment for his wound, his foot could not be saved.

"And that's enough war stories for this visit. Did your dad ever tell you about his brush with death?"

Mark sat stunned. His mouth hanging open.

"I'll take that as a no. Well, we'll have to talk about that another time. How about I take a look around the house and we can sit back down and talk turkey. You can tell me what you think and I'll give you my price recommendation. If you like what I tell you, we can get this place on the market."

"Sounds good. I can walk with you if you like."

"We can walk and talk as we go."

"Alright. You take the lead."

***

Back at the dining room table, Clayton showed Mark some comparable prices for homes sold in the surrounding neighborhood. Though not quite as high as he hoped, Mark agreed to a starting price that would, he hoped, bring a quick sale. Neither he nor his sisters needed any money from the estate, so disposing of the house and property held priority over profit. Clayton also mentioned that this type of property drew a number of local contractors looking to purchase, renovate, and place the house back on the market, hoping to turn a quick profit.

After signing the paperwork, Clayton casually quipped, "The house looks the same as when we used to play Euchre here many years ago. I don't think your dad changed anything in the house."

"You've been here before?"

Clayton laughed, then settled to a broad smile. "Me and half a dozen other guys. Lots of guys liked to play poker, but we held Euker tournaments. We didn't bet money, just drank beer and swapped war stories. Your dad was a good man and a good card player."

His smile remained, but his expression showed a sadness that Mark could clearly see. The mystery surrounding his father grew larger. Mark needed to know more about his father. Maybe the footlocker held some of the answers to his questions.

Chapter 8

With the real estate agreement signed along with a multitude of associated papers, Clayton Biggs drove away. Before leaving, he promised to do right by Mark and his sisters and get a quick sale on their father's property. He told Mark that his father mentioned to him how much he regretted not providing a loving home for his children. *He wished he had been a better father to you, Mark. I could tell by the look on his face and the way his body sagged when he told me, that he was truly sorry, but knew he had to pay the price for his negligence.* Clayton Biggs had smiled as he pulled away.

Mark stood alone in the driveway and watched as another person who knew his father far better than he left another puzzling clue. He looked at his watch – 12:55 p.m. No wonder his stomach growled. Tacos and beer sounded good. Mark locked up the house, hopped in the pickup truck and headed west down Monroe Street. The Original Margaritaville on the west end of town – just what the doctor ordered. A sign in front of the restaurant advertised Bike Week Ohio for the Memorial Day weekend and the following week.

He descended the steps into the dining area of the rustic restaurant. The view of the waterfall where the old grist mill once ground grain into flour for farmers was a favorite of locals and tourists alike. He took a seat at the bar even though patrons occupied just a handful of tables. After the attractive, thirtyish woman tending bar took his order for a draft beer and three hardshell tacos, he scanned the dining room. A woman about his age sat in a booth by the windows nearest the waterfall. A man with salt and pepper hair occupied the seat across from her. He could only see the man's back left side, so could not get a good idea of his age, but believed him to be in his early sixties. He briefly locked eyes with the woman. She smiled then looked back at the falls. Mark turned in his barstool to get a better view of the waterfall. He smiled in surprise when he thought he saw a large fish jump into the clear, cascading water.

The barmaid set his draft beer on a cardboard coaster in front of him and said, "Did you see that fish? He's been trying to get up that waterfall all morning." She smiled then said, "You're Mark Traver, right?"

The shock on Mark's face brightened the smile on hers. She started to say "You …"

Mark finished for her, "… look just like your dad. I've heard that a number of times in the last two days. How did you know my dad?"

"He was a regular here. Every Wednesday night I put his taco salad and beer on the table just about the same time he sat down. Really nice man. Sorry for your loss."

Mark hardly knew what to say, the dichotomy of the situation becoming overwhelming. How could these people be talking about the same man?

"Thank you, uh …"

"Jodie. I've been tending bar here for about twelve years and waited and bussed tables for five before that. Your dad was a regular long before I started. He would talk with anyone about anything. He always made me laugh." She paused for a moment then said, "When I was having a bad day, your dad found a way to cheer me up, make me smile. He didn't have any 'best friends' that I knew of, but he liked everybody and everybody liked him. By the way, you have his smile."

Mark blushed. He nodded then said "Thanks." He did not know what else to say. Jodie walked down the bar to tend to another customer. His mind shifted into overdrive, thinking about everyone's impression of his father. From every waking moment of his young life, he hated living in the same house as his parents. Neither his mother nor father smiled or said anything nice about anything. Now he heard multiple people tell stories about a pleasant man, a happy man, a helpful man, and he could not reconcile the differences from what he lived through to what people described.

What happened after Mark and his sisters moved away from their Jay Street home and the City of Sandusky? Would he find the answers in the stacks of letters that he held yesterday as he looked through his father's footlocker?

Jodie brought his food order and asked, "Can I get you anything else?"

"No. I think this is going to hit the spot." He paused, then asked Jodie, "Did Dad ever talk about his family?"

"Yes, he did." Jodie's smile faded a bit, then she continued, "He said he wished he treated his family better. He didn't like talking about it because he said it saddened him. He told me he wished he could have a do-over, but knew that wasn't possible."

She read Mark's sad, tense look and said, "That look on your face? That's the look he would get when he talked about you and your sisters; the one topic that brought him down."

Another patron asked Jodie for a refill and she headed down the bar. Mark took a long drink of his beer and bit into a taco. The taste put a smile on his face, but it quickly disappeared as he thought about Jodie's description of his father's regrets. They quickly became his regrets as well.

He turned to look for the woman and the man in the booth by the waterfall but the booth sat empty. Something about the woman's smile - he could not put his finger on it, but a twinge of familiarity pricked his mind. Mark shook his head and attacked his tacos and beer. He finished one more beer before completing his meal, then left a generous tip for Jodie.

He waved at the barmaid and said, "Thanks, Jodie. Nice meeting you."

She smiled and waved, "See you soon."

***

After Mark finished his lunch, he headed east on Venice Road, heading towards downtown Sandusky. The drive to Citizens Bank's main branch put Mark at the front doors just after 1:30 p.m. He made his way to a teller and asked if he could access his father's safety deposit box. After signing the cards and providing the key, the teller led him down one of the isles lined with steel doors. As they moved down the aisle, the teller read the numbers on the boxes, then stopped. This section contained boxes that were larger than most. The locked door measured about fourteen inches across and ten inches high. She inserted both keys and pulled the heavy door open. She pulled the bank's key from its slot and stepped aside while Mark pulled the bond box out of the stall. The box, about twenty inches long, appeared to weigh over thirty pounds, much heavier than Mark anticipated.

The teller smiled and quipped, "Must be a ton of gold in there." She frowned and covered her mouth, then said, "Sorry, I'm not supposed to make remarks like that."

Mark smiled, "No problem. I won't tell. Besides, you might be right." He looked around, not being familiar with the process of viewing the contents of the box.

She picked up on his hesitation and said, "Right this way, Mr. Traver."

Mark followed the young woman to a small room with walls painted a flat, light gray. There was nothing adorning the room: no pictures on the wall and no clock. She motioned to the only furniture in the room - a table and chair - then said, "You can lock this door from the inside. Take your time. When you're finished, just return the box to the proper location, close the access door, lock the door, and remove your key. You're all set. If you need help, just let me know."

Mark nodded in thanks and the teller left, closing the door behind her. He pushed the button that locked the door.

He sat at the table and opened the lid exposing the spacious interior of the box. Stacked inside were several envelopes of varying sizes; some 12-inch by 8-inch mailing envelopes, others number 10 white business envelopes. Under those, at least a dozen white gift boxes, the kind used to hold larger pieces of jewelry, were stacked. Mark took a deep breath and decided to pull everything from the box, one item at a time, and place them on the table. He started with the small envelopes, then the larger ones. He picked up the first box, surprised by the weight, and set it down on the table. He removed the top of the box and stared in awe at the contents.

Never in his life had he seen an American Eagle gold coin before, except on television advertisements. He certainly never saw twenty gold coins together. He took a deep breath and removed the next box and set it on the table beside the first. They looked identical. He removed the box top and stared at a second box of twenty gold coins. He removed all the boxes, twenty in total, each with twenty gold coins.

He sat, unable to think what to do next.

After sitting for several minutes to gather his thoughts, he looked in the bottom of the safety deposit box and noted two small envelopes, one with writing on the front, the other blank. He opened the blank envelope and pulled out two keys. He removed a small piece of paper with a note written on it.

It read:

> *If you are reading this note, I am either incapacitated or dead. The large, odd-shaped key is for the gun cabinet. The other key is for the lockbox inside the gun cabinet.*
>
> *Joe Traver*

Mark frowned. His father left no explanation why the keys held any significance or why he did not simply place them with the other keys his father's attorney provided. The writing on the other envelope said *To Allen Westridge*. Mark put the envelope with the note and two keys and the envelope addressed to Allen Westridge in his pocket.

Next, he opened the larger envelopes and read their contents. One held a copy of his father's will. He read just a portion of the cover page and placed it back into the envelope. The second, thicker envelope contained a copy of his father's financial plan. A third envelope contained the original revocable trust. Without reading further, he replaced the document in the envelope planning to take the documents with him to make copies. He placed the three envelopes aside. A business envelope sat at the bottom of the box. The envelope contained a single sheet of paper. Unfolding the paper, a spreadsheet had multiple rows and several columns. The left column had three-digit codes. APL, MSC, INT. He didn't understand the codes. In the next columns, were website and partial passwords. At the bottom of the spreadsheet, a series of instructions had been listed on how to access the accounts for each site. Without a computer close by, he decided to take the paper with him. He would look into the websites and accounts later.

He wondered about the accounts listed in the spreadsheet, his mind racing, thinking what could the information mean? A more sinister question came to mind. Was his father a thief or a bookie? Is that where all the money came from? The gold coins?

Just who the hell were you, Dad?

Chapter 9

After leaving the bank, Mark drove to the Jay Street house. As he pulled into the driveway, he looked towards the garage and decided to try the keys that he found in the safe deposit box. Before exiting the truck, his gaze was drawn to the small window near the peak of the A-frame above the second floor of the house. The footlocker, he knew, sat just below the window. He bowed his head and thought about his father and his often-stern expression as they sat at the dinner table in silence. Imagining that face with a smile, or his voice offering words of encouragement, just did not seem possible. His memories of life in this house included no thoughts of happiness, laughter, kind words, or deeds. As he conjured up images of his father and his mother, all he could remember were looks of what … bitterness? Contempt? He could not recall ever hearing them argue. *Hell, they never talked, besides idle chatter.*

As he stared at the window, he could not think of a time when his father or mother raised their voices in anger. If they hated each other, they did not allow their children to see it or hear about it. They slept in the same bed. They rode in the same car. They ate at the same dinner table. But they acted like strangers - two people with nothing in common, forced to coexist – like a life sentence.

They were married, Mark knew, but they acted differently from his friends' parents. He witnessed what loving homes looked like; the atmosphere, the emotion, the interaction with one another had a completely different feel. You could sense the love. You could also tell when his friends' parents were angry, sad, anxious, happy, or just tired. They openly praised their children and their accomplishments. They offered words of encouragement when their children made mistakes or expressed disappointment for not achieving a goal. Those houses were homes. They teemed with life and love.

Mark again thought that something must have happened in his parent's lives to cause such a glum atmosphere around the Traver household. He took a deep breath, left the truck, and headed towards the garage.

He opened the garage door and turned towards the door to the basement under the garage. He tried the first key. It worked smoothly without any difficulty; so smooth that Mark thought the locking mechanism might have been lubricated recently. He turned to look at the covered Mustang, smiled, then opened the basement door. He found a light switch and flipped it on. At the base of the steps, the basement below illuminated with bright lights, much brighter than the single bulb in the attic inside the house. The steps were constructed of two by eight inch pine. The wide staircase sported drywall on both sides which had been painted recently, a telling, strong scent of new paint evident. He made his way down to the foot of the steps and stopped, looking around the twenty-four-foot by twenty-four-foot space. Four bare bulbs were screwed into fixtures equally spaced in the eight-foot high ceiling, casting off bright light evenly around the space. Not a speck of wood dust could be found on the polished concrete floor. The cinder block walls were raw and bare, not painted. Nothing hung from them.

A workbench ran along the length of one wall. Several large tool storage lockers sat at one end of the room. Expensive wood-working power tools took up shelf space along the wall at the north end of the room. The south end of the room sported a series of deep shelves on which sat dozens of hand-crafted wall hangings. Each wall hanging had intricately carved sayings. *You are My Only True Love*, *Your Heart is My Home*, *Happy Anniversary*, were just a few examples. Again, Mark's mind grappled with the inconsistency with the man he knew and the man who created such works of art.

He looked to his right. A home-made wooden storage area

sat in the space under the steps he had just descended. A hasp kept the door closed, but did not have a lock. He walked up to the door, turned the handle on the hasp and pulled the door open to reveal a large, glossy black, steel gun cabinet - an expensive model.

Mark rubbed his forehead and looked at the lock. He pulled the keys from his pocket and inserted the odd-shaped key into the lock. As with the garage door lock, the key rotated easily. Mark turned a large handle on the door, heard the locking bars disengage, and pulled the heavy door open.

He did not know what to expect; based on the size and cost of the cabinet, maybe an arsenal of weapons, dozens of boxes of ammunition, pipe bombs. Well, maybe not pipe bombs. But seeing only two handguns, two long guns, ammunition for each, and a gun cleaning kit came as a surprise. One of the long guns had a broken stock, as if it had been hit against a tree or a rock. He looked closer and noticed an envelope near the cleaning kit. He opened the envelope and looked inside. A single folded sheet of paper with a cryptic note; *The bullet is in my footlocker.* Mark frowned. *What bullet?* He placed the note back into the envelope and put it back on the shelf. He turned and locked the gun cabinet.

Before heading upstairs and back into the house, he inspected the tool cabinets. Unlike the contents of the gun safe, his father's collection of tools impressed him. After spending another twenty minutes rummaging through tools and other workshop supplies, he headed out of the garage and back to the house.

As he exited the garage, he looked up at the bright blue, cloudless sky. The temperature remained just below sixty, but with only a slight breeze, the air felt good. He knew the temperature at home in Maitland, Florida would be a sub-tropical eighty degrees and the typical afternoon rain clouds would likely be forming. The crisp air in Ohio was a nice change, at least weather-wise.

Stopping at the refrigerator, he grabbed a beer, twisted off the cap, and took a drink. With his mind still spinning, he headed up the two flights of stairs to the attic. He stared at the footlocker, wondering if the letters between his parents held any answers to the growing number of questions in his mind.

Mark opened the footlocker again and pulled out much of the same materials as the previous day. He set the bundles of letters aside and looked through the stack of pictures from his father's military days. The photos of explosions taken from one of the bombers grabbed his attention. In the pictures he could see clouds of smoke billowing up from buildings, streets, and airfields.

He came across a thin folder with a single, faded sheet of paper. It looked like an essay with a title – A Terrifying Experience by Joseph Traver. He read the first sentence and could not set the paper down.

It read:

> In looking back on my Army Air Corps career, I see now that I was very fortunate.
>
> I reposted to Fort Hayes, Columbus, Ohio in April 1943, and within a day was sent to the Army Air Corps classification center in Nashville, Tennessee. The battery of tests to be taken were designed to select the people who were most qualified to be pilots, navigators, or bombardiers. I qualified for the first two and had a choice. I chose to be a navigator. I was moved again, this time to Monroe, Louisiana for preflight school, followed by advanced navigation school, on the other side of the same base, Selman Field.
>
> I graduated and received my wings in December 1943. In checking the assignment

sheet, I found that I was picked to be an instructor, which I was at Selman Field until October, 1944. Every other weekend I had to fly with a pick-up crew of two pilots and three navigators. We took "Proficiency Flights," which were designed to prepare us for combat when our time came.

In January, 1944, I learned that my wife gave birth to fraternal twins, Mark and Maryanne Traver. I cannot wait to meet my children in person, but my commitment to the military won't allow even a short visit home.

In November, 1944 I was sent to Langley Field, Virginia to pursue a course in radar in order to qualify as a Navigator/Radar Observer, which I successfully passed.

I received orders to board a plane leaving from Mitchell Field, New York to England via Gander, Newfoundland, Iceland, and Shannon, Ireland.

I was assigned to the 303rd Bomber Squadron based at Molesworth Air Base, England. The Navigator/Radar Observers, nicknamed Mickey Men, flew in the lead ship of a formation, and at that time in the war directed the other planes to the assigned target and when the weather clouded over, *even dropped bombs using radar. When the lead plane dropped its bombs the rest of the planes in the group also dropped theirs. It was called saturation bombing.*

On my first mission as we neared our target, the flack became thicker and one burst sent a lot of shrapnel through the nose section where I was seated. A piece came up between my legs, cut my flying suit, and bounced off the frame of the airplane over my head. My leg was burned but not seriously, and I did find and keep the piece of shrapnel. Obviously, I was terrified. I flew five additional missions over Germany, and then the war in Europe was over, thanks be to God.

Mark sat stunned, wondering if this experience caused his inability to be happy, loving, even cordial around his family. But, if true, what caused him to snap out of his misery and live a normal life? People he just met described Joe Traver as happy, cordial, even helpful. This revelation ratcheted up his desire to learn more about him. He looked into the footlocker again and noticed a small giftbox that had been next to the envelope with his father's story. He opened the box Sitting on a bed of cotton as if being displayed like an expensive piece of jewelry, sat a misshapen chunk of black metal with sharp edges – the shrapnel described in his father's story.

Sitting on the floor with the bundles of letters between his legs, he picked up the bundle from his mother to his father and untied the ribbon holding the letters together. He counted the envelopes; fifteen letters in total. The first letter was postmarked April 19, 1943. The last – January 2, 1945. As he looked at the postmarks on each envelope, he noticed that they were roughly one month apart. He wondered at the length of time between communications, then thought the post office might not have been as efficient back then as they are now.

He picked up the stack of letters from his father to his mother and went through the same exercise. His father wrote twenty-seven letters to his mother, the first postmarked May 11, 1943, around three weeks after his mother's letter to his father. The postmark of his father's last letter – May 1, 1945. That seemed like a long time from his mother's last letter to his father's reply. Then he noticed his father had written two more letters in reply to his mother's final letter. This struck Mark as odd, but he reasoned that his mother's letters may have been lost over time.

Mark picked up the first letter from his mother to his father and pulled the sheets from the envelope. A chill gripped him as he unfolded the sheets.

Chapter 10

Before Mark began to read the first letter to his father, he decided to read all the letters in chronological order. After reading his mother's letter, he would read his father's response. He believed that, reading them in such a manner might give him a better understanding of their relationship.

He unfolded the first letter postmarked April 19, 1943. There were two pages handwritten in beautiful cursive.

My Dear Joseph,

I hope this letter finds you in good health and not shaken by my news. I know that hearing of our situation just before your leaving for training to fight in this horrific war left you dismayed, to say the least. You had already made a courageous decision to follow your conscience, a decision that I know you did not make lightly.

When hearing my news, the look in your eyes took on many shades giving away the shock you must have experienced. But, in my opinion, you ultimately came to the right decision. I am so proud to be your wife. I love you now as I always have.

I will take care of myself for my health as well as the health of our child. It is far too early to know much about our baby's health, but I will write to you with updates as frequently as I am able. Just know our child will feel my love as well as yours.

I pray this horrible war will end soon and you will come home to us. Each day I will listen for good news that the German's have been defeated so our family can be reunited.

I apologize in the way I broke this news to you, but there was no other way. I did not know at the time that you had committed to military service. I pray knowing you will be a father in a little over eight months, will give you something to look forward to, something joyous to come home to.

My heart aches each day without you.

All my love to you,
Ada May.

Mark could hardly believe his eyes. The words expressed in his mother's letter sounded like a declaration of true love. His mother poured her heart out to his father. Thinking of his and his sister's birthdate, she would have been very early in her pregnancy, almost too early to know for certain that she was pregnant. But her words were confident and clear. She was pregnant with him and his sister, living proof that she had been right.

As he reread her words he scrutinized each sentence, looking for any clues to how their relationship derailed. His father had not known of her pregnancy prior to joining the military. The war had progressed to a critical stage, with Germany on the march, taking over country after country, laying waste to the European continent. Young men all over the country left their homes to join the war effort. He hoped to learn more about his father's decision to fight.

Mark was surprised that his mother had become pregnant prior to his parents' marriage. Being devout Catholics certainly put an added strain on their relationship with their parents, Mark's grandparents. From his mother's words, their wedding had been rushed so that his father could meet his military commitment. He wondered what his grandparents thought of the situation. Certainly, their friends would gossip. These days, no one would bat an eye.

Since his mother had not known of his father's commitment to the military, he wondered if there had been a break in their relationship. Joining the service certainly was a life-changing move. Not telling your fiancé about such a move seemed unlikely if all had been going well. Maybe his father's reply would provide answers.

He placed his mother's letter back in the envelope and set it aside. He paused before reaching for his father's first letter and tried to place himself in his father's shoes. At the time he received this letter, he would be at the beginning of his military training. How would he feel if he was on the path to being a father while also committed to join the war, perhaps placing himself in danger. He thought back on the terrifying moment described in his story of being burned by a piece of shrapnel from anti-aircraft guns. He knew his father's military commitment lasted a little over two years. At certain times he must have wondered if he would see his wife again, or ever see his children – at that point, for all he knew, just one child.

Mark lifted the first letter in the stack of letters to his mother, postmarked May 11, 1943. He carefully opened the flap, noticing the yellowing of the envelope. As with his mother's letter, the single page felt fragile. Unlike his mother's beautiful penmanship, his father wrote in block letters.

Dear Ada May,

I'm happy to hear from you and that you are taking care of the baby through caring for yourself. Certainly, the timing could have been better, as well as the circumstances, but that is behind us now. We both have important tasks in front of us. You must eat well, get rest, and follow the doctor's orders. You have been to the doctor, I trust?

I will do my part to end this war. You will receive money from my paycheck at regular intervals. I'm not sure when that will start, but I have filled out all the necessary paperwork to make that happen.

I took tests to see where I might best support the war effort. I was selected for flight training. When I finish my classes, I will be a navigator on a bomber. An actual assignment to a plane is over a year away. I pray the war is over before my first assignment. Time will tell.

Be safe, my love,

Joe

Mark noticed his father's letter seemed to lack passion,

but he quickly thought of his circumstances. He remembered his own fear of being sent to Vietnam. Two of his close friends joined the Navy to avoid being drafted into the Army, truly a difficult choice for those men in the sixties. The entire country seemed to be protesting the war. Though the United States lost nearly 60,000 men and women in that war, it did not compare to the scope of death and destruction during World War II. Men in the military back then must have believed that they were marching directly into hell.

With two major life changing events on his mind, Joseph Traver must have felt overwhelmed by the weight of responsibility that he faced. At the time he wrote this letter, he had to concentrate on his studies. He could not fault his father for being brief. He wondered if the lack of passion came from sleep deprivation, or the necessity to keep his attention on his training … or was there another, underlying reason?

Mark reread both letters, again wondering what had happened to cause their relationship to faulter. Given the events of the times, it is hard to imagine how people kept their sanity. But many did. Most families were able to put the war behind them. No one ever heard of Post Traumatic Stress Disorder after World War II, but certainly many men and women were affected by the horrors of war, either directly, or through a spouse or even a close friend.

He picked up the pictures of the bombs exploding on factories and air fields. He turned the pictures over. On one, he noticed the writing had been smeared, as if it had gotten wet. He could barely make out the note but finally pieced together the words *Unterluss Munitions Factory, April 4, 1945*. He recognized the handwriting as his father's because it matched the writing in his letter. He looked at the backs of the other pictures, but they had clear writing, nothing smeared. If the pictures had been together in the footlocker, they all should have gotten wet. But the smears looked more like drops of liquid, like from a wet glass … or tears.

Mark replaced the pictures in the top tray of the footlocker and began reading the letters again. About to open the second letter from his mother, he heard the doorbell ring. Setting the letter down, he quickly descended the stairs and headed for the front door. When he opened the door, Peggy Whipple and her husband stood on the stoop. They had a couple bags in their hands that looked like burgers and drinks. Randy had a six pack of Miller Lite in his left hand.

Mark smiled, "Hi, Peggy. Randy. Come on in"

Peggy said, "Hi, Mark. You said to stop by if we saw your truck. We thought you might want to take a dinner break. We've got burgers and chicken sandwiches. We weren't sure which ones you'd prefer, so we got both."

Mark smiled and waved them through into the living room. He looked at his watch, surprised by the late hour - 7:25 p.m.

"Thanks for coming over, and for the food. I've been so focused on some things that I lost track of time."

Peggy looked around, shook her head, then said, "Hadn't changed a single thing since I stopped cleaning. I asked if he wanted me to help him shop for some new furniture. I told him Randy and I would help pay for it. He laughed. He said he didn't need any charity. He said it in a friendly way, not like he was insulted."

Mark smiled and said, "Since I've been here, I found some things that assure me he didn't need money." He paused then asked, "Did Dad ever talk about my mom?"

Peggy looked up at the ceiling as if searching the tiles for an answer. "Not that I recall. I joked with him one day that he needed a woman's touch to spruce up the house, give it some charm and color. He smiled and said to me, 'I've been down that road once. That was enough for me.' That was the only thing he ever said about their relationship. I assumed he meant your mom."

Mark shrugged his shoulders. They spread the food out on the dining room table and the three of them twisted the tops off beers. Before Mark could take a drink, she said, "A toast to your father, Joe Traver, a member of the Greatest Generation."

They clinked bottle necks and drank. Then they

selected their choices for dinner and ate in silence for a few minutes.

Mark asked, "So what did Dad talk about? You mentioned when I met you at the store that you and he would talk for hours."

Peggy again looked up at the ceiling, then said, "He told me about his hobbies, politics, religion. He loved woodworking in his spare time. He made Randy and me several very cool signs for our den. He mentioned his children and grandchildren, how proud he was of you."

Mark thought *How could he have been proud of me? We never spoke after I left home.* He said, "I'm not searching for compliments or anything, but what did he say about me?"

Peggy looked at him with knowing eyes. In a steady voice she said, "He knew a lot about you. He somehow learned that you were financially successful, were a good father to 'his grandkids'" – she used her fingers to highlight the quote – "and that you were a loving husband. He envied your family relationship. He said you married a good woman, the best woman, in fact."

Mark's eyes were in danger of leaking tears as Peggy finished. She noted his discomfort and turned her attention to her sandwich. Mark rolled his neck and took a swallow of his beer.

The conversation shifted to what Mark planned to do with the house and the belongings; mostly idle chatter. In the course of their visit, Peggy and Randy confirmed that his father was a changed man from the one Mark once knew.

Chapter 11

Soon after Peggy and Randy Whipple left, Mark sat alone at the dinner table. Peggy had cleared the paper sacks, empty beer bottles and other debris from the table and thrown it in the trash can in the kitchen. He thanked the couple for coming by and asked that they come over anytime they saw the truck in the driveway. They replied that they would and left.

He looked closer at the dining room and its furnishings. An expensive-looking China cabinet dominated one wall while a matching butler anchored the opposite wall. The table and chairs rounded out the dining room suite of furniture that looked to be antiques. This appeared to be the only furniture of value in the house.

He stood and walked to the China cabinet noticing the layer of accumulated dust on every horizontal surface. His wife, Denise, would have started dusting, unable to tolerate the mess. Inside the glass doors, the dinnerware had obviously not been moved for quite some time. He would ask Peggy about it when he next spoke with her.

As he explored the cabinet further, he found dish towels, candles, place mats, cork screws, and assorted trinkets. He lifted some of the towels to get an idea of how many were stored in the drawer and found a plain white envelope the size of a greeting card with his father's name on the front. The unsealed envelope appeared to have been handled many times. He lifted the flap and pulled a note card from inside.

Before he could begin reading, the doorbell rang. He wondered if the Whipples left something behind. He slid the note back into the envelope, placed it on the China cabinet, and answered the door. To his surprise, an elderly woman stood on the stoop with a casserole dish in her hand. Recognition and a smile lit up Mark's face. The woman's gray hair flowed to her shoulders, but her facial features remained much the same as Mark remembered over forty years ago. Mrs. Abigail Holtzmiller, the Traver's next door neighbor, gave him the same bright smile he remembered when she would sneak him a glass of lemon soda pop when he played with his friends around the neighborhood. She would tell Mark to keep it their little secret.

"Mrs. Holtzmiller, how are you? Come in, please."

She stepped past him into the living room, still holding the dish. Her smile faded a bit as she offered her condolences. "Mark, I'm so sorry about your father. Please pass that along to your sisters. I spoke with Joseph the day before his passing. He seemed resolved, even ready to move on. He did not look ill, at least no more than any man approaching his nineties."

"Thank you, ma'am. Here, let me take that and put it in the kitchen. I'm sorry, but I just ate dinner."

"No problem, Dear. You put that in the fridge and eat it at your leisure. I figured you'd be busy with your father's affairs, and wouldn't have much time for driving all over town for a meal. If you need anything else, you let me know. I have an apple pie cooling on the kitchen counter. I'll bring you a piece tomorrow."

"You don't have to go to all that trouble."

"Mark, Dear, it's no trouble at all."

As he took the dish from her hands and headed for the kitchen, he said, "Have a seat in the dining room. It isn't safe to sit in here." He smiled as he nodded his head at the living room couch and chair that should have seen the landfill years ago.

While in the kitchen he hollered and asked if she would like something to drink. "I have beer," he joked.

She hollered back, "No, no. I can't stay long. I just wanted to see you again and bring you something to eat. I wish the circumstances were different. If I'd have thought, I'd have brought you a glass of pop for old time's sake."

Mark's laugh from the kitchen brought a smile to the woman's face. He came back to the living room and saw her looking around, through the doorways into the den and dining room. She remarked, "I see you have your hands full. Have you decided what to do with the house and property?"

Without hesitation, Mark replied, "We've already contracted with a realtor. Clayton Biggs. Do you know him?"

As they moved into the dining room, she smiled and replied. "I don't know him personally, but I hear he is one of the best in town, so you're probably in good hands with him and his company."

As she took a seat at the dining room table, her smile changed to an expression that conveyed caution before she spoke. "You never came home after you married, did you?"

Her question was more of a statement, though it held no malice behind it. Mark looked around the room, feeling uncomfortable with her question, but knowing she probably already knew the answer. He wanted to avoid eye contact but he finally met her gaze and said, "No. I never felt at home here." He paused, a question forming in his mind, but not sure if he should ask the elderly woman about his family business. He thought *What could it hurt?* "Mrs. Holtzmiller, do you know why my parents were so … I don't know … miserable around each other?"

"I'm sorry, Mark. I won't speak ill of the dead. Besides, it isn't my place to tell you, mainly because it would just be from my point of view … and gossipy. I do know what you mean, though. Had I been in your shoes, I might never have come back to this town or this house."

He stared at his visitor for a long moment, his expression turning serious. He asked, "Do you have time to talk? I don't want to impose. It would only be a few minutes."

With hesitation in her voice, she said, "Sure. But can I get that drink you offered first?"

"Yes ma'am. What would you like?"

"A beer as long as it isn't one of those IPA things." She smiled and he smiled back.

"All I have is Miller Lite."

Her smile broadened, "My brand."

On his way back from the kitchen he opened a beer for her and one for himself. Once seated, he began, "Did you notice a change in my father over the years?"

Abigail Holtzmiller took a deep breath and looked at the beer in her hand. Mark sensed that she wished to choose her words with caution, especially since declaring her desire to not talk unkindly about her former neighbors. She looked up and said, "Yes. Yes, I did. There were two major changes, and I can tell you, both changes shocked me."

Mark's eyes narrowed, then he asked, "Were they sudden changes or …"

Mark stopped in mid-sentence. He rubbed his chin and looked around the room, thinking how to pose his question. "Let me explain what I'm getting at. Since I've been back in town, people I've never met recognized me by my likeness to Dad. They'd say stuff like *You look just like your father. You have his smile.* His smile? I never saw Dad smile in the twenty-plus years I lived here."

"Mark, I'll tell you what I think, and, God forgive me if this is gossip, but your father's personality, no, his entire outlook on life, changed almost overnight."

She took a hardy pull on her beer then set the bottle down on the table. Her expression turned to one of sorrow, her eyebrows turning downward, the lines in her face becoming more pronounced. She looked as if her next words might never make it past her lips. Then she looked him straight in the eyes and said, "Within a few days of your mother's passing, your father became a new man. He would wave and say good morning when he left for work. He would go out after work and get home late. Not like two in the morning, mind you. But pretty late. I cannot tell you why or how. I just know it was as if someone turned a switch and he became a different man."

He looked at his old neighbor, doing everything he could to keep his jaw from hitting the table. Her description of his dad's demeanor mirrored what others had told him since he arrived in town. Abigail Holtzmiller's explanation of when Joseph Traver's personality changed provided the first clue of when that change occurred and the reason for his father's transformation. Had his mother's death freed him from some invisible, self-imposed prison cell? Had their relationship deteriorated to such an extent that he felt trapped by a vow? Did they do what other parents claim to have done and stayed together 'for the sake of their children?' If this had been their reasoning for staying together, they failed. Their self-inflicted, forced cohabitation may have caused more damage to him and his sisters than a divorce.

Seeing Mark's sadness, she placed her pale, veined hand over his. She said, "I wish it wasn't true, but I think your mom wanted out of the marriage. You know she committed suicide, right?"

Mark nodded, then said, "She sent me a copy of the obituary with a note stating as much. The obituary that I have wasn't clipped from the paper. It had been handwritten on regular paper. Mom wrote her own obituary - in beautiful cursive." He paused, thinking of his mother's handwriting in her letters.

She looked at him, recognizing that he had many questions running through his head. "What is it, Mark?"

"Nothing." He paused and they both took drinks of their beers. He asked, "How long did you live next to Mom and Dad?"

"I've lived in my house since I turned sixteen. I married very young. Anton, my husband, robbed the cradle. He was much older than me. He died in the war in 1943, just before you were born."

Mark said, "I'm so sorry. You never remarried?"

She scoffed at the idea. "My Anton. A good man and a good provider, but once he passed, I had no need or desire to remarry. He left me with a paid-off house and plenty of money. I never asked where it came from and don't care."

He smiled and said, "You'd be quite the catch." Then his smile faded. "I really appreciate your telling me this. It gives me some clue about what changed with Dad."

The old woman finished her beer and said, "I hope you learn enough to put your mind at ease. I didn't envy you kids growing up with your parents. I wish I could tell you more."

But Mark could tell, the old woman knew more than she had let on.

She slowly stood. He stood along with her and approached her. He gave her a gentle hug, saying, "Thank you for the casserole. I appreciate your frankness about my dad."

"Well, if I had a few more beers, who knows what I might have said."

They both laughed. Then Mark remembered something she had said. "You mentioned that there were two changes, but you only described one."

She smiled and said, "The second change happened several years ago. A woman, about your age, came to visit him. I saw him greet her at that door," she pointed to the front entrance to the house, "and he embraced her like a long-lost love. I saw tears in his eyes. She would take him out, to where, I don't know. But she visited him regularly until about a year or so ago. Then she stopped coming to see him. He never said why, but that seemed to drain him of any desire to live."

Chapter 12

When Abagail Holtzmiller left, Mark decided that the answers to his questions, which seemed to multiply with each new encounter, were in the letters in the footlocker. He threw the empty beer bottles into the trash, smiling at the knowledge of his elderly neighbor being a beer drinker. He took the steps to the second floor, then to the attic two at a time, anxious to get back to reading the letters exchanged between his parents. He sat in front of the footlocker, unconcerned about the dust all around him.

He had left off with his father's reply to his mother's first letter. Removing his mother's second letter, dated May 24, 1943, from the stack, he took a deep breath and lifted the envelope's flap. He unfolded the single-page letter and read:

My Dear Joseph,

I just returned from the doctor's office. I am happy to report that all is fine with our child. At least as far as the doctor could discern. It is still quite early. I am experiencing morning sickness. The nausea can be terrible, but I'm told by the doctor and my mother that this is quite normal at this stage. It will pass, they say, but not soon enough for me.

I hope you are doing well in your training. I hope these letters will not distract you. If they do, let me know.

I received the first check from your pay.

It will help, but it isn't much. You should not worry. We will get by. I am living with my parents until your return, which should help. They have said they can't provide financial help but I told them that allowing me to remain living at home would be all the assistance we need. They applaud your commitment to the war effort. They send their prayers that you'll return home soon, safely.

Until then, my love,

Ada May

Mark held the one-page letter and read it a second time. He again wondered at the hand-written expression of love coming from his mother. What could have possibly gone wrong between the time he and his sister were born to his earliest memories of childhood, where mother and father acted like strangers. He vowed to read on and picked up his father's response.

Postmarked June 10, 1943, he removed the letter. Again, his father's printed letter lacked the fluid cursive writing of his mother's. The block letters written in a choppy manner, the sentences not level from one side of the stationary to the other. He wondered if his father's exhaustion played a part in the lack of emotion.

My Dear Ada May,

I'm very pleased that you went to the doctor and he assured you that all was well with you and our baby. I'm anxious to hear of your progress. I hope your morning sickness ends soon. Such a terrible side-effect to an otherwise happy miracle.

I'm sorry that this note is so short. I must get some sleep. We are training nearly eighteen hours each day. But hopefully the war will be over sooner than later.

I can't wait to be with you again.

My love to you,

Joe

Mark could feel the exhaustion in his father's letter, the grueling hours training, the pressures of his situation most likely always on his mind. What a monstrous weight to be on the shoulders of a twenty-one year old. He thought back to his time when he feared being drafted and remembered how he and his friends talked about the Vietnam War and the horror stories they heard about soldiers being captured and tortured. When his friends joined the Navy and left for boot camp, he considered joining them, but decided to wait and see if his low draft number would allow him to avoid the conflict altogether. In the end, his number never came up, but he kept in touch with his friends. After boot camp at Great Lakes, Illinois, they received orders for duty aboard an air craft carrier. They traveled the world and never saw combat, though they did assist in the recovery of capsules and astronauts from several space program launches.

The short letter conveyed a sense of dread for coming events, knowing the pace of training would not slow. Each passing day moved his father closer to an assignment on a bomber and direct participation in the war. He shuddered at the thought of riding in an airplane loaded with bombs, knowing that an enemy aircraft could strafe the bomber and set off one of the bombs. He did not know if these thoughts ran through his father's mind, but what man could avoid dwelling on a violent death when placed in that situation?

Mark thought that at the time this letter was written, Hitler's war machine ramped up, intensifying and expanding into new fronts, advancing onto new continents. World leaders feared that they would not be able to stop the continued onslaught from the German Army, Navy, and Luftwaffe. His father not only had the weight of his training and coming assignment on his mind, he now had a family - a wife, and an unborn child - added to his responsibilities.

Could I have handled such a massive set of obligations? Mark shook his head, thinking that he needed a beer, but decided to move on to his mother's reply, dated June 30, 1943. The letter, three pages long, expressed some concern for the family's financial situation though his father could do nothing to help. His entire paycheck went to her to ensure that her and their coming child could survive.

Dear Joseph,

I pray this letter finds you well. I don't know how you are able to stand the strain of working all those hours, training with little sleep. Maybe the war will be over before you are ordered overseas. It is hard to imagine that God could allow such evil to exist in the world. I know I should not be thinking such thoughts. They should be of you returning to us safely. I pray every day for just that.

Our baby is growing inside of me. I have another appointment with the doctor in about a month. I have a little baby bump, but it is so slight that most people don't even notice. The morning sickness seems to have lessened, but is still as regular as the sunrise. According to the doctor, this is normal and I should not be concerned.

I am receiving your pay without incident. I am also receiving assistance from the church. They are having food drives and provide some food free of charge.

I only take what I need. Mother and father are helping, too. They are letting me stay here, but I am trying to find a cheap apartment for when you return home. That way we have our privacy and my parents won't feel obligated to help support us.

A couple of our friends are also helping. The women in town here are forming a support group so that if needs arise among any of us, the group can work together to meet those needs. The biggest needs are food, clothing, and gas for cars. Fuel is being rationed and there is talk about food rationing. Already, many materials are being diverted to the war effort for making munitions, ships, planes, and uniforms for troops.

I'm sorry for rambling on. I just miss you so much. I will continue to take good care of myself and our child. Please be safe and come home soon.

All my love,

Ada May

Mark's eyes watered, but he did not cry. He reread the letter from his mother, wondering how she could afford an apartment. He referred back to her previous letter noting that she could barely survive even with assistance from her parents. He wondered if she figured out a way to manage the income from his father's pay, or if he received a pay increase. But it was just over a month between letters. How could her circumstances have changed in such a short time? Maybe the church helped young mothers whose husbands had been called to military service, or friends of his parents offered help with rent. Without any real evidence to support these thoughts, he decided to keep reading.

His father's next letter to his mother, dated July 29, 1943, read much the same as his previous letter. The exhaustion in his words and the brevity of the letter gave every indication that he had little time to do or think of anything besides his training. Mark had no idea how long his father's training lasted or when an assignment to a bomber group came, but he could read between the lines. Exhaustion and tension dominated his father's life. Did he reach a breaking point along the way? Was his lack of outward emotion once he returned home from the war caused by the constant stress? With each letter, he gained some inkling, some additional piece of a puzzle, but the picture it represented remained a mystery.

He looked at his watch; nearing midnight on Friday, May 8, 2009. He had been in Sandusky for just two and a half days and learned more about his mother and father than he knew his entire lifetime.

He knew his mother ended her own life, but still had no evidence of a reason. In her letters, she professed love to his father. She struggled with finances and loneliness, which, under the circumstances, would affect most people in a similar manner. But she appeared to have dealt with both.

Mark looked around the attic. The tiny window yielded only darkness. The bulb which hung from an electric wire above him cast enough light for him to read the letters and see into the footlocker, but did not illuminate much else in the large, open area in the attic. He yawned, the long hours finally catching up to him. Then he thought about his father riding in the front of a freezing plane on his way to a bombing mission, and the cauldron of emotions he must have experienced during that time. He figured he owed it to his father to handle his affairs as professionally as possible. If he had to work long days, he would.

And he needed to satisfy his own curiosity. What went so horribly wrong in his parents' marriage? Why had his mother taken her own life? Did she believe that it would punish his father for some misstep in his life, or was she so miserable that she could no longer live with herself?

He took a long look at the footlocker and wondered; are the answers in there? He yawned again, knowing that he could not concentrate on the letters another minute. He stood and headed for his truck and back to the hotel room to try and get a good night's sleep. But sleep would not come easy as dreams of a war from long ago invaded his brain.

Chapter 13

The drive from his hotel room to Jay Street offered little in the way of a distraction from the task in front of him. Mark picked up breakfast and coffee at a drive through restaurant on Route 250 and headed west towards Jay Street. The appraiser would be at the house at 10:00 a.m. to determine the market value of the property; a requirement of any bank offering to finance a sale. No other visitors were expected, but considering how the past two days had gone, he figured some new surprise would pop up.

He pulled the truck onto the cracked driveway and parked. As he exited the truck, a white sedan pulled in behind him, his first surprise of the day. He smiled when his son, Elliot, and his grandson, Marcus, exited the car. Elliot walked up to his dad with a smile and an extended hand and said, "We thought you could use the company and maybe an extra hand or two."

Mark took his son's hand and pulled him into a hug. When they broke free, he turned to Marcus and said, "Come here, kid." He embraced his grandson in a tight hug then asked, "When did you get so tall? I saw you last year. You must have grown a foot or more."

Marcus, his only grandson, stood nearly five inches taller than his father and grandfather. At seventeen, he had the build of a basketball player or a cross-country runner. He participated in both sports, but preferred baseball, excelling at pitching and hitting. The last time Mark had seen his grandson, he sported braces and a mild case of acne. Now, both were gone and he had blossomed into a handsome young man with light brown wavy hair and dark blue eyes. He favored his mother's side of the family, but his square jaw and smile mirrored his grandfather.

With the face of a proud father Elliot said, "That was two years ago, Dad. He's really sprouted since then."

"Is that right? Two years? Wow. Your grandmother and I have to venture up here more often. Any serious girlfriends?"

Marcus blushed as he shook his head and said, "A few, but none too serious."

Mark smiled and said, "Let's head inside." He said to Elliot, "I thought you were supposed to monitor testing this weekend."

They continued to make their way into the house. Elliot responded, "I called in a favor and one of my fellow profs is stepping in for me."

As they made their way through the living room, Elliot and Marcus looked around at the dingey, ancient furniture. Marcus asked with a dismayed look on his face, "Great grandpa lived here? The place is a … not a dump, but wow. The furniture looks dangerous to sit on."

Mark smiled. Kids his age had no filters when they spoke. This generation never seemed to hold back on their thoughts or feelings. He replied, "Most of this will probably end up in the landfill. There are a few good pieces, but not much. Let's go to the dining room. You can watch me eat my breakfast. You need anything to drink? I can make some coffee."

"No, Dad, we're good. We ate on the way up."

They sat and made small talk about Marcus' plans for the summer and his upcoming senior year. He already planned to attend Ohio State, but, with one more year of high school ahead, he said that his dad reminded him to concentrate on being a senior; to enjoy that final year.

Elliot asked Mark, "What have you done so far?"

He finished swallowing the last bite of his breakfast sandwich and washed it down with black coffee, then replied, "I signed a contract to put the house on the market, scheduled the appraiser – he'll be here this morning – and the auctioneer will be here Monday morning. Then we clean the place out and, hopefully, someone will buy it."

"How long do you figure it will take to finalize everything?"

"The earliest is about ten days. If there're any snags, who

knows? It could drag on for quite a while. But your grandpa's lawyer thinks this should be snag-free. Dad didn't have much in the way of complications. No wife, no relatives fighting over money or belongings. You both can look around and see if there's anything you want."

Elliot looked around the dining room into the living room then said, "If everything looks like this furniture, there's nothing I really want. Have you seen anything of real value besides the dining room suite?"

Mark smiled, thinking of the Mustang in the garage and the gold coins from the safety deposit box. Then he thought of the footlocker.

"There are a few things that surprised me. There's a vintage Ford Mustang in the garage, fixed up like showroom condition."

The younger men's faces both lit up. "Seriously? Wow."

"And he collected gold coins. They have to be appraised, but that's pretty valuable. Your aunts will get their share of everything."

Elliot frowned, and after a few moments of silence said, "Why aren't they here helping you?"

Mark took a deep breath and looked at the ceiling then said, "I really don't know."

He took a moment to gather his thoughts before continuing. His son and grandson had never met the elder Traver. Mark made sure of it. Over the past two days, he wondered if his actions were selfish. His perceptions of his father were jaded by his first-hand experience living with the man for twenty years. Of course, he remembered very little of the first four or five years. Now a different perception of the same man began forming in his mind; a man, who, by all accounts, had completely changed. He had yet to find what triggered the change. Mrs. Holzmiller provided some clues and insight, but he needed more evidence to collaborate what she told him.

"You know we never visited your grandpa," he looked at Elliot then at Marcus, "your great-grandpa, when you were growing up. I had my reasons for keeping you from meeting him. I believed that my reasons were justified. Joe Traver … he was a cold-hearted man. At least, that's what I believed all my life. In the last two days since I've been here, I've met people who painted a completely different picture of him." He struggled to continue. "The experiences they described with him … like they were talking about someone else. But your aunts, like me, only remember the gloomy side of growing up in this house. They hated Dad." He paused a moment, took a deep breath, then said, "I did, too."

Mark's eyes welled up and he turned his head away. The burst of emotion pounced on him as the tears ran down his cheeks. He quickly rubbed them away with the backs of his hands, then grabbed the used napkins from his breakfast and dried his eyes. "Sorry about that."

Elliot and Marcus sat stunned, not knowing what to say. Finally, Marcus said, "Grandpa, I had no idea what Great Grandpa Traver was like. I wondered why we never stopped that time we came up here to the amusement park. That had to suck. I guess Dad's not so bad after all."

They all laughed. Elliot shook his head as his eyes looked up at the ceiling in mock prayer. Marcus' comment broke the tension that each man felt.

Elliot broke the silence, "What can we do to help you, Dad?"

Mark rubbed his nose, then said, "Let's look around the house and garage. You let me know if there's anything here you want. Your aunts have already told me they want nothing except to see the estate settled and the paperwork finished. So, if you see anything, let me know so the auctioneer doesn't line it up to sell. I figure most of the things you'll be interested in are in the garage."

They stood and as Mark lead the way, his grandson, Marcus, noticed a white envelope on the China cabinet. He picked it up and pulled the card from the envelope and read the note in silence. When finished, he called to his grandfather and asked, "Hey gramps, who is Emma Franks?"

Mark turned and saw that Marcus held the note he had not had the chance to read. "I don't know. I just found it in that drawer yesterday. Why?"

"She thanked great-granddad for visiting her mother. She says that she had never seen her mom so excited and happy. He must have been a real charmer."

Mark walked over to Marcus who handed him the note and envelope. He noticed the signature – Emma Franks. Not recognizing the name, he raised his eyebrows and shrugged at the new and surprising revelation.

He placed the note back in the envelope and set it back on the China cabinet, then led the young men out of the house towards the garage.

They spent the next forty-five minutes in the garage basement looking at tools, crafts, guns, and ammunition. Elliot was not much of a craftsman. He preferred spending his time in an office environment, working on papers and writing. The men decided that they would sell all the expensive shop tools. Marcus grabbed a drill and a few other hand tools and tossed them in a leather bag.

Looking inside the gun cabinet, Elliot said, "Not interested, Dad. I have a pistol for home protection and we don't want any more guns around the house. I'd be up the creek if I came home with another one. I'm sure Sandy would have a cow if I brought one home for Marcus."

"I understand. Denise won't like it, but I might take the pistols."

Marcus pointed into the cabinet and asked, "What happened to that rifle?"

They all looked at the long gun with the damaged stock. Mark pulled it from the cabinet and showed them the scarred wood near where the stock had splintered.

Mark said, "I don't know. Looks like someone smashed it against a tree or a rock or something. That'll end up in the trash, I'm sure."

Mark put the rifle back in the cabinet, locked it then they headed up the stairs.

Standing next to the Mustang, admiring the car's showroom condition, Marcus surprised his father and grandfather by saying, "Granddad, unless you plan to keep it, I think you should sell the Mustang." Turning to his father he said, "I don't want it, do you?"

Elliot said, "Not really. I'm not much of a car enthusiast. That's something a collector would want." He turned to his father, "Are you planning to keep it?"

Mark rubbed his chin, wondering if his wife might like to tool around central Florida in a classic Mustang. "I'll talk with your mom about it. She might have an opinion on that."

Elliot smiled and said, "I can see Mom riding around town in this thing. Good plan to talk with her. You know what they say – *Happy wife, happy life*."

Marcus rolled his eyes at the saying.

As they stood there, they heard a car door shut. Mark looked at his watch. It was time for his meeting.

"It's the appraiser. I have to talk with him for a few minutes. If you want, you can look around and see if there's anything else that interests you."

They nodded as Mark left the garage and walked towards the front of the house to greet the appraiser.

***

Mark spoke with Simon Wilkes, the appraiser, for about ten minutes. He thought Simon looked more like an accountant than an appraiser. Simon said he would not need Mark to follow him around, but if he needed to ask any questions, he would find him later. Mark said he would not leave for lunch until they spoke. Simon said thanks and they shook hands. Then Simon began his tour around the house, taking notes, and snapping pictures.

Mark found Elliot and Marcus in the attic standing in front of the footlocker looking at the pictures of bombs exploding. Marcus seemed in awe of the photos and asked, "Hey, Grandpa, are these real?"

Mark said, "Yeah, I'm 99% sure, anyway. You can read on the back of the pictures what was bombed and when."

Marcus flipped the picture he held and read, "Friday, April 4, 1945, munitions factory, Unterluss, Germany. It's kind of hard to read. The writing is a bit blurred."

He flipped the picture back over and looked at the smoke rising from the buildings. It appeared to his untrained eye that the mission had been a success.

"How did Great Grandpa get these?"

"Good question. Your Great Grandpa dropped those bombs from a B-17 bomber during World War II. He never spoke of the war to me or your aunts. I don't know if he ever said anything to your grandmother either. I just found out about all this in the last two days."

The younger Travers looked at Mark with stunned expressions. Silence filled the attic. Finally, Mark said, "I've been going through his footlocker. I'm learning things about my dad that I never knew."

Chapter 14

Mark told Elliot and Marcus about the footlocker and what he discovered so far. He mentioned the letters sent back and forth between his parents during Joe Traver's overseas deployment, and that he had just begun reading them. Impressed with the footlocker's contents, Marcus seemed to focus his attention on his great-grandfather's medals. He marveled at the weight and pristine condition of the awards, and that they had been stored with such care. He took a picture of each medal, planning to research what each one represented. Fascinated, he wanted to dig into the footlocker's contents further.

Just before noon, Simon Wilkes hollered up the stairs to Mark and said, "I'm finishing up. I wanted to ask a couple questions before I go."

"Alright, Simon, I'll be right down."

He turned to Elliot and Marcus and said, "Come on down when you finish rummaging through the footlocker. Try to not disturb the stacks of letters. They're in order by date. I need them to stay that way."

Elliot raised an eyebrow, wondering what his father learned over the last two days. He could not have read too many letters based on the things that he already accomplished on the estate. He replied, "Okay, Dad. We won't even touch them. If you find anything interesting, you can let us know."

Mark hustled down the steps to speak with the appraiser as the younger Travers turned their attention back to the footlocker. Marcus leafed through the pictures and found an envelope with his and his sisters yearly school pictures and copies of their report cards. He smiled at his grades, then laughed when he saw that his sister's grades were as good, or better than his. He showed his father the envelope's contents.

Elliot said, "I sent them to your great-granddad thinking that he would be proud of his family. I never heard back from him. He kept them here with his most prized possessions, so I have to believe that he was proud of you both."

Marcus looked at other envelopes, then frowned. "There's not very much here about my cousins. I would have thought that Aunt Maryanne and Aunt Caroline would send more pictures or something." He fell silent for a moment, then said, "They must have really hated great-grandpa."

The two men fell silent, beginning to wonder about the man who was their flesh and blood, but whom they never met.

***

Mark found Simon Wilkes standing inside the front door. His stone face did not convey anything good or bad relative to the value of his father's property. When Mark asked if the appraiser had finished, Simon replied that he needed to fill in a few forms and do some property comparisons, but that it would not take long to produce a final report.

"I'll send copies to Mr. Westridge. He will provide copies to you, your siblings, and your real estate agent."

"Can you give me a ballpark figure?"

"I really can't. We just don't do that anymore. We don't want to be held liable for tossing out a figure that we think might be close, then the owners aren't happy with the final report."

Mark shrugged his shoulders, not really concerned with the price. He asked, "When did you think your final report might be ready?"

Simon scrunched his face in thought and said, "It should be delivered to Mr. Westridge by Wednesday. You can contact him about mid-day. He can just tell you the final figure over the phone. Have you contracted with a real estate agent yet?"

"Yes. Clayton Biggs."

Simon almost smiled then said, "Clayton is good. If he has suggested a list price, I suspect that he'll be close to the figure that will ultimately be in my report."

"He said he would get back to me after you did your inspection, so I'll hear from him soon."

Simon asked, "Have you contracted with an auctioneer yet?"

"No. They'll be here Monday morning."

"I'll be watching the papers for the date. I saw your dad's tools. I may want to bid on a few things. Woodworking is one of my serious hobbies. Your dad has some great shop tools down there." He smiled then added, "How about that Mustang?"

Mark smiled. "I haven't decided what to do with that. I might keep it."

"I had to ask. That's a beautiful car."

The men shook hands and Simon hopped into his Mercedes and drove off.

****

When the appraiser left, Mark offered to take his son and grandson out for lunch at Berardi's Family Diner, a favorite of the locals. The parking lot neared capacity, but Mark figured it would be worth the wait. From his lunch experience the day before, he observed the quick turnover rate for diners. The staff did not rush you out the door, but once you left, dirty dishes did not sit long on the tables.

After being seated in the back dining area – Mark and his grandson on one side of the table, Elliot on the other side – the same waitress who had waited on Mark yesterday took their drink order and recommended the daily special; perch dinner. Even though Mark had a perch sandwich for dinner two days earlier, they all ordered the special, Marcus opting for a side salad instead of French fries. Once she served their drinks and left, he began to tell them of life in the Traver household. As the story unfolded for the younger Travers, what they heard left them speechless. They found it hard to believe that the elder Traver, their own flesh and blood, could be so cold.

Then Mark told them of the things he learned, albeit second hand, that his father had made a complete about-face. People who had spoken with Mark, those who knew his father, painted a picture of a happy, smiling man; a man seemingly without a care in the world.

Marcus asked, "What happened to great-grandma?"

Mark stopped instantly, a beer halfway to his mouth. He slowly set the bottle down and cleared his throat. He asked, "What do you know about your great-grandmother?"

Marcus shrugged his shoulders and, after a long pause, said, "Nothing. Literally, not one thing."

Mark looked at Elliot. He had a blank stare on his face as he shrugged his shoulders. Neither of them had a clue about Ada May Traver.

"Oh, boy. Your Great-grandma Ada May lived until she was forty-seven years old." He took a deep breath then continued. "Shortly after your Aunt Caroline moved out of the house, she killed herself."

Both younger Travers drew in deep breaths, shocked by the revelation. Elliot said, "Oh, God. Seriously?"

"I'm afraid so."

He asked, "Where did she do it?"

"In the basement of the Jay Street house. There's a room down there that used to be what is called the coal room. Before gas furnaces became available, everyone used coal to heat their homes. Delivery companies would shovel coal into the room through a metal door in the house's foundation. This happened long after Dad put in a gas furnace. By that time, the room wasn't being used for anything. Nobody knows why she did it."

Elliot said, "From what you said about living there, maybe she just couldn't take the doom and gloom atmosphere in the house. With you, Aunt Maryanne and Aunt Caroline gone, maybe she couldn't stand the thought of living alone with granddad."

Marcus just shook his head, deep in thought.

Their waitress showed up with their food and noticed the glum faces. With a bright smile she said, "Come on, guys. The food isn't that bad."

They laughed at the joke which helped to lighten the mood around the table.

After she left, Mark said, "No more negative talk. Let's enjoy these Lake Erie perch sandwiches. Are you planning to head back to Columbus later?"

Elliot said, "Is there anything we can help you with before we leave? It sounds like most of the grunt work will be handled by the auctioneer."

"That's true. But I want you to know I really appreciate you both coming up and offering to help. If you want, take another look around the house and see if there's anything else you might like. Dad's only hobbies seem to be working on cars and wood-working, so most everything of real value would be tools."

Elliot said, "We'll take a look around before we head out. In the mean time, if you think of anything else we can help with, let us know. I mean that."

Marcus nodded agreement.

They finished their dinners, Mark paying the bill over his son's objection. Once back at the house, the young men looked through the house. Marcus noticed the bookshelf in the den. He leafed through a couple books and said to Mark and Elliot, "I can't believe Great Grandpa was a J. T. Skipjack fan. He's my favorite author. I'd take a few books but I've read them all."

By mid-afternoon, the three men stood in the driveway, saying their goodbyes, with promises to stay in touch. As the younger Travers drove away, Mark had to take deep breaths to control his emotions.

***

Back in the attic, Mark picked up the next letter in the exchange between his mother and father. The one-page letter from his father to his mother, dated July 29, again had little in the way of emotion. It appeared to be a replay of his previous letter, describing the long hours, the difficulty of the course work, and hoping that she and their child remained healthy. He again commented that she should continue to see the doctor as a precaution.

Mark frowned. He wondered if the brevity indicated the level of stress that his father experienced. Even the words sounded as if fatigue had taken over. The idea of being assigned to a bomber, flying over enemy territory, dropping bombs on factories where civilians worked had to weigh on every airman's mind. He put the letter away and looked for his mother's reply.

The letter dated August 24, 1943 from Ada May had four pages. Her perfect handwriting conveyed great news.

My Dearest Joseph,

I miss you so much, darling. I pray every day and every night for your safe return. I can hear the exhaustion in your letters. The training must be extreme, but the world is in peril now. This hell, pardon my French, cannot go on. I know you must do your part, as you've committed to do. Just be safe and come home to us.

Our child is really growing now. There is no hiding my condition, as my bump strains and stretches my skin. I still have some morning nausea, but it is not as extreme as before and subsides quickly. I have an appointment with the doctor next week. I'm sure all will be fine. I can feel the baby move inside me at times. It is comforting, feeling the energy of a new life within me.

I have other news. When you come home, we will have our own home. I have rented a small home on Jay Street on the west side of town. It is not too far from downtown. Once the baby is born, I'll be able to walk the distance with a stroller to shop and enjoy the park and the Boy with the Boot fountain.

Ada May's letter went on in a cheerful tone. The prospect of moving into a new home away from her parents appeared to boost her mood. Then she wrote something that Mark did not expect.

I spoke with your dear friend, Lyle O'Conner, today. He asked about your health and about your training and when you were to be assigned to a mission. He has been a tremendous help in arranging the rental on Jay Street. He sends his regards.

That's all for now. I love you and miss you. Please come home safe.

Ada May

Mark wondered how his father might have taken the news that an old friend of his helped his wife in finding and moving into a new home. Could this be part of the rift that had formed between his parents?

Lyle O'Conner … *where did I hear that name?*

The hunting accident.

Chapter 15

After reading his mother's last letter, Mark had to go downstairs and get a beer. As he took sips from the longneck bottle, he walked through the first floor of the house, taking in as many details as possible. Every piece of furniture, from the couch with the large flower pattern, to the dark brown and orange, mis-matched chairs and all the scratched and scarred end tables and coffee table, looked like candidates for the landfill. He doubted the auctioneer would even consider putting them up for bid. Mark would wait to have that discussion when he arrived Monday morning.

He walked into what his father probably considered a den or family room. An old nineteen-inch, boxy TV sat on a pressboard cart in one corner of the room. The plaster walls displayed cracks that ran at odd angles from near the ceiling to the lower part of window casings on the front and side walls. All the cracks had been patched and painted over. The faded, light blue paint sported a layer of dust, some of which had been captured by cob webs that occupied every corner in the room.

Mark opened the drawer on an old roll-top desk. He found a handful of household bills in separate stacks; one for paid bills, the other for bills coming due. A checkbook sat next to the two stacks. He looked at the next available check and compared it to the check register and smiled. He knew few people who actively maintained their check registers, but Joe Traver did. This surprised him since Peggy Whipple had said his father seemed to be losing his will to live. *I guess Dad considered some things to be important in life, even to the end.* Mark looked through the drawer and cubby holes, looking for anything of value or any other surprises. There were none.

Mark moved into the kitchen, looking through cupboards and drawers. Aside from some newer looking pots and pans, nothing out of the ordinary popped up. He moved on to the laundry room then upstairs to each bedroom. Again, nothing of significance caught Mark's eye. Joseph Traver had few clothes; a few pairs of pants, one pair of dress shoes, and one pair of sneakers. The clothes in his dresser barely filled two drawers. He had no jewelry excepting an old Timex watch with a gold-plated wrist-band. In the closet he had one sports coat with an Air Force pin attached to the lapel, two pairs of pants and one dress shirt that had not been worn in ages.

In the master bath, Mark noted the usual toiletries. Nothing out of the ordinary. His father wore no cologne or after shave. He used shaving cream from an aerosol can and cavity control toothpaste. As did Mark, he used Old Spice original style deodorant. In the bathroom closet, an extra bath towel with matching hand towel and wash cloth sat alone on a shelf. The remaining shelves sat empty.

The one surprising aspect of the master bath; it had recently been remodeled. A vanity, sink, medicine cabinet, toilet, and tiled walk-in shower showed very little wear. The coating of paint appeared to be fresh. The entire space had been cleaned recently, a sharp contrast to the rest of the house. Mark wondered if the remodel had been for safety reasons as his father aged, or if the bathroom had suffered a plumbing failure requiring the upgrade. He might never know the answer.

Mark scratched his head, walked out into the hallway at the top of the stairs and sat on the top step. He had very little to show for his two-hour tour of the house. From Mark's perspective, his dad spent most of his time while at home in the garage or in the basement under the garage, either working on his car or his woodworking crafts.

He looked at his watch, surprised at the time; 6:45 p.m. He decided he wanted pizza for dinner. Walking downstairs to the kitchen he remembered that he had seen coupons for local businesses in one of the drawers. He pulled another beer from the refrigerator and unscrewed the top. He found the drawer and saw that there were coupons for two different pizza restaurants. He flipped a coin. Pizza House West won the toss. He called and asked for a medium deluxe pizza and a small chef's salad with ranch dressing for delivery. He was surprised at the low price and the quick delivery time. Completing arrangements for dinner, he moved to the dining room. The envelope with the note that his grandson had read before they left for lunch caught his attention. He pulled the note from the envelope as he sat at the table.

Dear Mr. Traver,

It was a sincere pleasure meeting you and getting to know you in person. Prior to your visits, mother, with a gleam in her eyes, spoke of you often. She had many fond memories of the man who befriended her at a time when most everyone around her treated her as if she might be contagious or a German spy. You helped guide her through a difficult time in her life so many years ago.

She mentioned that you had joined the Army Air Corps in 1943 and she never saw you again. When she off-handedly wondered if you had survived the war, I decided to find out more about you. Imagine my surprise to learn that you lived within twenty minutes of my mother. I was so pleased that you accepted my invitation and took the time to visit mother. Your visits, I believe, extended her life and made these last years her most joyous.

Thank you again, from the bottom of my heart. I hope to one day meet your son. From what you have told me, and knowing that he is in your family tree, he must be a fine man.

I wish I could repay you for the joy you have given our family, but the kindness you showed my mother was beyond measure. The gift of your time, the time that you spent with my mother, was simply priceless.

God bless you, Mr. Traver.
Most Sincerely,
Emma Franks

Mark sat, stunned by the note in his hands. He wondered when his father had known Emma Franks' mother and if their relationship may have caused friction in his parents' relationship. Mark thought back to his mother's first letter to his father after he had reported for military training. His mother remarked that "the circumstances of their marriage not being ideal." Did she give his father an ultimatum; either me or the other woman? Maybe Emma's mother had a strong accent, or perhaps she did not deny it when asked about her German citizenship.

Mark reread the note then set it on the China cabinet. He felt alone, wishing that he had asked his son and grandson to stay … for company, if nothing else. He had been in Sandusky for just over two days. He missed his wife. The urge to call her overwhelmed him but he wanted time to clear his mind and settle his emotions. Too much information swirled in his brain, much more than he could sort out and compartmentalize.

Taking a long pull on his beer, he pressed a button on his cell phone; the speed-dial number for his wife, Denise. When she answered with a soft and sultry, "Hello, Darling," he nearly broke down in tears, but managed to maintain control.

"Hi, Sweetheart."

"Is everything alright? You sound … stressed."

"I'm fine, honey." Hearing her soft, soothing voice helped calm him. He said, "Elliot and Marcus were here earlier. They offered to stay and help with the estate, but there really isn't much to do right now. I think the auctioneer will handle most of the grunt work."

"Elliot called just a little while ago. He said you were … I think he said, confused about your dad. You heard some things from his friends and neighbors?"

Mark smiled and said, "Elliot snitched on me? The rat."

Denise replied, "He's worried about you. He thinks you're blaming yourself for isolating your dad, not introducing him to the rest of the family."

"Well, he's probably not wrong. Honey, it's like these

people are describing a complete stranger, some good Samaritan."

"I told Elliot about the times when we visited the house just before we married and how uncomfortable I was just sitting there with you, your mom, and your dad; how they never spoke to each other or us. I hated going to your parent's house. We never told the kids about that so they have no idea what kind of life you lived before moving out. I let him know that you weren't exaggerating. He didn't blame you or anything like that. I think he's really worried about you."

Torn between laughing and crying, Mark said, "I'll call him later. I appreciate his concern."

"Have you been eating?"

In a sarcastic tone, he said, "Yes, Mom." Then in his normal conversational voice said, "I have a pizza coming anytime now. And I have beer in the fridge."

A loud knock sounded on the front door. He continued to talk with his wife as he made his way to the vestibule. He said, "Hang on for a second, honey, I think my pizza is here."

He put the phone and his beer on an end table next to a chair by the vestibule. He pulled out his wallet, took out enough cash for the bill plus a generous tip, and opened the door. A bearded man of about forty stood on the stoop with an insulated delivery pouch and a small grocery bag.

"Mr. Traver. Medium deluxe and a small chef's salad?"

"That's right. Come on in."

They entered the living room and Mark helped get the pizza out of the pouch. Mark expected the man to take the money and turn to leave, but instead he said, "You're Mark, right?"

Mark eyed him with a bit of suspicion. "That's right."

"You look exactly like your dad, if you shave twenty years off him." He paused as if gathering his thoughts then said, "I want you to know, he was one of my favorite delivery stops. He ordered from us about once a month." A sad look came over this total stranger as he said in a bit of a weepy voice, "We're going to miss him."

Mark's jaw nearly hit the floor. He started to wonder who in town did not know his dad? Shaking his head slightly, he said in a choked-up voice, "Thank you."

He held out the cash for the order but the delivery man waved him off. "We all decided that this one's on all of us. Call us again if you need anything. We all mean that." He paused again and said, "We'll look for the funeral notice in the paper. We all want to say our good-byes."

As the man turned, Mark asked, "What's your name?"

"Jay Miller. Our owner's name is Danny Balken. He was a friend of your dad. They played cards together and he went hunting with your dad once."

Mark had to clear his throat before saying, "Thanks, Jay … really, thanks."

He closed the door behind Jay, looked up at the ceiling, feelings of guilt beginning to creep into his mind. Had he really been fair to his father? He blamed his father for the conditions around the Traver household as he and his sisters grew to adulthood? Should he have confronted his parents and asked them why they were always so miserable around each other? During most of that time, he and his sisters were just kids. Who were they to bring up such a potentially explosive topic?

Mark almost forgot that his wife was on the phone. He hoped she had not hung up. He picked up the phone and asked, "Honey, you still there?"

"What was that all about? I couldn't hear most of the conversation, but it sounded like the pizza delivery guy knew your dad?"

"Yeah. It's getting really weird, honey." Mark paused then said, "Maybe you should come up. You can see this for yourself."

"I'll see when I can get a flight."

"Let me know. I'll pick you up when you get in."

When the call disconnected, Mark ate then headed to the attic. He hoped those letters in the footlocker held the answers he sought.

Chapter 16

Sunday morning, May 10, proved to be everything the weatherman on Fox News out of Cleveland, Ohio said it would be. A cloudless sky with a bright sun rising in the east promised a rising temperature later in the day, but a cool, crisp start during the mid-morning hours.

Mark ate at the breakfast buffet offered by the hotel. He steered clear of the "D" shaped omelets and opted for two cups of coffee, an English muffin with peanut butter and honey, and a banana. Being up early on a Sunday morning proved to be a habit Mark followed, even on this trip. The constant churning of thoughts in his mind made the early rise at 6:00 a.m. easier than at home. Being newly retired, he could not break the cycle of waking at an early hour while staying awake until near midnight. He figured that he averaged between five to six hours sleep, below the federal government's recommended seven or more hours, but his routine proved hard to break.

The previous nights abbreviated sleep had been fueled by his discussions with Jay Miller, the pizza delivery man, and with his wife, Denise. He hoped to hear about her flight plans later today. He told her to avoid a Monday morning flight, that it would conflict with his meeting with the auctioneer. Flights today, or Monday afternoon would be ideal.

Mark attended Mass at Holy Angels Catholic Church, less than a mile from the Jay Street house. He parked at the house and walked to the church, taking a route that took him past several kid's ballparks, the Cholera Cemetery, Pizza House West, an old antiques-curiosities shop, and a bar that was in business even when he lived in town. The morning walk proved relaxing, an elixir to help him think clearly about all that he had learned since arriving in town Wednesday afternoon.

He thought back to his childhood when he and his friends would play pick-up baseball games at the ball diamonds, or run through the Cholera Cemetery, having no knowledge of the cholera outbreak of 1849, which decimated the city's population. Nearly ten percent of the inhabitants of Sandusky perished with many more fleeing the area.

The previous night, he read several more letters between his parents. The length and tone of the letters settled into a mundane exchange, more of a news update than messages of affection and devotion between two lovers.

The only thing in the letters that raised Mark's curiosity; his mother again mentioned Lyle O'Conner as being helpful in getting her moved and settled into the new house. Her words appeared to Mark to be a bit too enthusiastic about his assistance. In his reply, Mark's father asked why Lyle remained at home while all his friends were out fighting the war. That made Mark wonder if future letters might become more tense. He again recalled that his father's attorney described how Lyle O'Conner had died in a hunting accident and that his father had been "cleared" in the incident. He wondered just how friendly Lyle O'Conner became with his mother during his father's absence.

He reached the church and admired the structure from across the street. The church building looked much the same as he remembered, built of quarried sandstone with a severely pitched roof. The beauty of the church came from the stained-glass windows on the sides and front of the structure. Mark knew that the appearance of the windows from the outside did not do justice to the way they looked from inside the sanctuary when light shined through the windows. The splendor of colors and the beautiful images the saints depicted ignited a person's senses. One could not help but to look in awe at the stain-glass images portrayed in each window.

He made his way across Tiffin Avenue and followed other church-goers into the new entrance to the left of the original building. During the 1990s a renovation connected the church and the gym, adding church offices and a gathering room to the campus. Mark smiled as he noted the new construction blended well with the older sandstone of the original church and the newer brick of the gymnasium.

As he walked in along with a small crowd of people, a greeter smiled and reached out a hand and said, "Welcome to Holy Angels, Mark."

Mark stopped and asked, "How do you know my name?" He paused but before the man could answer, he said, "Don't tell me. I look just like my father."

The man wore a name tag – Danny Balken. "Well, yeah, you do. He was a good friend. We're dedicating a Mass to him on Wednesday if you'd like to attend."

"I'd like that. You're the owner of Pizza House West. Right?"

"Yeah. Jay told me he spoke with you last night."

"If you have time in the next few days, I'd like to talk with you about my father."

With a bright smile, Danny replied, "I'd like that." He reached into his sports coat and handed Mark a card. "Call me anytime."

Mark took the card, looked at it briefly and shook Danny's hand again as the pace of churchgoers behind him entering the sanctuary increased. He pocketed the card and moved into the church. He took his seat in a pew near the back of the church and knelt. He thought about his dad and asked God to be kind to his father's soul. He thought about his wife, then his children and grandchildren, his sisters, nieces, and nephews. He wondered if his relationship with his sisters could be resurrected, not that a good relationship with them ever existed. He said a short prayer for peace, not in the world, or even in the country … but in his heart and mind. He took a deep breath, made the Sign of the Cross and sat back in the old oak pew. He noted that they were the same pews he sat in as a child when he attended school at Holy Angels Elementary. He smiled at the thought.

A hand lightly touched his shoulder. He turned and looked into the elderly face of the priest in his green robes. He appeared to be in his late eighties. An altar boy and girl held tall candles, nervously looking around. Behind them, a layman held the challis, a beautiful gold goblet, in front of his chest, preparing to walk up the main aisle of the sanctuary.

"Hello, Mark," the priest said in a baritone voice that carried a bit over the din of the crowd. "I'm Father Nicholas Shultz. You can call me Father Nick."

Mark started to stand to shake the priest's hand, but he said, "No, stay seated. You'll be standing, kneeling, and sitting enough in a little bit." The music for the beginning of the ceremony started, a guitarist and singer belting out a tune that Mark did not recognize. Father Nick said, "I know you're busy with your father's estate, but can you stick around for a few minutes after Mass? You can just wait for me here if you like."

"Sure, Father. I can do that."

"Wonderful."

He turned to the altar attendants, smiled, and said, "Let's rock and roll."

The children smiled as the procession moved down the aisle in a slow gait as the ceremony began. Mark watched the crowd around him, not remembering when to stand, sit, or kneel. He noticed that many of the responses were different since his last attendance in church many decades ago. But he muddled his way through the Mass, not too embarrassed by anything he said out of synch with the rest of the congregation.

At the end of Mass, he remained seated in the pew as the crowd paraded towards the exit. Several patrons stopped and offered condolences, a few making comments on what a fine man his father had been. Others asked about funeral arrangements. Mark still awaited word regarding his father's interment from Dylan Hart, so he could not give anyone a definitive answer.

A few minutes after the last patron left the sanctuary, Father Nick walked back in from the hall to the church entrance. He smiled and said, "I'm glad you joined us today,

Mark. Let me get into my street clothes and we can chat for a little bit."

Mark followed the priest to the front of the church by the altar. In just a few minutes, Father Nick came out of the room and they walked to the parish home. The priest gestured to a comfortable chair in a room that looked more like a den than a priest's office. After offering a drink, which Mark declined, the priest told Mark what a tremendous asset his father had been to the parish. A top tier donor, and a volunteer for many programs, at least in his younger years.

"Your father fostered many friendships. Did you know that he helped pay the heating bill for a family who fell on hard times when the economy took a bad turn? The father lost his job and they just couldn't make ends meet. The Parish helped with food and some other necessities, but your dad insisted that he pay that bill. He would not accept repayment from the family. He told them to help someone else in need if the opportunity ever arose and they were able to help."

Mark sat in silence as Father Nick told the story about his dad. He did not know what to say. The priest went on to tell Mark a few more stories of his father's good deeds. Then he said, "I know your home situation was not … ideal when you were growing up. I was a new priest at that time, ordained for just a few months. Holy Angels was my first assignment. I spoke with your father and mother about life in the Traver home, separately and together. They both described the same situation, though from different perspectives, of course. But they both knew that the environment you grew up in was unhealthy – not from a physical standpoint. I have every reason to believe that you and your sisters did not suffer physically. But from a mental health standpoint, by today's standards, it might have bordered on child abuse."

Mark sat stunned. He wondered how many others knew about his home life. What exactly had his parents said and to whom did they say it?

Mark asked, "So, do you know why Mom and Dad were always so miserable?"

"I can only surmise, based on what each told me." Father Nick remained silent. Mark had time to think about what he heard, then the priest asked, "Do you know how your mother died?"

"Yes." He took a deep breath an anguished expression overtaking his face, his body tensing. "She sent me a letter describing what she planned to do. By the time I received the letter, she had already done exactly what she wrote in her letter. The envelope also contained her hand-written obituary. Apparently, she wrote it before she killed herself."

Father Nick looked down at the floor. He said, "She went to confession the day she died. I cannot divulge what she confessed, but I did everything within my power and within the rules of my vocation to keep her from committing a mortal sin. Nothing I did or said changed her mind." A moment of silence ensued, then the priest said, "I am supremely sorry, Mark, for all that you and your sisters endured. I have been praying that your parent's mistakes did not ruin your lives."

Mark simply nodded. He stood, thanked Father Schultz for his time, and walked back to the Jay Street house, the short trip far less pleasant than the walk to the church. He barely noticed the cars, the trees, the cats that played in a driveway along Tiffin Avenue. The cool breeze chilled him as he passed the ice cream store. The aroma of pizza sauce rode the air from Pizza House West.

He hoped that his wife booked a flight for this evening. He needed the company and, maybe another set of eyes to sift through the calamity of his family's life.

Chapter 17

After arriving at the Jay Street House, Mark immediately climbed the steps to the attic, the words of Father Schultz still pinging around in his head. The priest knew that Mark's parents' relationship suffered and he knew why, but he could not provide the details, or even his personal opinion, as to the cause. Again, he wondered who else knew of the family's dysfunction. He and his sisters knew because they lived through it, but did the neighbors? According to Mrs. Holtzmiller, she knew that something was not right at the Traver house, but reluctant to come out and tell everything that she knew. Would the letters between his parents provide the answers? So far, they appeared to be nothing more than normal communications between husband and wife.

Mark grabbed the two bundles of letters and headed downstairs to the dining room, tension causing his muscles to tighten. He wondered if his wife purchased her ticket for the trip from Florida to Ohio. He knew she would call as soon as she made the arrangements. He nearly slipped on the stairs as his concentration shifted back to the letters in his hands. After regaining his balance, he took the last three steps slowly, then turned into the dining room. He took a seat and placed the bundles of envelopes on the table then stepped into the kitchen and grabbed a beer. Returning to the dining room, he looked through the stacks and found the letter from his father dated December 27, 1943, the last letter that he read. His father had requested emergency leave to be home for the birth of his child, but the request had been denied. No one would be granted leave during the German's offensive.

Mark picked up the next letter from his mother, dated January 17, 1944, three days after his and Maryanne's birthday.

My Dearest Joseph,

Congratulations daddy. That's right, you are a father. I gave birth to a healthy baby girl on January 14. She is beautiful with a head full of hair. She already opens her eyes and looks around. She is eating well and has already gained a few ounces. The doctor expects that we'll be going home today or tomorrow. I have to line up some help for the next week or so, but after that, I should be able to handle things on my own. I have received gifts of diapers, towels, and clothes for our little girl.

Mark stopped, confused, and reread the first paragraph. There was no mention of a second baby, a baby boy … him. He rolled his head around on his shoulders, trying to loosen the tightness that had formed in the back of his neck.

How can this be? He read the first part of the letter a third time, still in disbelief. He continued to read on.

We should discuss names. I've thought of several. I especially like Maryanne. What do you think? If you have other ideas, please let me know as soon as possible. I have to fill in the birth certificate information soon.

I'm so sorry that you were not able to get leave and come home for your daughter's birth, but I know you will be here as soon as you're able. This gives you another reason to stay safe and return home to us as soon as possible, as soon as you are able.

The letter continued, putting her husband's mind at ease about financial matters. According to his mother, money was no longer an issue. She did not elaborate. The letter closed with:

I love you and miss you every day. Our little girl will keep me company until your return.

Ada May

After several minutes, Mark read the letter again in its entirety, wondering if he had misread his mother's words. But he had not. The words did not change. So, where did he come from? Was he delivered several days later, a secret baby, refusing to come out along with his sister? That seemed far-fetched.

He picked up the next letter in the sequence from his father dated January 31, 1944. He unfolded the one-page reply.

My Dear Ada May,

I am so pleased to hear of the birth of our dear daughter, Maryanne. The name you selected is perfect. I'm sure she is as precious and perfect as you described. It is so wonderful that she is healthy and growing and alert. I can't wait to see her in person.

School is becoming more intense, but that can wait for another time. It is time to celebrate and be filled with joy at our growing family.

Love,

Joe

Mark reread his father's reply again, wondering if his father's classes zapped him of his energy. The lack of passion along with the brevity of the letter had Mark thinking. His father must be getting closer to assignment to a bomber group actively engaged in the war. He thought back to the pictures of his father with the flight crews, standing in front of a monstrous B-17 flying fortress. He now faced the added pressure of a newborn to pull his mind away from his studies. Being in his early twenties, that level of anxiety had to be overwhelming. Mark wondered how he could put together a string of sentences, much less show his wife just how much he loved her.

He took a drink from his beer, thinking about his mother's letter, still troubled by the knowledge that his mother gave birth to only one baby. He wanted to keep reading the letters, but decided he needed a break. He looked at his watch. Time to try some of Mrs. Holtzmiller's casserole. He pushed his chair back and stood, noticing the next letter from his mother on top of the pile. He looked at the date – January 31 – the same date as his father's reply. *Mom sent this letter before she received dad's last letter. They crossed in the mail.* He picked up the envelope, pulled out the single page letter, unfolded it and began reading. There was no salutation:

That woman, Ingrid Engel, came by the house today. She handed me a baby boy swaddled in blankets and said he is your son. She had the original birth certificate naming you as the father. She said she was sorry but she was in no position to care for the child and since you were now married and had a child near the same age, that you would take responsibility for the boy and give him a loving home. She said his name is Mark.

His name will remain Mark. She gave birth to your son on January 17. He is healthy from everything I can see.

Oh God, Joseph. How could you? You swore to me that this girl just needed a friend! How will I explain this to our friends and neighbors? To my family? To yours?

Since this is not the child's fault and he is apparently your son, I will care for him as long as necessary.

Ada May

Mark collapsed back into the chair, stunned and near tears. He reread the letter, tears blurring his eyes. Everything he assumed about his entire life changed in an instant. He now knew with sudden clarity why his parents acted like adversaries. How could his father have functioned under this new pressure? How did he father a child – *him* - out of wedlock? Did he have an affair? Thinking back on previous letters between his parents, they seemed happy under the current situation, him off to fight a war, her alone, either pregnant or with an infant child. In her first letter, his mother alluded to the circumstances of their marriage. He did not understand what she meant. Certainly, she did not realize that she would be placed in a position of taking care of another woman's child.

Not hers. She was never my real mother. No wonder she never really acknowledged me. She must have hated that I lived in her home, the son of another woman. How had she tolerated me all those years ... the way I treated her? It is amazing that she hadn't turned around and blurted out the truth ... that my real mother abandoned me to a complete stranger.

Exhausted by the onslaught of information, Mark folded his arms on the table and laid his head down. He fell asleep thinking about his parents. He now knew the reason for the discord in his early family life. His mind needed a break.

While he slept, his brain continued to churn, grinding through information that ran opposed to everything he thought he previously knew. He dreamed about riding along in a B-17 bomber, heading towards the enemy targets with a load of bombs. He looked aft in the planes belly, observing the payload that they would soon drop on the German war machine, hoping to cause sufficient damage to get the Nazis to surrender.

He looked out the front of the plane at the glass dome that gave him a bird's eye view of the land in front of the plane and below. As he watched, enemy antiaircraft fire picked up, ordinance exploded in front of their plane, causing the whole fuselage of the aircraft to quake. Swarms of enemy fighters filled the sky. One of the bombers in their group took a hit and exploded, falling from the sky.

Mark pictured himself manning the machine guns in the navigator's bay of the aircraft and began firing at a Messerschmidt as it made a run at one of the American bombers. Mark's movements felt as if he had lead blankets over his arms. He could not seem to get his aim ahead of the fighters. Then he saw a fighter coming straight at him, bearing down on his plane. The German's guns began to strafe his plane, an emergency bell sounded in his ears. The Pilot yelled over his headset, Mayday! Mayday! The bell sounded again, louder this time.

He awoke with a start, his head jerking off the table. His cell phone rang a third time. He took a deep breath and looked at the screen. His wife, Denise.

He swiped across the screen and in a shaky voice said, "Hello."

"You sound terrible. Did I wake you?"

"Yeah. Yeah, you did."

"Well, the cavalry's coming. I have my ticket for a flight tomorrow. I'll be landing in Cleveland at 2:30 p.m. Delta."

"I'll be there, Dear. I'll pick you up at the 'arrivals' doors. Just call when you have your luggage in hand."

"Mark, you don't sound like yourself. What's going on?"

"I'll tell you all about it on the drive to Sandusky. It explains a lot. At the same time, I don't know, hon … I just don't know."

"I love you, Sweetheart. I'm on my way."

"I love you, too. See you tomorrow."

Chapter 18

Mark Traver sat at his father's dining room table for nearly an hour, an overwhelming dread draining his energy. What he believed about his family history lay in shambles in the letters on the table in front of him. He had known his biological father. They lived in the same house together, though they never really interacted well as father and son. But his biological mother's identity? A complete mystery. Maybe the letters between his father and his – step mother, stand-in mother *What should I call her now?* - held further clues, but his desire to read them waned, his brain now on overload, a touch of depression settling in.

He stood and stepped into the kitchen to grab another beer, but he finished the last beer earlier with lunch. Thinking a walk in the cool, spring breeze might do his frame of mind some good, he exited the house and headed the three blocks towards Dick's Carryout. On the way, a man and a woman smiled and waved from across the street. He waved back and wondered if they had known his father and if they knew the secrets that were just now revealed to him. He shook his head, telling himself he sounded like a conspiracy theorist.

Approaching the store, he noted the State of Ohio Licensed Liquor Outlet sign. He thought that a bottle of Seagrams V.O. might be the medicine he needed right now. He walked into the store, the bright fluorescent lights nearly hurting his eyes. He walked into the back room where liquor lined the shelves. He picked up a fifth of the booze, then went to the cooler and selected a six-pack of lemon soda (called pop, since he was in Ohio) and a twelve pack of Miller Lite. He walked up to the counter just as Peggy Whipple came out of the cooler to man the register.

With a smile, she said, "Hi, Mark." She noted the drawn expression on his face, then saw the beer and booze on the counter. "Problems with the estate?"

Mark looked up and forced a smile. He raised his eyebrows and thought for a moment, then said, "I wish it was that simple." He took a deep breath then said, "I just found out something … well, I don't want to say too much right now."

Peggy looked down at the whiskey and asked, "I didn't know you were a drinker."

"I'm usually not." He paused, his face twisting as if he had just swallowed a lemon, then said, "Maybe this isn't such a great idea."

Peggy smiled. "I just met you and I'm not judging. Randy and I can come over if you need some help going through stuff … or just to visit."

Mark smiled, a little weight lifting from his shoulders. He picked up the whiskey bottle and turned as if to return it. Peggy said, "Leave it. I'll take it back. You still want the pop?"

"No, thanks. And, Peggy, thank you. I think that might have been a big mistake."

"Listen, your dad helped Randy and me when we were having a rough spot in our marriage." She paused as if weighing her next words, then said, "He told me that he and your mom made some mistakes in their marriage and it cost him dearly. He wanted to help us not make similar mistakes." She cleared her throat and seemed to choke up a bit then said, "He really helped us see things clearly. I don't know where we'd be right now if not for your dad."

As Peggy rang up the beer, Mark wondered what Peggy knew of his family's history. Would she know that his mother was not his biological mother? He asked, "How about if I treat you and Randy to dinner tonight? I'll order something in. Is there a good Mexican restaurant in town?"

"We'll take care of it. Anything special, or anything that you don't want?"

"As long as it isn't too spicy, I'm good."

Peggy smiled and said, "Okay, we'll be there around six."

He did not even have to force the smile on his face this time.

***

Seeing Peggy at the store helped restore some of the energy he lost reading his mother's letter. Back at the Jay Street house, Mark sat at the dinner table and picked up the next letter from his father, dated February 14, 1944; Valentines Day. He expected that it would not be filled with hearts, love, and kisses. He slowly unfolded the three-page letter and read:

Dear Ada May,

I hardly know what to say. I had no idea that Ingrid had become pregnant, or that she would meet with you, especially to saddle you with another child, one that is not yours. I am so sorry that you have been further burdened with a second child, but even more that you now must face your family, my family, and your friends with an explanation of this unexpected child. But it gives me even more reason to get home to you, safe.

I know you must be quite angry and hurt, but remember that we were not together for nearly three months prior to our hastily arranged marriage. You found out that you were pregnant with Maryanne and came to me, asking that I do "the right thing" and take responsibility for our child, which I was happy to do. I still loved you and still do to this day.

You must also remember that it was you who broke off our engagement based on rumors and gossip of my "relationship" with Ingrid. I had no intention of becoming intimately involved with her. I just wanted to help a frightened girl gain her footing in a strange country full of hateful people. She was as much a victim of Hitler's war as the rest of the world. Her parents sent her to America to get away from that madman, to keep her safe. What she found was a country full of people who blamed her for the war. It was unfair. I only wanted to help her find people who empathized with her, who would help protect her from being deported back to a country she feared. She had hopes that her parents could join her here in the United States, but she lost contact with them. She was alone without any support.

I cannot and will not apologize for befriending her. When you sent me away, Ingrid returned the support that I had offered her. Naturally, we became close. It was because of the void in my heart that you created.

We must put that behind us now. There is too much at stake to allow this to tear us apart again. I must complete my studies and take on whatever assignment the Army Air Corps gives me. I cannot afford any distractions. My life, and the lives of those whom will be my crewmates depends on it.

Please assure me that you will care for infant Mark the same as you will care for Maryanne. I know this is asking so much more than I can put into words. You will have to set aside your animosity towards me for what you see as a betrayal. Please, please do it for us and for our children. I believe it is for the best. I hope you can see that as well.

All my love,

Joe

Mark reread the letter again, moved by his father's words. He believed they fell on deaf ears, based on the way his parents lived during his youth. Not only did his mother not treat him with love, she treated his sisters, her biological daughters, as badly as him.

He looked for his mother's letter in response, but none existed. The next letter in the chronologic order was again from his father to his mother.

Dear Ada May,

It worries me that you have not replied to my last letter. I know you are hurt, angry, overwhelmed — maybe all of these feelings and more – but I hope that you are taking my advice and treating both our children with love and care.

Please, Ada May, our love can endure if we let it. We must do what is right for the children, but more importantly, we must do what is right for us.

All my love,

Joe

Mark wondered if there might be a letter missing from the bundle. According to his father's letter above, his mother did not reply. He decided to look in the footlocker and see if there might be letters that slipped from the bundles. He did not remember seeing anything out of place, but he thought it best to check.

He looked at his watch – 5:14 p.m. Peggy and Randy should be over in about forty-five minutes. That should be plenty of time to take a quick inventory of the items in the footlocker. He bounded up the steps and leaned over the trunk. Removing the tray, the boxes of medals, and the larger envelopes, he did not see any stray envelopes. But something caught his eye.

A leather tab in the front center at the bottom of the footlocker stood out about an inch from the inner wall. Mark pulled the tab, but it did not move. He pulled harder and the entire bottom of the footlocker began to slide upward. He removed the remaining contents of the trunk, reached down and gave the leather tab a strong pull. A false bottom lifted and swung to the back side of the trunk. This exposed a two-inch-deep compartment, which held another bundle of letters and a ten-inch by twelve-inch envelope with no writing on the outside.

Mark picked up the new bundle of letters and read the envelope on top. Dated May 5, 1943, the letter to his father was from Ingrid Engel, Mark's biological mother.

The doorbell rang. Mark took a deep breath, placed the bundle of letters back in the footlocker, and headed downstairs to answer the door. Peggy and Randy stood on the stoop with bags from El Grande Patron, the Mexican restaurant, in hand.

Peggy said, "They were quick with our order. We hope it's okay that we're early."

Mark smiled and waved them in. He said, "Put the bags on the dining room table, grab a beer, and make yourselves at home. We have a lot to talk about."

This surprised both of his guests who looked at him with a questioning expression. They moved past him.

Peggy headed for the dining room. Randy said, "I'll grab the beer. From the look on your face, this ought to be good."

They ate, cleared the table, then sat for hours, talking about the Traver family. Mark surmised that they suspected something was off with his parents' relationship, though they were too young to experience it first-hand. Their view developed from what Joseph Traver told them during their own marital difficulties.

Randy smiled and said, "Your old man, he opened my eyes to what I couldn't see was right in front of me." He looked at Peggy and smiled, then turned back to Mark. "You know, the little things in life are irritating. The more the little things build up without being resolved, they turn into big things, at least that's how we saw them. In reality, it's just a bunch of little crap that, if you use your head, is easy to resolve." He turned back to Peggy again. "After your dad taught us how to clear out the junk, we fell in love all over again."

Peggy blushed and took her husband's hand. "It's true. We don't let the little things build up anymore. We're brutally honest with each other. And we say some things that would surprise most couples, maybe even shock them, but you have to get it out in the open. You do that, it's smooth sailing. It's not *all* fun and games, but life sure gets better."

Randy said, "Your dad taught us that. He said it was based on his and your mother's experience. He told us how bad life was when you lived here with them. I'm sorry for that. I hope life with your own family isn't like that."

"You'll be able to hear it first-hand. Denise is flying up. I'm picking her up at the airport in Cleveland tomorrow afternoon.

Randy and Peggy both smiled. She said, "I can't wait to meet her."

Chapter 19

Mark arrived at the Jay Street house by 8:30 a.m., one half hour before his meeting with the auctioneer. The morning sky sported thin, gray clouds that posed no rain threat, but caused the morning to appear darker than yesterday at this time. The air smelled fresh with a comfortable level of humidity. According to the auctioneer, Arthur Wexley, his work would take about two hours, but if he needed more time, he could come back another day to finish the job. Most of the time would be spent cataloguing the larger items, and anything of significant value. Mark let him know that he had to leave for Cleveland Hopkins Airport by 1:30 p.m. to pick up his wife, whose flight would be arriving at 2:30 p.m. if all went according to schedule.

At 8:40 a.m., Mark stood in the ancient kitchen preparing to add water to the new coffee maker he had purchased the day after he arrived in Sandusky. After filling the pot and shutting the cold-water spigot, water continued to drip. He tried to shut the valve tighter, but the drip persisted. *The sooner we get this place sold the better.* He shook his head and started to pour water into the coffee machine when his cell phone's ringtone sounded. He looked at the screen and saw a familiar number, but he could not remember the owner. He answered, "Mark Traver."

"Hi, Mark, Clayton Biggs here."

The realtor. *I just signed the papers the other day.*

"Hey, Clayton. How are you?"

"I'm good. I have good news, at least I hope it's good. We have an offer on the property. I'd like to present it to you today, if possible."

Mark shook his head in surprise. He took a deep breath. "What do you mean 'you hope' it's good news?"

"I can explain that when we meet."

"Okay. When did you have in mind?"

"I'm ten minutes away if you're at the house. I can be there before 9:00."

"Yeah, yeah, great. That'll work. I'm at the house now. I'll have a cup of coffee waiting for you. The auctioneer will be here about that same time. I hope you don't mind working around his meeting."

The realtor chuckled. "That won't be a problem. And coffee would be great. See you in a few minutes."

The realtor beat the auctioneer by two minutes. Mark settled Clayton in at the dining room table with a fresh cup of coffee when the doorbell rang. Right on time, Arthur Wexley stood on the stoop, a folder under his arm, looking more like a home remodel contractor than an auctioneer. He introduced himself in a baritone voice that Mark thought fit the man perfectly for his profession. Wexley said, "We spoke on the phone, but it is nice to meet you in person. Please call me Art. I'm sorry about the circumstances with your father's death, but that's not unusual in my line of work."

He could picture the man conducting an auction while walking around the house, not needing a microphone as his voice boomed out over a crowd. Short and stout in stature, the man did not smile or frown, but projected an air of neutrality. Mark invited Wexley into the living room and they shook hands. He hovered over the auctioneer by about five inches which made it easy for him to see the bald patch at the top-back side of the man's head as he looked around the room, already surveying the furniture. The thick salt and pepper hair that adorned the sides of his head stood out, nearly covering his ears.

"Thanks, Art. I appreciate your working me in on short notice."

"Not a problem, Mark. It's what we do. What I'll do today is perform the inventory of goods. The larger items, like furniture, lawn equipment, kitchen appliances, I'll record and determine the fair market value for each item. These are used items, so you can't expect much from their sale, but if there are other items of value, we will contact dealers who specialize in those areas. Examples are gold coins, rare coin collections, cars, particularly older cars. The small things, like hand tools, we'll get a ballpark figure and sell those in lots."

"Sounds good to me, Art. Most of the furniture is worn out, as you can see." He gestured around the living room at the decrepit furniture. "But there are some things in the garage that will have more value. Do you need me to walk around with you?"

"No, no. I'll go room by room and take stock of everything. Anyplace that you want me to avoid?"

"Nope. You have free reign. Let me get the keys to the garage. If you have any questions, I'll be in the dining room or up in the attic."

"Before I leave, I'll have you sign an agreement to officially hire me."

They shook hands again and Art Wexley opened his notebook and began writing. Mark turned and made his way to the kitchen where he scooped up the garage keys. Back in the living room, he handed them to Art as he made his way towards the den. Then he walked back to the dining room where Clayton Biggs had a short stack of papers sitting next to a folder on the table. He stood, but Mark motioned him back to his seat.

"More coffee?"

"No thanks. I get too wired if I have more than a couple cups in the morning. Then I crash by midafternoon." He gestured to the top form on the table. "Let me show you this offer."

Mark sat next to the realtor. Clayton lifted one sheet off the stack and said, "I'm required to present this offer within twenty-four hours. I just received it this morning, so I'm getting this to you faster than necessary."

Mark raised a questioning eyebrow.

"The reason I wanted to get this to you is because I know you don't want to spend a lot of time in Ohio and it isn't a bad offer. Follow along with me. I'll stop at the important points."

Clayton walked Mark through the entirety of the offer. They were not offering the full asking price, but it was not a low-ball offer. The reason for Clayton's rush to get the offer to Mark? The buyer would pay cash, bypassing many of the standard time-consuming steps in the closing process. The potential buyer hoped to have a closing within three weeks.

Mark sat back in his chair, took a deep breath, and rubbed his face with both hands, trying to think if that would be possible from his perspective.

He asked Clayton, "Do you know what their plans are for the property? I'm not being nosey. I'm just wondering about their motivation for the quick closing."

"The folks making the offer are flippers. They take distressed properties or properties that they can buy at a bargain, renovate them, then put them back on the market and, hopefully, turn a profit. This offer is higher than I thought it would be. I've dealt with them before. They're very reliable and good at what they do."

Mark rubbed his chin, deep in thought. Clayton let him think.

"Can I counter the offer?"

"You can counter the offer in any way you want. You can ask for more time, you can ask for a higher price, you can ask if they want to keep the appliances. Pretty much anything."

"How long do I have to respond to the offer?"

"Twenty-four hours." Clayton paused, giving Mark more time to contemplate the offer.

Mark rubbed his chin, deep in thought, then picked up his coffee cup and took a sip. He said, "Here's what I want to do. I need to let my sisters know about the offer and I want to contact Allen Westridge, Dad's attorney, to see if he has any concerns."

Clayton nodded. "I know Allen. That's a good idea."

"Once I make those calls, I'll contact you, probably late this afternoon."

"Just between you and me, are you considering accepting the offer or making a counter offer?"

"Except the quick closing, I don't have any concerns with the offer, so yeah, I'm thinking about accepting. But keep that between us for now."

"Yes, sir. I will do that. Nothing is final until you sign the acceptance, so take your time, but not too much time. I just need your initials acknowledging that I presented the offer to you." He pointed to a short line on the offer form. "And here is a copy for you. Look it over again and call me if you have any other questions."

Clayton gathered the papers and stuffed them back into his folder. They stood and shook hands with Mark again promising to contact him later in the day.

When Clayton left, Mark heard Alex heading out the back door, heading for the garage. He looked at his watch. 9:20. The meeting with Clayton took very little time. He looked at the letters between his parents and found the last letter from his father. He read where his father explained to his mother that they were separated when he and Ingrid began to fall for each other.

Ingrid Engel … his biological mother. How frightened she must have been; a very young German girl in a hostile, foreign country, with no friends. Anyone whom she met viewed her as a potential enemy. Only onc man offered her a friendly, helping hand.

Had his father erred putting this relationship with Ingrid ahead of his long-time courtship with the woman he believed to be his mother for all his life? Or maybe the error had been trying to go back and take responsibility for Ada May's pregnancy and do the honorable thing according to the church. His father must have felt trapped with no way out. His life changed from having no commitments to three unbreakable commitments in less than two days. Did he learn about Ingrid's pregnancy before leaving for the military? He swore that he did not. Did he use his military commitment to get away from his mistakes? Did he believe that the pregnancies were mistakes?

Mark heard the back door of the house open, then Art Wexley called out his name. He called out from the dining room, "I'm in here."

He put the letter back in the envelope and placed it back on the correct stack. As Art entered the dining room, his father's words still rattled around in his brain. *We were not together for nearly three months ... It was you who broke off our engagement ...*

When Art walked into the dining room, he looked at the China cabinet and remarked, "The China cabinet with the rest of the dining room suite should bring a pretty good price. Solid cherry, in beautiful condition."

Mark smiled, knowing that not much else of significant value existed in his father's estate, especially at an auction. But he knew that having someone with professional experience handle the sale was the most expedient way to dispose of the property. Between the house and land, and the personal belongings, he hoped that the bulk of the estate would be settled before he headed home to Florida.

"So, what do you think?"

"I can't guarantee anything, but we'll do out best to sell everything. I have a couple questions."

"Shoot."

"The Mustang. Are you keeping it or do you want to sell it?"

Mark rubbed his chin, then replied, "I'll have to call you later today on that. My wife will be here this afternoon and I have to ask her what she thinks."

"Okay. How about the woodworking tools, especially the high-end saws, planer, joiner. You know, all the professional grade tools?"

"All that goes."

"Then there's the gun cabinet. Are there any guns that you'd like to sell?"

Mark scratched his head as he thought. He said, "There are a couple hand guns and one rifle and ammunition. I think I'd like to sell those and the cabinet itself. Can you sell them at auction?"

"Give me the particulars on the make and model for each and an inventory of the ammunition. Call me and I'll get back to you. We might handle those separate from the auction, but it won't require a separate contract. Same terms."

"Alright, Art. Sounds good."

Mark thought about the broken rifle and decided he needed to remove it from the cabinet and dispose of it. No one would buy a broken gun, would they?

"Oh, I almost forgot. In the attic, there's an old military footlocker. You might get a good price for it from a military enthusiast. Are you interested in selling it?"

Mark thought of all the memories packed away in that footlocker. The things he learned about his family in just four days and the secrets that might lie ahead, with a grim look he said, "No. No, I'm keeping it."

Art nodded and said, "Alright. I think we're set for now. I'd like to schedule the auction for twelve days from now. Will Saturday, May 23rd work for you?"

Mark nodded, signed the contract, and watched as Art Wexley drove away. He locked up the house and headed out to Route 101 then turned east on Route 2 towards Cleveland Hopkins Airport. It was amazing to him how quickly the leaves seemed to erupt from the trees' canopics compared to when he took the same route into Sandusky just days earlier. He could hardly wait to see his wife. It had been a long five days.

Chapter 20

The flight landed on time and without incident. Mark met his wife, Denise, inside the arrivals terminal after she collected her suitcase at baggage claim. When he saw her come up the escalator and smile his way, he moved quickly to embrace her in a passionate bear-hug. Surprised by the public display of affection, she raised her eyebrows in wonder. He rarely held her hand in public. When he pulled back to look her in the eyes, her smile melted his heart. His broad smile contrasted with the tears that welled in his eyes, but did not spill onto his cheeks.

"Who are you? My husband was supposed to pick me up." she remarked playfully.

He laughed at her joke and rubbed the tears from his eyes with the backs of his hands. "He's in here somewhere." He paused, looking at her, his smile etched upon his face. "I'm just happy you're here. Let's get out of here." They stood arm-in-arm as the mobile walkway moved them along.

He asked, "You hungry?"

"Famished. I ate a piece of toast and jelly this morning before leaving for the airport. It is so much more convenient flying from Sanford than Orlando International."

Mark placed her suitcase in the area behind the passenger seat of the Silverado's extended cab. Before exiting the airport, Mark leaned over and gave her a passionate kiss, surprising her again. He paid the parking toll and turned towards the airport exit.

"I sure have missed you," Mark said as they approached the light at Route 237.

"You've only been gone five days, Dear."

"I know. It seems like a lot longer than that." He paused.

He turned to his wife briefly just as the light turned green. From the look on her face, she noticed the tension his body projected. He did not know where to start, the volume of overwhelming news from his five days in Sandusky sent his brain into overdrive.

She looked at Mark as he drove along Brookpark Road, heading towards the interchange with I-480. Once on the highway heading towards the turnpike, she asked, "What's happening with the estate?

He said, "The real estate agent and the auctioneer were both at the house this morning. We have an offer on the house already. It isn't a great offer, but it's all cash, so it will be quick. That reminds me, I have to call the realtor this afternoon. Before that, I have to call Dad's attorney, and I should call Maryanne and Caroline."

"That's wonderful, especially if the buyer can avoid all the hassle dealing with the banks. Did the auctioneer say anything at the house was worth selling? You said most of the furniture was headed for the landfill."

"He seems to think we can sell most everything. He did say that we shouldn't get our hopes up on the amount of money the sale will net. There is the Mustang." He smiled and briefly looked her way. "Did you want to keep it?"

She beamed. "I could be *Mustang Sally* driving around Maitland. But we have time to talk about it. What else is worth anything?"

"Tools. Dad has some very expensive wood-working tools. A couple guns."

"We don't want those."

"I agree. He also has a bunch of gold coins. I haven't found any investment information but there are a couple envelopes in the desk in the den I haven't opened yet." He paused then said, "Wait until you see the house. What a mess. I told you about Peggy Whipple whom I met at Dick's Carryout.

She used to clean for Dad, but he told her to stop a year or so ago. She said he just seemed to have lost the will to live."

Denise did not answer for a time, appearing deep in thought. Then she said, "You already told me about the letters. Did they have any clues why your dad turned so glum?"

With one hand on the wheel, he rubbed his face with the other. "Yeah. And I found more letters … from . . . I don't know, his girlfriend?"

Denise's jaw fell open in shock. She regained her composure and asked, "What? Girlfriend?"

Mark's smile at her reaction had a backdrop of sadness. "That's nothing. Wait 'til you hear the punchline." He drew in a deep breath, looked around at the traffic on the highway then turned to her and slowly said, "Her name's Ingrid. She's my biological mother."

Denise's eyes widened in a look that would have been comical had the topic not been of such consequence.

Denise opened her mouth to speak, but nothing came out. She tried a second time with the same result. She finally blurted out in a shrill voice, "What?"

"God as my witness. That's what the letters say."

"Is she Maryanne's mother, too? I thought you were twins."

"Nope. Maryanne's mom is, well, who I thought my mom was, until yesterday. Mom and Dad separated before he signed up to go into the military. A couple days before he left for his first duty station, Mom came to him and told him she was pregnant. So, he married her. I think he figured he had to since it was his child." He stopped and looked at the flow of traffic as they approached the toll gates for the Ohio Turnpike. He stopped, grabbed the ticket, then merged with westbound traffic. He continued the story. "They married at the Erie County Courthouse, not in the church, then Dad headed for Louisianna for duty. That's when the letters started."

Denise sat, stunned by the news. She said, "You found letters from Ingrid to your dad. Did you find any letters from your dad to Ingrid?"

"No. The letters from Ingrid … it seems so weird calling her by her first name … were hidden in a compartment in the bottom of the footlocker."

"Do you think your dad was trying to hide the letters? Your mom's been dead for a long time."

Mark shrugged. They were silent for a while as they approached the Route 57 exit from the turnpike. After exiting the turnpike, Mark turned into the parking lot of a small diner in a strip mall that had a pawn shop, a Dollar General, a tattoo parlor, and a tobacco shop. They entered the diner, the aroma of a variety of spices filling the air. They were seated at a booth against the wall furthest from the entrance. At 3:30 p.m., they were the only patrons in the place. A few tables sported dirty dishes that were not yet cleared.

After ordering from the lunch menu, Denise looked Mark in the eyes and said, "No wonder you're all flustered. You told me about all the folks in Sandusky who sang your dad's high praises. I met your dad and your mom before we married. It gave me the creeps whenever we were at your house."

Mark smiled at his wife. "You ain't seen nothing yet, sweetie." He began to speak again but closed his mouth, thinking of what to tell her next, then said, "I went to church yesterday. I spoke with the priest, Father Shultz, about Dad's funeral service. He said Dad helped a family with their heating bill when they ran into some financial problems. Said Dad wouldn't let them repay him. He helped out at church quite a bit." Mark paused as their waitress delivered their food, then resumed. "Mom and Dad attended some counselling sessions with Father Shultz, a newly ordained priest at that time. I think he's approaching ninety now. He said he knew about our family situation, that Mom and Dad admitted they were miserable and the atmosphere was terrible for us kids."

"Did he know your mom killed herself?"

"Yeah. He said she went to confession just before she did it. He couldn't tell me what she confessed, of course, but he worried about how our home life affected us over the years."

"Did he know about the letter and the hand-written obituary she sent to you?"

"No, not until I told him, but it sounds like she confessed her plans to him. He said he did everything within his power to keep her from going through with it, but nothing worked … obviously. Anyway, I have to call the funeral director and get Dad's funeral planned. And I have to call the realtor and accept the offer on the house."

They finished their lunch in silence, then headed for the rented truck. Mark opened the door for Denise, then gave her another hug before she climbed into the cab. In moments, they were back on the road, merging with traffic on Route 2 west, just half an hour from Sandusky. Mark made the call to Clayton Biggs and accepted the offer on the house. He put off the call to his sisters. They seemed indifferent to anything about the estate, so they should have no objections.

***

Before they entered the Jay Street house, Mark led Denise to the detached garage and uncovered the blue 1964 Mustang. She walked around the car in awe of the beautiful restoration job. Everything about the car screamed *immaculate*. Mark knew she would be impressed. He did not care one way or another if she decided to keep the classic car. With a little work, adequate space existed in their garage in Maitland. They would have to clean out some boxes that spilled over into the extra car bay at home. Her smile remained radiant, her expression close to giddy. In the end, she said, "I think we should take it for a ride around the neighborhood, then find a buyer here."

"You're sure that's what you want to do? We could keep it then sell it in Florida."

She took a few more seconds to consider his suggestion then said, "Nope. Sell it. It would just be a constant reminder of what you lived through here. It could cause friction between you and your sisters. I know they say they don't want anything of your dad's but you know how those things go. It's your decision, though. Now you know what I think."

Mark looked up at the garage's ceiling. When he looked back down, Denise waited for his response. "You're right. I'll let Art know. Find a good buyer."

They headed for the house. They walked into the dining room where the letters between his parents sat on the dining room table. He scooped them up, careful to keep them in order, and turned Denise towards the stairway.

Denise took in the house as they went. She said, "I can't believe how everything is exactly the way I remember it. It's older and dustier now, but your dad didn't change a thing, as far as I can tell."

"You're right."

After taking the two flights of steps to the attic, they settled in front of the footlocker. Mark placed the two bundles of letters on the floor between them. Denise looked nervous quickly moving her eyes between Mark and the letters. She took a series of deep breaths then said, "I don't know why I'm so nervous."

"Maybe you're not sure it's right going through someone else's mail, even though they're dead? Trust me, I felt the same way before I started reading them."

"How do you want to do this?"

Over the next five hours, Mark and Denise Traver read through letters to and from Joe and Ada May Traver intermixed with letters Joe had received from Ingrid Engel. They read the letters out loud to each other. Mark read the letters from his father and Denise read the letters from Ada May and Ingrid. They agreed on that format so that the letters carried the voice of the feminine and masculine writers.

The contrast of the back and forth between Ada May and Joe and the letters from Ingrid could not be misinterpreted. Joe's letters to Ada May read like a weather report, or a journal of his daily activities with very little detail. The words appeared contrived, even forced. Ada May's return letters lacked passion. There seemed to be no compassion for Joe's situation, learning to navigate a monstrous plane to deliver death and destruction to a civilian population.

Ingrid's letters to Joe conveyed every possible, positive, passionate emotion. Her letters contained little pressed flowers and heart cutouts. She never mentioned being pregnant until the second to last letter. Ingrid and Joe were clearly and passionately in love. Even to Ingrid's last letter, where she told Joe that she had given up her child, Mark, to Ada May, conveyed the heartbreak she experienced in not being able to care for their child.

Then came letters to Ingrid from Joe that were stamped *Returned to Sender* … unopened.

Chapter 21

The sun had just breeched the horizon to the east, the clear skies promising warmer temperatures than the previous week. Sitting in the rental truck in the parking lot of House of Doughnuts on West Perkins Avenue, Denise gave Mark an inquisitive look. He sat in the driver's seat and handed a box of doughnuts and two cups of hot coffee to her to set on the floor before they headed to the Jay Street house. He felt her eyes on him and looked up. He smiled, then raised his hands and his shoulders as if to ask *What?*

"I'm just wondering what's gotten into you since you left Florida last week. You were so full of … energy last night."

"Me? I think it was you. You egged me on, teasing me."

"Ha! You didn't need any encouragement."

"Are you complaining?"

"Hardly. Maybe we should take a few days apart more often?"

Mark gave her a fake stern look then started the ignition. "I don't think I could take another five days like that. Though I am a little sore this morning."

"Should we head back to the hotel room for breakfast?"

"Jeez, woman. I need some recovery time. What's that song, *I Ain't as Good as I Once Was?*"

"Well, you were pretty darn good last night."

Mark's smile softened and took on a serious, no kidding look. "I love you. I have from the first moment I laid eyes on you."

He leaned across the console and kissed her, maintaining contact with her lips for several seconds. A horn honked behind them as a car tried to maneuver into a nearby parking space in the compact parking lot. The driver smiled and waved as he stepped out of his car, heading for the front door of the popular doughnut shop.

Mark said, "We better get out of here before someone calls the police."

"Let 'em." Denise leaned in closer for another kiss before settling back in her seat and buckling her seat belt.

Back at the house, Mark brought the bundles of envelopes from the attic and placed them on the dining room table. He and Denise sat side-by-side, having just finished a doughnut and about half a cup of coffee each. Denise appeared anxious to delve into the next letter from Ada May. Last night, they stopped at the letters from Joe to Ingrid that had been *Returned to Sender* unopened.

Denise picked up the envelope dated April 28, 1944. She looked at the prior letter in the bunch. She looked at Mark and said, "Almost three months before your mother answered your dad. He must have gone through hell wondering about the goings-on at home. I think he may have feared for your life."

Mark took another bite of Boston Crème and a sip of coffee, trying to relax. The previous night's passion with his wife helped him get the best sleep in many years. Now the anxiety began to ratchet up once more.

He said, "I can't imagine what was going through his mind. He'd been in some very intense training. Now he learned he fathered two children, from different mothers. I'm sure he yearned to meet his newborn children, regardless of the turmoil mom felt." Mark paused, his eyes drifting off. He quietly said, "Mom ... I still think of her that way, even under the circumstances. I mean, I never knew my real mother, my biological mother. She gave me away." He took a deep breath. "Who does that?"

"I know you just found out about Ingrid, but have you thought about trying to find out what happened to her? It sounds like she found herself in a real pickle and your dad was her salvation, at least for a while. Then she ended up possibly in a worse situation than prior to meeting your dad. I expect that she felt beyond desperate."

Mark nodded. "You're right. It's easy for me to sit here and judge. But, just thinking of the war, how crazy things were everywhere in the world. She must have been frightened out of her mind. I wonder where her parents were? She doesn't mention them in her letters, at least none that we've read so far."

Denise took a deep breath and held up the envelope she had been holding. She said, "This is from Ada May to your dad. The date is April 28, 1944, about three months after her last letter, the one where she tells Joe about receiving you from Ingrid."

He looked down at the table then said, 'Let's roll."

Denise pulled the letter from the envelope and began reading the one page note out loud.

Joseph,

I have prayed over this and I've come to a decision. We will raise the children as fraternal twins. Some people already know that I gave birth to only one baby, but most know nothing about that. Maryanne and Mark will never know of this. I will treat them as equals as best as I can. I know there is nothing you can do about this so I will do what is right. We have to look to the future and hope that this damn war will end soon and you can come home to us.

Both children are healthy and happy. I will update you as best I can as they grow together.

Ada May

Denise quickly re-read the letter in silence. She looked up at Mark who sat dumfounded, his mouth hanging open. The wheels in his head churned away at the letter's content.

Denise ventured a wisecrack, "You can just feel the love emanating from her letter."

Mark closed his mouth and shook his head. "At some point along the way, she must have cracked. I really think she wanted to do exactly what she said, to love my sister and me both, but she just couldn't keep up the charade. She never loved me, but I think her hate for me and what I represented also affected Maryanne, and later, Caroline."

Denise looked at him, deep in thought. She said, "Maybe there's more to it. We have a lot of letters to go through. What did your dad say?"

Mark picked up the next envelope. He looked at the date – May 23, 1944 – nearly a month later. He unfolded the letter and began reading.

Dear Ada May,

I agree with your decision and thank you. Raising the children as twins is the best decision, given the circumstances. I know this places added pressure on you. Our parents must wonder about the newest addition to our family, how this came to be. Assure them that both children are a welcome and loving addition to our family. No need to try and explain further.

At your first opportunity, please take pictures of the children and send them to me. I need something to help me get through the training, which is intense. But I have to do my part. I have less than one year of training remaining, then I expect to be assigned to a bomber squadron. This is what I have been trained to do. I hope the war ends before I deploy, but if I must, I will do my best to play a small part in the demise of Hitler and his military machine.

Sending my love to you and the children.

Joe

Denise looked glum when Mark finished reading the letter. Mark saw in her eyes that she felt the lack of passion in the letter, the feeling that they were both trapped in a marriage devoid of love. Mark knew the feeling continued on even after his younger sister, Caroline's birth. The atmosphere never changed for his entire childhood. The vow to love each child equally did not happen. Instead, throughout their childhood, he and his sisters experienced equal measures of misery and despair. Had they not seen what other households were like, they might have carried that misery into their own homes as adults.

They read the next four letters, which sounded like a weather report more than an exchange between a young, loving couple who missed each other. Ada May spoke of the children's health and how they were growing. Joseph expressed his thanks for the updates and described the difficulty of his training. Mundane would have painted a positive slant to the letters.

Then came a surprise; a letter from Ingrid to Joe, dated September 19, 1944.

My Dear Joseph,

I am sorry that I have not read any of your letters as I want to limit my heartache to that which I already feel. I am afraid that if I read your letters, my heart will break into a million pieces, to the point where I can no longer breathe. I do not wish that to be on your conscience. I have already caused enough grief in your life. I do not wish to add more.

I have news from my parents. They are both alive, but their circumstances are not good. My mother has been forced to work in a munitions plant in Unterluss, a small town in northern Germany. The plant is close to my home. Mother was able to get a letter to me, telling me that I must not return to Germany. Bombing raids by the American and English forces are increasing. It appears to be turning the tide of the German war effort, but Hitler will not give up. He keeps reassuring the people that we are winning, that the enemy is on the run, and are desperate. Most Germans just want the war to end.

My father was drafted into the regular German Army. He was shipped off to north Africa. My mother has not heard from him for nearly three months. I fear he will not survive.

I am living with a kind German couple. I will not tell you where. You have enough to worry about as it is. They are treating me like family. This will be my last letter. I just wanted to let you know that I am sorry for the way we left things. I love you. I love our son. I have dreams of us living in a fine house, raising our son and his siblings, leading a normal life. If only things were different. If only …

I will always cherish the time we spent together, the love we shared. It was a time I needed someone to hold on to, someone to assure me that life would get better. And for a time, it did.

I pray you can live the good life that you so deserve and I pray our son can share those times with you, his father. God bless you, my love, and God bless little Mark.

All my love,

Ingrid

As Denise finished reading the letter, tears that had threatened to cloud her eyes rolled down her cheek. She looked over at Mark. He rubbed his eyes with the palms of his hands. He cleared his throat, but said nothing.

The silence dragged on for several moments, then Mark said in a shaky whisper, "We have to find out what's become of her."

Chapter 22

By mid-morning, Mark and Denise read three more letters. The first letter from Ada May, dated October 17, 1944, described how baby Mark is walking and getting into everything he can reach. Maryanne is content to sit and let her mother bring her toys. The contrast between Mark and his sister brought a smile to his face. Denise continued reading. Both children are saying a few words and both are healthy and happy. Ada May remained financially stable, able to meet financial obligations. She did not expound on the subject of money.

Denise noted, once again, the letter lacked passion. Ada May might as well have been a babysitter or nanny. She also noted the time span between letters to and from Mark's parents were getting longer.

Mark picked up his father's reply dated November 23, 1944. He read the letter aloud but it may as well have been a photo copy of his previous letter, stating the difficulty of the training, when he expected to be deployed to a squadron overseas. He requested more pictures of the children.

After Mark placed Joe's letter back into the envelope, Denise picked up the next letter from Ada May. As she read the letter, the boring drivel continued. She almost put the letter back in the envelope without reading to the end when she noted the remark about Lyle O'Conner and how helpful he has been to her.

Mark had been looking around the room, barely paying attention to his wife, until he heard the name. He frowned then said, "Can you read that again?"

I don't know how I would survive without Lyle's help. He's been so supportive.

Denise looked at Mark who still frowned. He stood and walked into the kitchen then asked, "Do you want anything to drink?"

"No, thank you."

Mark's phone, sitting on the dining room table, rang. "Can you grab that for me, sweetie?"

Denise grabbed the phone and swiped across the screen. "Mark's phone."

After a brief pause, a man asked in a tenuous voice, "Is Mark there?"

"Yes, he is. Just a second."

Mark reentered the dining room and took the phone from his wife. "This is Mark."

"Hi, Mark. Simon Wilkes. I have the final appraisal report. I've sent a copy to Clayton Biggs and Allen Westridge."

"Thanks, Simon. I don't know if you've talked with Clayton, but we have an offer on the property."

"I did and the offer is consistent with the appraised value, so I don't think you'll have any issues with the sale, especially with the all-cash offer."

"Thanks for the call, Simon. Is that it?"

"Did you schedule an auction for the household goods yet?"

"Yes. Saturday, May 23."

"Hmm. I might have to see if I can get over there. I might try to get that radial arm saw. Anyway, good luck with the sale of the house and property. It sounds like everything is moving along."

"Thanks again."

After the call, Mark walked back to the kitchen and pulled a beer from the refrigerator, thought about it, then put the beer back and closed the door. Back in the dining room he said, "Let's go grab some lunch. We're going to Daly's, downtown."

Before she could rise from her chair, Mark's phone rang again. Allen Westridge's name appeared on the screen. Mark sat down and swiped the screen.

"Hello, Allen. What can I do for you?"

The attorney took a long, loud, labored breath, then said, "Just checking in, getting some billable hours." He paused as if waiting for laughter, then continued, "A little attorney humor to break the ice. I heard from Clayton Biggs and I was bored, so I thought I'd call and tell you that you don't have to tell me about every little thing that happens. But you can call if you want. Have you found anything interesting since arriving in our little town?"

Mark thought for a moment before answering, then replied, "Well, yeah. I have. Did you know that my dad had a girlfriend while he and mom were married?"

Allen cleared his throat, then said, "Well, Mark, I can't hear you real well. I think I better hang up and try again."

"Allen, don't hang up on me. I have a feeling that you know more than you're letting on."

"Mark, I am sworn to secrecy and I won't break my promise. But your mom and dad's relationship had a few bumps. Before your dad died, he said you might be calling me, asking what I know. He said that everything you need to know is in the footlocker." Allen began coughing loudly and deeply, so much so that Mark wondered if he should hang up and call 911. Just as he prepared to do it, Allen came back on the line. "I hope I didn't bust your eardrum. But, to get back to what I know; I know that you should let the dead be dead and do what you can for the living. If you come across anything that you need legal advice on, give me a call. Don't wait too long. I lost another client yesterday, but hell, he'd been in a nursing home for three years. He lived two years longer than the doctors gave him."

"Allen, how well did you know Lyle O'Conner?"

"Well enough to go on hunting trips with him for a few years. He, your father, and I were best friends for many years."

"Did he and my mom ..."

"Sorry, Mark. I have an incoming call that I must take."

The line went dead. Mark looked at his phone, then looked at Denise. She raised her eyebrows, then her shoulders.

She had heard the entire conversation. Without discussing it, she agreed with her husband; Allen Westridge knew a lot more than he divulged, which was not much.

Before Mark could say anything, his phone rang again. Dylan Hart, Funeral Director at Hart Funeral Services.

"Hello, Dylan."

"Mr. Traver."

"Please, call me Mark."

"Alright, Mark. I called to let you know that I spoke with Father Shultz at Holy Angels. He said we should put our heads together and come up with a date for your father's funeral service. I have taken possession of his remains. All I need is a preferred date for the service."

Mark scratched his head and said, "The only date that is a no-go is May 23. We have the auction scheduled for that Saturday."

"Okay. We don't have anything scheduled for the Thursday before that, May 21. Today is the twelfth, so that give us nine days. Do you have an obituary ready for the Register?"

The Sandusky Register needed a few days advance notice before printing an obituary. Mark had not given his father's obituary any thought except noting that it had to be done.

"No, I don't. We'll get one together, though I'm not sure what to say."

"Your dad was in World War II, if I recall when I spoke with him about his prepaid plan. You should include something about him being a member of *the Greatest Generation*. Also, he did a lot of community work. I know that from reading the papers and from some things Father Shultz told me."

"Okay, Dylan. I'll get something put together."

"If you get writer's block, let me know, I can help get some of it organized. Or you can just look at the obits in the Register and follow how they have it laid out."

"Okay. I'll get back to you about the date later today. And thanks for calling."

"Hey, Mark, it is my pleasure. I know you have a lot to do to wrap things up here in town. We'll talk soon."

As the line went dead, the doorbell rang. Mark looked up at the ceiling and rolled his eyes. Denise stood and headed for the front door. Mark fell in step behind her. When she opened the door, Peggy and Randy Whipple stood on the stoop.

On seeing Denise, Peggy smiled and nearly yelled, "You must be Mark's wife, Denise! We've heard so much about you."

Denise smiled and said, "Yes, I am. I hope some of it was good."

Over her shoulder, Mark said, "Hi Peggy. Hi Randy. Come on in."

Peggy laughed as she and Randy stepped into the living room. They were dressed in shorts and tee shirts, the temperature reaching the mid-seventies. "All good, Denise. Trust me."

"We were just getting ready to head to Daly's for lunch. Want to join us?"

Peggy replied, "We would, but we have plans. We saw the truck and wanted to meet Denise. Maybe we can stop by later and visit."

Mark and Denise looked at each other and smiled. Mark said, "That would be terrific. We can order a pizza or subs. I'll pick up some beer. Maybe a bottle of wine."

Peggy said, "Don't worry about the drinks. I'll pick something up from the drive-through."

After a few minutes of getting to know Denise, everyone hugged and said their good-byes. The Whipples left, then Mark and Denise headed for Daly's.

***

Mark and Denise finished their lunches from a window seat at Daly's in downtown Sandusky. Mark had a good view of the Sandusky Bay just beyond Schade Mylander Plaza. The Jet Express had just docked, arriving from one of the Lake Erie Islands. He smiled, thinking that a trip to the islands with his wife might be a way to shed some of the stress that seemed to consume him each morning. He turned to Denise who had been smiling as she watched his face.

"Penny for your thoughts?"

Mark said, "How would you like to take a trip to Put-in-Bay?"

"Great. When do we leave?"

He laughed. "As soon as we can wrap up this estate business. We can …"

Mark did not finish. Two women approached and stopped right next to their table; one of the ladies appeared to be in her sixties, around Mark and Denise's age. The other was near, if not over, ninety. They were arm-in-arm, the younger lady seeming to provide support or to help balance the older woman. Their facial features appeared similar, leading Mark to believe that they were mother and daughter.

When the younger woman spoke, Mark's brain signaled a twinge of recognition. "We apologize for interrupting your lunch, but are you Mark Traver?"

Mark stood, nodded, and said, "Yes, I am. This is my wife, Denise."

The woman smiled. "I'm Catherine Sims. We went to school together at Sandusky High School."

Mark remembered her now. She had been a shy, pretty girl. They had several classes together, though they did not run in the same circle of friends.

She continued, "This is my mother, Millie O'Conner."

Mark nodded and said, "Hello, Mrs. O'Conner."

The moment he said her last name, his brain sent up alarm bells. He looked briefly back at Denise, whose face showed alarm behind the smile she desperately tried to maintain.

Catherine Sims asked, "We're so sorry about your father. Would you have time to talk for a bit?"

Mark thought about any meetings that he had scheduled. Realizing his wide opened afternoon would not provide an excuse, he said, "Sure, let's find a table away from the crowd."

Chapter 23

Mark flagged down their waitress and asked if she could find an open table for the four of them with some degree of privacy. She smiled and motioned for them to follow her. She led them to the back of the dining area and offered a table with four seats where no other diners were close by. Before she departed, she asked if they needed anything. Mark looked to the three women. Denise commented that coffee would be nice. Catherine agreed. Mildred shook her head but quietly asked for a glass of water. Mark told their waitress three coffees and a water, asked her to add it to his bill, and offered his thanks.

Mark liked the atmosphere in Daly's, with the beautiful brick walls, the antique tiled ceiling, the classic bar with a sports bar atmosphere. But they also had separate sections for more intimate gatherings.

After their waitress departed, Mark turned to Catherine and asked if she remembered what classes they attended together. A brief chat about high school ensued. After their waitress delivered coffee and water and left again, Catherine turned to her mother, then back to Mark and Denise and said, "Mother and your mother," she looked at Mark, "were best friends in high school."

Mark sat back in his chair, a look of surprise on his face. He turned to Denise who had a similar reaction. He turned to Mildred. The old woman's expression had not changed. Downturned lips remained etched on her pale, wrinkled face. If the friendship remained happy or turned sour, Mark could not tell by looking at her. He wondered if the friendship lasted until his mother's final hours when she took her own life.

In a cautious tone, he asked, "Were you related to Lyle O'Conner?"

She slowly opened her mouth, her expression not changing, but a sadness appeared in her eyes. She said in a scratchy, barely audible voice, "He was my husband." She opened her mouth as if to say more, but she turned away slightly, looking at the wall behind Mark. After a moment, she again met Mark's gaze and said, "I'm sorry, but you look so much like your father."

He smiled and replied, "I've heard that several times since I arrived Thursday."

An awkward silence ensued. He did not know what to say next. Just this morning, he heard Allen Westridge say that he, Lyle, and his dad were best friends. Now Mildred O'Conner sat across from him, her daughter telling him that her mother and Ada May were best friends. He also knew that Lyle had helped his mother in some way that she had not fully explained in her letters to his father. She never mentioned her "best friend," Mildred. Had the relationship between Ada May and Lyle become too close and caused a rift in their friendship?

He took a deep breath and asked, "Can you tell me about my father and mother and their relationship back then?"

Her stoic expression remained, "Back then covers a lot of time. Do you mean before you were born?"

"Well, yes. That would be a good place to start."

The old woman's eyes seemed to drift back in time as she conjured up memories from seventy years prior. Her face took on what Mark believed might have been the closest thing to a smile that she could muster. She began to speak.

"Ada May and I were best friends, as Catherine told you. We did everything together. We studied, went to school events, were in the school choir, read the same books. We liked the same boys. My parents hated it when I started dating. They said Ada May was a bad influence on me, but it really wasn't like that. We egged each other on.

"She liked your dad very much." She locked eyes with Mark. "I did, too.

"We had a competition of sorts to see who could get him to ask them to the school dance. Your mother won. I settled for second best." She looked at her daughter and said, "Sorry, sweetie, but your dad wasn't my first choice."

Catherine smiled, blushed, turned away, and took a sip of coffee.

Mildred continued, "After that dance, I became obsessed with your dad. I wanted to get the last laugh, but somehow, your mom had a hold on Joseph. They fell in love. Again, I settled, and spent all my free time with Lyle. It wasn't all that bad. Lyle, Allen, and your dad were always together, at least when Joseph and Lyle weren't alone with us girls.

"Around that time, the war started to get noticed in America. One by one, young men signed up to fight overseas. Joseph and Lyle were in their second year in college. I'd go visit Lyle when I could. Your mom had a job so she could only go with me once in a while to visit Joe. The guys hung out together at college until Joe met this German girl … then everything changed."

Mark inhaled, wondering if Mildred O'Conner, the widow of the man who had died while on a hunting trip with his father, had all the answers to his questions about his family. He wanted to interrupt her and ask pointed questions, but he waited, thinking that she might not need prodding. She seemed perfectly happy to tell her story.

After a sip of water and what Mark perceived to be a moment's reflection, she continued, "Her name was Ingrid. Joe said she was just a friend, but she somehow got her hooks into Joe … but good."

The old woman's eyes glossed a bit, threatening to spill tears. But her voice began to show a touch of anger, though her face remained unchanged. When she reached for her water glass again, her hand shook. Mark could not tell if this was due to her age or if her change in mood had any effect on her muscle control. Denise and Catherine seemed to notice the shaking as well, but neither of them said anything about it.

Mildred continued after taking a drink. "It wasn't long and Joe was spending most of his free time with Ingrid. He even introduced the girl to us; your mother and me, that is. We took an immediate dislike to her. Her goal was so obvious. She planned to steal Joe away from Ada May."

Mark asked, "Is that when my mother broke up with my dad?"

For the first time, the old woman's expression changed from a stone-like fixture to anger. If her eyes were lasers, she would have burned holes in his head.

"Your mother never broke up with Joseph. Once that girl got her hooks in Joe, he never spent time with Ada May. She begged him to break away from that girl, that she had evil intentions. She had some sob story about being shipped to America. She said her parents wanted to keep her safe from the war in Germany. The war wasn't in Germany! It was her people who started the war! They were ravaging the entire European continent, making life a living hell for everyone else! And this little hussy had the nerve to play the poor little innocent German girl. She stole your father's heart. Then she dumped your father and he came crawling back to Ada May. Thank goodness for your sake, and your sister's."

Mark listened and tried to square what Mildred said with what he had read in the letters between his father and mother. While the players were all the same, the story had a completely different spin. Obviously, Mildred O'Conner had no idea that Ingrid had given birth to him, that Ada May was not his biological mother. If they were such good friends, how could she have not known that he and Maryanne were not born on the same day to the same woman? Part of her version of events stirred resentment in his mind. Could it be that Mildred's recollection of the story was true? He looked at Catherine who shrugged her shoulders such that her mother could not see her. Mark wondered if she had heard the story before, or if she had heard different versions of the story as her mother aged.

Mark asked, "Did you and Mom remain friends?"

The question seemed to deflate her body. She hung her head and, in a voice almost too quiet to hear, said, "No. Not long after your father left for military service, your mother's pregnancy took a toll on her. She lived with her parents - your grandparents - and spent all her time worrying about the health of her unborn children. Your grandfather wouldn't allow me to visit her. It turns out that I was pregnant with Catherine at that same time. Lyle and I were married as soon as I found out I was pregnant and moved into an apartment on the east side of town. I couldn't make the trip to visit, anyway. Lyle worked long hours at the munitions plant – lots of overtime. He was so tired when he came home. Our relationship suffered because of it. The war affected everyone in one way or another. I heard that Ada May rented a house on the west side of town, but we never reconnected."

She expressed no shame for her admission that she became pregnant before she and Lyle were married. Mark and Denise both glanced at Catherine who looked back without embarrassment. She must have known this tidbit of information already.

Mark wondered why Lyle had not joined the military like all his friends, but was hesitant to ask. Mildred saved him the trouble.

"When Joseph announced that he had signed up for the Army Air Corps, he asked Lyle if he planned to join. Lyle told Joe that, yes, he planned to see the recruiter the next day. Several days came and went. Finally, Joe had to leave for Louisianna and Lyle had yet to sign up. Lyle told me that Joseph was a fool to join, that the man had a child on the way. How could he abandon his family like that. Lyle swore to me that he would not leave me stranded."

Mark took a deep breath, then a sip of warm coffee. He thought about Mildred's version of his parent's issues and the role Ingrid played. Mark had read the letters from Ingrid to his father. They seemed genuine, but without having been there, he could not judge the authenticity of Ingrid's feelings.

Mark again looked at Catherine and asked, "Do you have any brothers or sisters?"

With a smile, she replied, "No. I'm an only child."

Mark looked at her face. Recognition flashed in his mind. He thought it most likely that he remembered her from their high school years, but he could not shake the feeling that his mind might be playing tricks on him.

After a long period of awkward silence, Catherine asked, "Mom, are you ready to head home?"

Mildred O'Conner took a long, deep breath. She just nodded and moved to stand. Mark went around the table and assisted her, pulling her chair out while supporting her right arm. Catherine did the same from her left side. They said their goodbyes.

Mark and Denise waited until Mildred and Catherine were out on the sidewalk, walking slowly along Columbus Avenue. Catherine looked back through the window and waved.

Mark turned to Denise and said, "Catherine could be Maryanne's twin sister."

Denise slowly nodded in agreement.

Chapter 24

Mark and Denise walked into the Jay Street house just after 3:30 p.m., still dumbfounded by Mildred O'Conner and her recollection of the friendship between her and his mother, as well as the crush she had on his father. She sounded like a gossipy high school girl, telling her secrets, competing with her best friend for the affection of some cute boy. When some other girl came into the picture, she tried to ostracize the intruder, advising all her friends that they should not like the girl because of her family, her upbringing, her ethnicity, her relationship with the evil warmongers. The German girl invaded their little group and, according to Mildred, was the source of all their ills. Had the subject not been so serious, her stories might have been comical. But world affairs back in the 1940s were anything but funny. Clearly, adult life consumed them all at an early age. Between the changes from high school to college, the unplanned pregnancies, and the war, events took an ugly turn, an about-face from the relatively easy life they had been living. They were dealt cards they knew not how to play, the situations they encountered immensely complex. They were ill-equipped to handle them.

Denise asked Mark if he believed Catherine O'Conner Sims might be Maryanne's half-sister, the implication being that Mildred's husband impregnated Mark's mother. Like many people who recently entered Mark's life and compared his likeness to his father's, Catherine's physical appearance seemed too similar to Maryanne's to ignore. They could easily pass for twins. Mark wanted to ask Catherine if she remembered Maryanne from school, but thought better of it.

He already faced more than his share of issues since arriving in Sandusky.

"I don't know. They sure do look alike."

Then Denise asked if he believed Mildred O'Conner's version of events. They certainly did not align with what they read in the letters between his mother and father, and those to his father from Ingrid.

Ever since Mildred and Catherine left Daly's, Mark thought about the disparity in the tale spun by an old woman and the letters that were written so many years ago. The letters were penned by people living the very real events of those days. Without delay, he said, "Not everything. I think she believes it, but I'm sure over time her mind has molded her memories into what is most comfortable for her to believe. She admitted her bias. She competed with my mom for Dad's attention and affection … and lost. That had to be a big blow to her ego. Then she admitted to *settling* for Catherine's dad, right in front of her. That stung, don't you think?"

"I guess it depends on Catherine's relationship with her father. Maybe she didn't get along with her dad."

Mark looked up at the ceiling in thought, noticing the cob webs where the walls met the ceiling, then said, "She would have been about nine or ten when her dad died in the hunting accident. If they were close, that must have been devastating, making her mother's comment even more cruel. But it's been a long time, and time heals."

Denise yawned. Mark smiled at his wife and asked if she needed a nap.

"The thought crossed my mind. These last twenty-four hours have been like being caught in a tornado."

"That's how I've felt since arriving." Mark rolled his head around to loosen the tension in his neck. When he first heard of his father's death, he thought dispensing with Joe Traver's worldly goods would be a cinch. Just hire an auctioneer, a realtor, and work with his father's lawyer and be done with it. He did not count on finding letters that exposed deep, dark family secrets. He did not know that his father, whom until the last few days, he considered a real bastard, earned the respect of so many of the townspeople. Much of what he thought he knew of his father was blown away by the recollections of so many who knew him. The stories people told just seemed like a series of fairy tales, works of fiction, as if they described the life of a complete stranger. At some point over the last five days, the work of disposition of the estate became secondary to learning the truth of his family's history.

But most of all, he had no idea that he would discover that the first twenty-plus years of his life had been a lie, that the mother he knew all his life was not who she portrayed herself to be. Not only that, the sister he thought to be his fraternal twin was his half-sister or maybe not related to him by blood at all.

He thought about the woman named Ingrid, his biological mother. What became of her? Did she return to Germany after the war and look for her parents? Did they survive the war? The realization hit him that this man and woman, Ingrid's parents, were his grandparents. His eyes popped wide at the thought.

Between thinking of the tasks that he still needed to perform for the estate and the earth-shattering news of his ancestry, coupled with the extra cups of coffee at lunch, his brain kept churning, chugging through the overload of data. He thought that maybe he should record the information that kept pouring in.

Thinking of writing things down, he remembered that he better get started on his father's obituary. He wondered if Denise might help him with that task.

"Hey, Sweety, do you think you could help me with Dad's obit? I'm at a loss for what to write."

"Sure. Is there a pad of paper around anywhere? I have a pen in my purse."

While Denise looked for paper to begin recording Joseph Traver's obituary, Mark remembered the ten by twelve envelope he found in the bottom of the foot locker. He looked around the dining room, trying to remember if he brought the envelope down from the attic, or if he left it in the bottom compartment of the footlocker. He did not see the envelope among the other letters. He asked Denise if she remembered seeing a ten by twelve envelope, but she replied no.

Mark bounded up the stairs, pulled the top tray that contained the old pictures up, and set it aside. He emptied the footlocker, then opened the bottom compartment and found the envelope where he found the letters from Ingrid to Joe. He returned to the dining room and placed the envelope on the table next to the bundles of letters just as Denise returned to the room with paper and pen. She sat down, ready to begin writing.

Mark opened a copy of the Sandusky Register on the table to a page with multiple obituaries. He looked through two that filled two columns, each about four inches long. He gave the paper to Denise and said, "I guess you could kind-of follow the general format in these two." He pointed to the recent obituaries.

"Let me look these over. I think I can get the basics down. We can fill in more details as we go."

Mark watched for a moment, then, as Denise continued to write, his attention shifted to the large envelope he had retrieved from the footlocker. His curiosity got the best of him. He ripped open the top and peered inside. The large envelope contained three white, business sized envelopes and a folded piece of notebook paper. He dumped the contents onto the dining room table.

Each of the three envelopes was sealed. His full name was written on one envelope. The other envelopes were addressed to his sisters; one to Maryanne Traver Campbell, the other to Caroline Traver Eastman. The single page folded paper contained two paragraphs in his father's less than stellar penmanship. He looked over at Denise who continued writing.

He read the note:

Mark, Maryanne, Caroline,

Whoever finds these letters, please deliver the remaining letters to your siblings. I expect that by the time you read this, I have died. Please do not read each other's messages as they are my personal words meant only for each of you individually. If, after reading them, you wish to share your thoughts, that is your prerogative.

I am sorry that your mother and I could not provide you with the happy home so many of your friends enjoyed. The enclosed letters should explain many things. It will not excuse your mother's and my behaviors. I know that our actions had an impact on your lives, but I also know that all of you learned from our mistakes, even though you didn't know the scope of our failings. I pray your families weather the storms of life better than your parents did.

Joseph

Mark inhaled so loudly that Denise stopped writing and looked at Mark. She must have been startled at what she saw because she asked, "What now?"

He simply handed her the note.

She read it twice then looked at Mark. The color drained from her face, fearful of what the letter from Mark's father might say.

She asked, "Are you going to open it?"

Mark took a deep breath and said, "Yeah. Yeah, I am, but not right now." He paused and looked at the paper where Denise had written some notes and asked, "How's it coming?"

She moved her chair closer and pulled the tablet of paper with her. Before she said anything, she put her hands on Mark's cheeks and pulled his face to hers and gave him a soft kiss on the lips. The tension drained away from his neck all the way down to his feet. He kissed her back, and put his arms around her, pulling her as tight as he dared from their awkward positions on the dining room chairs.

He pulled back slightly and whispered, "Thanks. I needed that."

"Me, too." She paused then quietly said, "How about we head back to the hotel and take a break for a few hours?"

Mark smiled and nodded as they stood and headed for the door.

***

Mark and Denise spent two hours back at the hotel. They made love, slowly and gently, concentrating on each other's needs and desires, expressing their unconditional love for each other between kisses and caresses. When they finished showering and dressing, the clock read 6:08 p.m.

Mark asked, "Hungry?"

"A little. Want to order something and pick it up on the way back to the house?"

"You read my mind."

By the time they picked up food from El Grand Patron on the west end of town, and made their way to Jay Street, it was past 7:00 p.m. They walked into the dining room and, as they set the bags of food on the table, Mark noticed the envelope addressed to him sitting in the middle of the table. He turned to Denise who saw his reaction.

Seeing the letter sent Mark's mood into a tailspin, and he did not know why. *The past is past. Nothing in that letter will change it. What could it hurt?* But the old feeling that gripped this household some fifty to sixty years ago seemed to seep out of the walls, the ceiling, the furniture, and close in around him. A chill ran up his spine.

Denise asked, "Should we eat first?"

"Uh, yeah … yeah, we should."

He grabbed the envelopes and the note and pushed them further down the table to make room for their dinner. The tension that they shed earlier with their lovemaking and cuddling crept up on Mark as he slowly ate his enchilada and chips, and drank his beer.

"Maybe we should just work on the obituary after we finish eating. The letter can wait."

Denise nodded, but Mark could see that she did not believe he could or would wait.

Chapter 25

Sitting at the dining room table, Mark's mood continued to spiral downward. He looked from the obituary to the bundles of letters, then to the note and three letters addressed to him and his sisters. At a loss where to start, he sat back and covered his face with his hands, hoping to hide the despair he felt from his wife, but to no avail. She stepped behind him, gripped his shoulders, and began massaging his tight muscles. At her touch, he felt a bit of tension slip away, but his mind still worked overtime, his thoughts pinging like a pinball.

Denise whispered in his ear, "It's getting late. Maybe we should call it a day and get some sleep. I mean, really sleep this time."

Despite still feeling the stress, he smiled, lowering the anxiety level one more notch. He knew Denise, with good intentions, analyzed the situation correctly. The best thing for him would be to leave everything as it stood and get some rest. He didn't know how many more surprises he could take.

The letter addressed to him kept beckoning him to open the envelope and read. Then he remembered letters between his parents remained unread.

He said, "Let's read the last few letters. I can leave my dad's letter until tomorrow."

Even as he said it, he was not sure he could sleep a wink without opening the letter and reading the personal note from the grave. But Denise stopped rubbing his shoulders and said, "Good idea. There are just a few letters left. Where did we leave off?"

Mark leafed through the stack and lifted the next letter in line dated December 19, 1944; less than one week before Christmas.

My Dear Ada May,

I miss you and the children. I hope you all have a Merry Christmas and a hopeful, happy New Year. I pray that the war is coming to an end. It appears that the tide is turning since our troops landed in Normandy. The German Army is faltering now that a fierce, worldwide resistance has risen.

I expect to receive orders within the next three months. I hope and pray that the end of the war is near by then. Maybe I'll be spared actual combat, but that is in God's hands and I will do what needs to be done.

My wish is that this is the last Christmas and New Year that we will be apart. I can't wait to see you again and meet our children in the flesh.

All my love,

Joseph

Denise took a deep breath and lifted the next envelope from the bundle. Dated January 2, 1945, she removed the one-page letter.

Dear Joseph,

Happy New Year. Of all the things I pray for, I mostly pray for peace and your safe return home from this dreadful war. Every day, I look for news that Hitler has surrendered. Every day, I look for your letter saying that you have been *discharged and are on your way home. We are here, awaiting your return.*

God bless you and keep you safe.

Love,

Ada May

The letters did little to relieve Mark's tension, but they neared the last letters in the bundles. Mark hoped that there were no more surprises. That alone would be a relief.

He picked up the next letter expecting to see a return message from his father, but instead, held a letter to his father from Ingrid, dated January 3, 1944.

His eyebrows raised. He looked at Denise who noted his surprise. He said, "It's from Ingrid."

He handed the envelope to Denise who removed the single page note and read:

My Beloved Joseph,

I miss you so. This last year without hearing from you has been torture. I know it was of my own doing, and necessary, but perhaps foolhardy. I ache each day to hear your words, to see your face, to feel your light touch on my face. How could I have cut you out of my life? It was necessary so that you could live your life to the fullest with your wife and children. I could not live with the guilt had I caused such a complete disruption in your life.

This note is to simply wish you a Happy New Year for 1945. I pray for an end to the war, for the destruction of that evil man, Adolf Hitler and his henchmen.

But most of all, I pray that you remain safe so that you're able to return to your wife and family. They will need you as you will need them.

If only things were different, my love. If only ...

Ingrid

Denise continued to stare at the letter, not trusting herself to look at Mark. She reread the letter, taking in the implications of Ingrid having been so passionately in love, but having to walk away from the relationship. Her heart ached for this woman who might be dead. If alive, she would certainly be in her mid-to-late eighties.

She finally looked at her husband. They locked eyes. They reached for each other and hugged fiercely, feeling and knowing the precious love that they shared. Tears welled in their eyes and they both sniffed back moisture threatening to seep from their noses. The sniffs were so in synch that they laughed, breaking the moment.

Mark spoke first. "I can't get over how much Ingrid loved Dad."

Denise wiped the tears from her eyes with the backs of her hands. She asked, "I wonder what became of her? I wonder if she ever moved past her relationship with your dad and found someone else to share her life with? I imagine that, at that time, available men were few. Most were fighting in the war. Maybe when the war ended and men returned home, she maybe found someone." She paused, then said, "But can you imagine the men returning home after seeing their friends and fellow soldiers killed by German soldiers, then meeting a German girl? How would they react?"

Mark nodded. "That would be a tough environment, I'd bet. We may never know what happened. I wouldn't even know where to start searching for her. I mean, I'd really like to find her. She is my real mother, after all."

A few minutes of silence followed, then Mark looked towards the notes for the obituary and the letters to him and his sisters. A chill ran down his spine. He turned back to the bundle of letters. Only four remained.

Mark picked up the next letter addressed to Ada May and was surprised at the date: March 6, 1945. It had been over two months after the last letter from Ada May. He pulled the letter from the envelope and read:

Dear Ada May,

I hope all is well at home. I haven't received any letters from you. I expect that if you sent them, they are lost in the postal system somewhere.

I expect to receive orders to a bomber group any day now. I won't have time to write when I receive orders but will let you know when I get settled at my new duty station, most likely somewhere in England.

Kiss the children for me. Give them my love.

I love you.

Joseph

Mark looked at the date from Ada May's previous letter. It had been over two months since the last letter from his mother to his father. That letter was brief and lacked emotion. He wondered why his mother had not written his father for so long. He looked at the last three letters that remained unread. Not one was from Ada May. He frowned, wondering if his mother experienced some sort of mental crisis. He looked at Denise who shrugged her shoulders, apparently the same question on her mind.

He opened the envelope dated March 30, 1945 and unfolded the one-page letter.

Dear Ada May,

I received orders today. I must report to Molesworth Air Base in England by April 4. I will catch a military flight over. Please say a prayer for all of us trying our best to end the war.

I will send another letter when time permits.

I love you·

Joseph

Mark moved quickly to the next letter. The date – May 7, 1945.

Dear Ada May,

Praise God, the war is over· I am coming home· I hope to be in Sandusky in two or three days, God willing·

I'm coming home!

I love you·

Joseph

Mark looked up, a tentative smile on his face. His father was coming home to his wife and two children. At sixteen months, Mark had no recollection of his father's homecoming. He did not know if he came home to a hero's welcome or if that is the time their homelife began to fall apart.

Denise held the last envelope, dated May 11, 1945. "It's from Ingrid."

Mark's expression turned from a cautious smile to surprise, as if an unwelcome relative showed up unannounced. He took a deep breath and said, "I'm afraid of what it might say. Maybe she changed her mind and decided to go after Dad and that caused the friction at home."

"Only one way to find out."

Denise pulled the letter from the envelope and unfolded the single page.

My Darling Joseph,

I can't believe it is finally over and you made it home safely. When I heard the news that Germany had surrendered, I was cautiously overjoyed, that is until I received word that you were home with your family. It is a miracle and I am so happy for you, your wife, and your children. Now you can lead a normal, happy life.

I am in hiding now with the same family whom I wrote about some time ago. They have been so wonderful and supportive. I don't know how I would have made it through this difficult time without them.

And, of course, I could not have survived without your love and support before you were torn from me. I will always cherish our time together and the love we shared. We may never again meet in this life, but I know we will see each other in the afterlife. Until then, my love.

If only times were different. If only …

All my love,

Ingrid

ps. I received word that my mother died April 4 while working in a factory in Unterluss. Father was killed in Northern Africa by an Allied soldier, God rest their souls.

When Mark heard the postscript about Ingrid's mother dying on April 4 at a factory in Unterluss, his mouth dropped open and his face lost all color. He stood and ran from the room and headed up the stairs, taking two steps at a time. He nearly stumbled as he made his way into the attic. He opened the footlocker and pulled the stack of black and white pictures from the top tray. He quickly leafed through the photos and abruptly stopped. The picture he held showed bombs exploding, destroying a large building; a factory. He turned the photo over and read the barely legible caption; *Munitions factory, Unterluss, Germany, April 4, 1945.*

Mark collapsed onto the floor and broke down, sobbing, realizing that his father may have killed Ingrid's mother, his grandmother.

He looked at the picture and noticed dried spots that distorted the handwritten entry. He suspected they may have been made by his father's tears.

Denise came up behind him and put her arms around her husband. She did not say a word. She just held him tightly.

Chapter 26

Mark and Denise intended to sleep in after the energy draining day Tuesday. The weather started out haze-gray with a chilly drizzle that the Chief Meteorologist from Cleveland Fox Nightly News said would eventually turn into a downpour by 11:00 a.m., then clear out by early afternoon. Mark tossed and turned for most of the night, waking Denise multiple times. They both were unable to sleep beyond 6:30 a.m. Mark decided to shower first. He then dressed in blue jeans and a tee shirt and headed to the hotel's morning continental breakfast buffet while Denise showered. He poured two coffees in a paper-plastic hybrid cup and headed back to the room. As he settled into the chair at the work table, Denise exited the bathroom, hair still damp, in a robe.

She smiled, trying to keep the mood light, and asked, "So, what kind of crazy Traver family secrets are we going to learn today?"

Mark just shook his head and smiled, though the smile lacked authenticity. He could not shake the late-night discovery about the death of Ingrid's mother and his father's potential role in her death. Prior to that revelation, Mark believed that there could not possibly be anything more bizarre than learning about his true ancestry. Now, he feared delving into that history any further. How much more could there be? The more he learned about his family, the more he thought he understood the gloomy mood throughout their house. He wondered why his parents had not just separated. If they stayed together for the sake of Mark and his sisters, he believed that decision was a mistake. It may have been what drove Ada May to kill herself.

Mark turned towards Denise as she watched him, her eyes asking the question *What part of the Traver saga has you so tied up in knots?* When Mark locked eyes with her, she threw open her robe and gave him a full-frontal flash. He smiled and shook his head.

"Just trying to break you out of your moody head."

"It worked." He smiled and stood, stretched, then asked, "What would you like for breakfast on this fine, Ohio morning?"

He took a sip of coffee then looked at it as if he had taken a bite out of a lemon, the coffee having cooled close to room temperature.

"Let me get dressed. We could just grab something light from the breakfast bar. A bagel or English muffins."

Mark said, "Okay. Yeah, that'll work. I think I saw peanut butter and honey. I can work with that."

Twenty minutes later, they sat quietly eating their breakfasts. The fresh, hot coffee turned out better than the cup Mark took back to the room.

He said, "Let's take another run at this obituary. I'd like to finish it today and take it to the Register. I'm not sure it's doable, but we can give it a try."

"Think positive, Mark. We can do it. Things are looking up. Every one thing we finish, it's another checkmark on the list."

The drive to the Jay Street house took fifteen minutes. The rain picked up causing Mark to take it slow down Perkins Avenue, the truck tires splashing water up over the curb along the way. They sat in the car for several minutes while a serious downpour lost its energy, then they made a dash for the door. As soon as they shed their coats and sat at the dining room table, the doorbell rang. When Mark answered, Peggy and Randy Whipple shook off the water from their rain gear. Mark smiled and invited them in.

Peggy said, "I don't have to work until later today, so we thought we'd stop in for a visit, if that's okay."

"That's great," Mark replied. "Denise is in the dining room. Make yourselves at home."

After greetings, with the Whipples seated at the dining room table, Peggy, noted the pad of paper and asked, "Whatcha working on?"

Mark asked from the kitchen, "Can I get you coffee or anything to drink?"

Peggy said, "Coffee would be great; one each, black."

"Coming right up."

Denise said, "We're writing Joe's obituary."

Peggy perked up, smiling as if Denise had suggested a game of cards or charades. "Can we help?"

"Sure."

Mark returned with two steaming coffees. Peggy and Randy moved their chairs to either side of his wife. He set the mugs down in front of their guests and smiled. As Denise led them through what she wrote so far, Peggy suggested that they add more detail to the section on his military years. She said many of the people in town appreciate their veterans, especially those from World War II.

Peggy said, "Your dad didn't talk about the war without being encouraged. When we would have our talks, he would try to avoid the subject. He wasn't shy about telling stories from his past, it just seemed like it caused him pain to talk about it. I don't know … I think it bothered him that he dropped bombs on people who were … defenseless. Those weren't his words, but I could kind of read between the lines. He did like talking about the friends he made while in the service."

As Peggy spoke, Mark thought about his father reading Ingrid's note at the bottom of her last letter. He wondered if that guilt tormented him, why he hated to talk about his part in the war. Mark knew his father could not have known about Ingrid's mother. Even if he knew in advance, he could not have altered the events of that day. He received his orders. Destroy the Unterluss munitions factory, a major cog in Hitler's war machine.

"Mark, honey, are you with us?" Denise asked.

"Sorry. Lost in thought. So, what did we decide?"

Denise said, "I told Peggy about the information that your father left in the footlocker and she suggested that we piece together the timing of his service, the military schools that he attended, the duty stations, and the missions he flew. We could add a section just for those three or so years."

Mark forced a smile and said he agreed, though his mind remained scattered in a dozen different directions.

Denise continued, "They also suggested that we talk with Danny Balken about the civic groups he worked with. Did you know he founded at least two low-income assistance programs?"

That caught Mark's attention. "I met Danny at Holy Angels on Sunday. I have his number right here." He reached for his wallet and pulled out Danny's card. He dialed his personal number. Danny answered on the first ring. He was helping check in supplies at the restaurant and said he could be at the Jay Street house in ten minutes. He pulled up to the curb in six.

Mark greeted him at the door and ushered him into the dining room where, while tipping his Cleveland ballcap to everyone, another round of greetings was exchanged. He declined Mark's offer of coffee.

He asked, "What's up?"

Mark explained that they were writing his dad's obituary, hoping that Danny could help with identifying some of the civic groups in which his father participated.

Danny said, "Let me see what you've got."

He sat at the table, set his ballcap on the chair next to him, and read over several sheets of Denise's notes. As he read, Danny nodded, smiled, hummed a bit, and smiled more. He set the notes down on the table.

He looked at Mark and then at each of them in turn and said, "All good stuff. How about you give me a few minutes and I'll add a few lines."

They all nodded and started talking while Danny went to work. After ten minutes, the four looked at Danny expectantly as he continued to scribble away. Once every few minutes, he would stop, put the pen to his chin, look at the ceiling, smile, then continue writing. Finally, he put the pen down, stood, and stretched.

Looking at Mark, he said, "Take a look."

Mark read through ten pages of notes. If true, his father participated in seven different organizations. He had been president, vice president, and secretary in several and, according to Danny, had been a top financial contributor to most. As Mark continued to read on, the surprise on his face must have shown because Denise and the others stopped talking and were staring at him.

He finally looked up and asked Danny, "Is all this true and verifiable?"

"Every word. I was a member with him in every one of those groups. I'm a pretty generous guy. Not bragging. I've just been fortunate in business and I received a nice inheritance from my parents when they passed. I like to share what I have with others. But your dad … he …" Danny faltered, choking a bit on his words … "your dad was just so generous. Not only financially. He worked his butt off. When any one of those groups had a fund-raiser, like a dinner, or a fair, your dad raised his hand first to volunteer. And he knew how to get people to jump in and help. He made you feel good about giving of your time and your money. But he recognized when people couldn't afford the financial part and just asked that they come do what they could, or just come and enjoy the event. There was just something about him. You wish you could bottle it and sprinkle it on others."

Peggy and Randy nodded their heads in agreement. Randy said, "That's right. Everybody respected your dad. Like Danny said, just something about him made you want to jump in and help. He just made you feel good about yourself, your family, your community."

Mark did not know what to say. He turned to his wife and smiled, tears fighting to escape, but he fought them back, turning to his new friends, nodding his head in thanks.

Randy looked at his cell phone and said, "Peg, we gotta run. You have to get ready for work. I have to be at George's in an hour." As Peggy stood, he turned to Mark and Denise and said, "I hope this helped. I know you're under some stress here, but if there's anything we can do to help, and I mean this sincerely, anything, you let us know. We'll do whatever we can."

Mark and Denise stood and approached their friends, gave them both hugs and saw them to the front door. When they turned, Danny donned his ballcap and, with a broad smile, said, "Like Randy said, I hope this helped. This is too much for the two of you. Call me if you need anything." He turned, then paused and turned back. "Don't go anywhere for lunch. My guys will have something over for you in about half an hour. My treat."

Before they could object, Danny Balken closed the door behind him.

Mark turned to Denise and said, "I guess we better put the finished product together. This is going to cost a fortune to publish."

The front door opened. Danny Balken said, "Before I forget, I'm paying for the obituary. I'll call Max Westridge on my way back to the restaurant."

The door closed again as their jaws dropped.

Chapter 27

True to his word, Danny Balken's crew from Pizza House West delivered a lunchtime feast to the Jay Street house. The spread included two types of submarine sandwiches, two dozen chicken wings with two sauces, a medium cheesy bread and marinara sauce, a chef's salad and drinks. The driver, a young, shaggy-haired kid about high school age, would not accept money even for a tip. He commented that Danny took care of everything.

Stuffed after barely putting a dent in the abundance of food, Mark sat back looking around the table, wondering if they would need to go out for dinner later. Denise saved him from making a decision. "There's enough food in the refrigerator for several days, between today's left-overs and the casserole still in the refrigerator from Abigail Holtzmiller."

Mark's attention was again drawn to the letters to him and his sisters. He looked at Denise who knew Mark could not hold out any longer. The letter from his father drew him in like a magnet. Anticipation mixed with dread as he reached across the table and drew all three letters close to him. He lifted the one with his name and held it to his forehead, as if the act might cause the letter's content to magically transmit to his brain. When nothing happened, he pulled out his pocket knife and sliced through the top of the envelope.

No evil cloud of doom escaped. He did not feel dread or gloom from his past. He took a deep breath and pulled the multi-page letter from the envelope, unfolded the pages and spread them on the table.

Denise asked, "Do you want to read this alone?"

Without looking at her, he said, "No. I want you to read it with me. We're in this together, no matter what."

She pulled her chair close to his, leaning her head on his shoulder, her blondish-gray hair tickling his neck. He took another deep breath and slowly let it out.

He read:

Dear Mark,

If you are reading this letter, I am dead, or in a state where I should be. I hope by writing this letter to you, and similar letters to your sisters, that I can give you some explanation, not excuses, to why your mother and I did not provide all of you with the life you deserved. That's too sugary. We sucked at parenting. We let our problems get in the way of providing the homelife you all deserved.

I hardly know where to start. If you've read the letters between your mother and me, and those that I received from Ingrid Engel, you already know that your mother is not your biological mother. Ingrid is.

Your mother broke off our relationship well over two months before I joined the military. We rarely saw each other during that period. Two days before I had to leave for my first duty station, your mother (Ada May) contacted me and broke the news that she was pregnant and that I was the father. She had not told her folks yet, but begged me to marry her. Being Catholic, and since I believed that I was the father of her child, I decided to do right by her, what was expected of me, and we were married the next day at the Erie County Courthouse.

This was an easy decision from a moral perspective. I fathered a child, so I took responsibility for the child. It was an extremely difficult, personal decision because I had fallen deeply in love with Ingrid Engel, a German girl alone in our country. She had been bullied by nearly everyone in our classes at college. Most of our classmates were men. Not many women attended college back then. But I befriended her while still engaged to Ada May. Our friendship became a point of contention between Ada May and me. Her friends advised her to break off our engagement, and she did.

Since Ada May broke off our engagement, my relationship with Ingrid grew stronger and we fell in love. I did not intend to fall so hard for her or for her to become pregnant. I did not know she had become pregnant until Ada May's letter from January 1945. Ingrid had no one to turn to for help, so she went to

Ada May and turned you over to her. She must have felt justified doing so. After all, Ada May had stolen me from her.

That brings me to another topic, one that will be most difficult for you and your sisters to hear. But you need to hear it from me.

I shot and killed Lyle O'Conner. It was no accident. Lyle and I were best friends all through school. When I signed up for the military, he said he planned to sign up, too. But he didn't. Instead, he stayed at home and played the field of women whose husbands and boyfriends joined the military to fight the war. Lyle started a relationship with Ada May after she ended our engagement, while he was engaged to Mildred Parker, Ada May's best friend in high school. I am not your sister, Maryanne's biological father. The timing of our separation and the timing of her pregnancy does not add up. I also discovered that Ada May's and Lyle's relationship carried on long after I arrived home from the war. So long, in fact, that Lyle is also Caroline's biological father.

I confronted him about this while on our hunting trip. At first, he denied it. Then he admitted it, even bragged about it. He taunted me, called me a coward for leaving Ada May in a difficult position, that he just helped her in a time of need. I couldn't believe it. He called me a coward! He stayed home taking advantage of lonely women while his friends put their lives in jeopardy. What a bastard. He dared me to do something about it. So, I did.

Allen Westridge witnessed the entire scene. He even tried to intervene, but I told him to stay out of it. He was on my side and viewed Lyle's bragging with disdain. Allen joined the military around the same time as I, so he held little sympathy for Lyle. When the police came and questioned us about Lyle's death, Allen swore that it was an accident. The police believed it and wrote it off as that, a hunting accident. Allen and I agreed to take this to our graves. When I wrote this letter, Allen was still alive. Please don't push him on this. It was the right thing to do. I have prayed for forgiveness every day since. I hope God is in a forgiving mood when he considers my lifetime deeds, in total, after my death.

Your mother hated me from the moment I returned from England. I think she believed I would not survive the war, that my plane would be shot out of the sky, or some other calamity. I knew something in our relationship changed when I stopped getting letters from her. She never responded to me after wishing me a happy New Year. When I arrived home, we barely spoke. Having figured out that Maryanne was not my child, I wondered if she would ask for a divorce, even after trapping me into marriage. By that time, Lyle and his fiancé, Mildred, had married and she had nowhere to go for support. I never confronted her about her relationship with Lyle. She trapped herself, and me, into a loveless marriage.

After Caroline moved out, your mother could not tolerate the lie that we had been living. Maybe she and I should have sought counselling beyond that provided by Father Schultz. Maybe, as a good Christian, I should have forgiven her. I could not bring myself to do that. But instead, she found out where I kept my guns and where I kept the key to the gun cabinet. You know the result.

When she killed herself, I felt lonely, but not remorse, the loneliness just a continuation of the feelings that I had for over twenty-five years. Should you ever be inclined to visit her final resting place, after her cremation, I scattered her ashes at Oakland Cemetery along Pipe Creek. There is no marker.

The real victims of our actions were you, Maryanne, Caroline, and your children. The church teaches us that divorce is a sin. I think the greater sin is the hell we put you kids through for all your young lives. That's why I am so proud, so amazed at the success that you, Maryanne, and Caroline experienced raising your kids. Yes, I kept tabs on you and how your life progressed even though I made no direct contact with you. I believed that, if you wanted me to be a part of yours and your family's lives, you would have contacted me. That your sisters and you did not, tells me how deeply I hurt all of you. I deserved every bit of yours and your sisters' scorn.

I am so very, deeply sorry for the hurt I caused you. As father and son, we should have developed a relationship, a good relationship, regardless of the rift between Ada May and me. I should have found a way to put that aside and be a good father to you. I blame myself for everything that transpired. Ada May's faults do not absolve me of my *responsibilities as a father· I know the blame sits squarely on my shoulders·*

I am hardly one in a position to give advice, but here goes· Love your family with all your heart and mind· Don't let anything stand in the way of that· No matter what material things you accumulate, nothing is as important as the love of, and for, them·

I am not seeking forgiveness· I am not seeking absolution· I just wanted you to know the facts as I see them and hope that you have learned from my mistakes· From what I have seen, you certainly have·

God bless you and your beautiful family, Mark·

I love you son,

Joe

By the time Mark read his father's name, his eyes watered and his hands quivered slightly. Through his reading of the letter, Denise rubbed his back, then put a hand on his arm, the emotion of the moment engulfing them both.

Chapter 28

Mid-afternoon on Wednesday, Mark and Denise had the dining room lights on to overcome the darkness from the damp, drab day. A hard rain that earlier soaked the streets fizzled away to a mist. The mood from the day and the letter from Mark's father settled into their hearts and minds. Just when they thought nothing could be more demoralizing than the remarks from Mildred O'Conner the previous afternoon, they learned that Mark's father had killed a man, Mildred's husband, in cold blood: maybe justified, maybe not. But the unvarnished truth hit Mark hard. The roller-coaster ride that had been his father's life continued and it pulled Mark into a dizzying cycle.

After reading the letter a second time, Mark turned to his wife, wrapped his arms around her, and pulled her to him in a tight hug. They stayed that way for several minutes. Denise kissed Mark softly on the lips, lingering for several seconds. She put her hands on either side of his face and locked eyes with him. She remained silent, the message passing to her husband that she supported him and loved him unconditionally. Slowly, she stood and began to clear the table of the large volume of leftovers, courtesy of Danny Balken and Pizza House West.

As she entered the kitchen and began loading the food into the refrigerator, she called over her shoulder, "Do you want another beer?"

Before he could answer, the doorbell rang.

"Hold off on that beer, honey."

Mark stood, walked to the front door, and opened it, surprised to see Catherine O'Conner Sims on the stoop. She turned to Mark, forced a tentative smile, and said, "I hope I'm not intruding."

"No, not at all. Come in."

Mark stepped aside and motioned for Catherine to enter. He asked her to follow him into the dining room, noting that she surveyed the dilapidated living room furniture as she passed. Once they entered the dining room, he pointed to a chair, inviting her to have a seat. When they both sat, he asked, "What brings you by?"

Before she could speak, Denise returned from the kitchen and said, "Hi Catherine. Can I get you anything? Coffee, water, pop, a beer?"

"Water would be nice, thanks."

Mark called to her, "I'll take that beer now, if you don't mind."

Denise acknowledged Mark's request and returned with drinks.

Catherine asked Mark, "How's the estate coming along?"

Mark raised his eyes to the ceiling and thought for a moment before responding. "It's coming. It's a slow process, but I think everything's falling into place."

"Do you have a date for the funeral? I think Mom would like to attend, if that's alright."

Even though the request surprised him, he replied, "I don't see why not. Sure. The funeral is set for 10:00 a.m. Thursday, May twenty-first, at Holy Angels. Dad will be cremated and his ashes will be interred at Calvary Cemetery. We're still working on the wake after the graveside service. I think the Bereavement Committee at the church will provide a lunch."

"That sounds nice."

An awkward silence ensued. Catherine looked as if she struggled with what she wished to say next, looking down at the table, holding her water glass tight. She looked up. "Mom is getting up in age."

Mark and Denise nodded slightly, not knowing the intention of Catherine's visit and what direction the conversation might head. She continued, "Her stories from long ago have changed over time." She cleared her throat. "When Dad died in that hunting accident, I was young, just a little kid really, like ten. I cried my eyes out for days."

Catherine's mention of the "hunting accident" caused Mark to tense. He flicked a glance at Denise. He caught the concern in her eyes, wondering if Catherine knew any details of the incident. If she did, she did not show it.

She continued, "Mom tried to console me, but she couldn't. I blamed her." She took a deep, trembling breath. "Can you believe it? I blamed her for Dad getting killed over two hundred miles from home."

Catherine began to cry. Denise grabbed her purse. Like a Girl Scout, always prepared, she handed Catherine a travel package of tissues. Mark and Denise remained silent as their guest wiped her eyes and took a healthy drink of water.

When she continued, her eyes were red and puffy, but her tears subsided. "Before Dad died, I'd hear them fighting, arguing so loud I'm sure the neighbors heard. The police were called to our house a couple times that I remember. Mom accused Dad of cheating on her … with her best friend."

Catherine's eyes met Mark's. She continued. "He didn't even deny it. I remember him saying that his cheating was her fault. Her fault!" She paused, the silence deafening. "What's worse, back then, I sided with Dad. I hated mom for making him cheat on her. Of course, now I know that was all bullshit … pardon my language."

Denise quietly said, "That's alright. Go on."

"Mom blamed Dad, of course. When I reached my teens, she confided in me that she knew he cheated on her even before they married. She would catch him in a lie. She'd argue, yell, even threaten to take me and leave him. He'd swear up and down that he would stop, that he still loved her and her only. The other women meant nothing to him. Then she'd forgive him. All his sins forgiven, until the next time, then it started all over again. It only encouraged him to cheat more. Over time, after Dad died, she came up with this story about some German girl who caused all their troubles. At the time, she couldn't keep her thoughts straight and her stories changed. At first, I thought she made the whole thing up, but she spoke with such certainty. How could I not believe her?" She laughed as she wiped the tears from her eyes again. "I don't know why I'm telling you all this. It sounds gossipy even as I say it."

Mark and Denise remained silent for a spell, then Mark asked, "Why did she blame this German girl?"

Catherine took another deep breath, trying to control her emotions, then looked directly at Mark. "According to mom, this girl - I never learned her name – she somehow seduced your dad, stole him away from your mom. Mom said she acted like the poor victim, claiming that everyone picked on her. Her parents were still in Germany. They sent her over here to go to school. Most of her classmates, mainly the few female classmates, hated her, because she was pretty, but also because of her accent. The war, according to Mom, was getting scary. Hitler took over country after country, sometimes without a fight. So, naturally, when this girl showed up, everyone became suspicious of her, like she was some kind of spy, or something.

"Mom said that your dad felt sorry for her. He started to protect her from the abuse. According to Mom, this girl faked the whole 'poor me' scenario to win him over."

She paused, wiped her eyes with a tissue, then asked, "Could I get that beer now?"

Denise smiled, nodded, and stepped into the kitchen, returning with an opened bottle of beer. She handed it to Catherine, who thanked her, and took a quick drink, then continued.

"Mom encouraged your mom to break off her engagement. She said your dad didn't deserve her, that she could do better. I wondered from the way mom told her side of the story if she devised secret plans to make a move on your dad. You heard her last night. She settled for my dad. I think she loved your dad, and she was as jealous of your mom as she was of the German girl."

Mark eyed Catherine, wondering if she hoped to hear something from him that would validate or refute her mother's stories. He asked, "Do you know why your mother believed the German girl caused my parent's breakup? We've been reading some letters between my parents and there's nothing that we can see that indicates Ingrid – that's the German girl's name, by the way – was the instigator."

"Remember, this is my mom talking. She said your dad spent so much time with … Ingrid … that it left him little time for your mom. She felt lonely, abandoned. She gave your dad an ultimatum; either stop seeing "that girl" or we're through. But he wouldn't abandon Ingrid to fend for herself, so your mom broke off their engagement. She didn't know then that she was pregnant. Your mom, I mean."

Mark took a deep breath, wondering if Catherine knew more about family relationships than she let on. He wondered how many others in town knew that Mark and Maryanne were not twins. As he looked at Catherine's face, the resemblance to his sister, Maryanne so striking, he again wondered about the possible biological relationship between his sister and the woman seated at the table. "Have you ever met my sisters, Maryanne and Caroline?"

"No. why do you ask?"

"No reason. Just curious."

He hoped Catherine believed the lie. He asked, "What do you know about the hunting accident and how your father died?"

"Just that he had been hunting with friends. Your dad and another man were on the trip and one of the guns accidentally discharged. The bullet hit dad in the chest. They were a long way from any city, so help couldn't get there in time to save him."

Mark lowered his eyes so she could not see the relief in his expression. He took a deep breath and said, "I'm sorry. It must have been awful for you, then to go through your teen years without a father."

Mark shook his head, not knowing what else to say, especially in light of his learning the truth about Lyle O'Conner's death just moments before her arrival at the Jay Street house.

Denise said, "Your name is Sims. So, you're married?"

"I was. My husband died from cancer. He was a firefighter for the City of Huron. He's been gone now for nineteen years. I have a steady live-in but I'll never marry again."

Catherine took another drink of beer, then said, "I just wanted you to know that you should take what my mother said with a grain of salt. Her memory is failing. I think she's modifying her recollections to fit what she wished had happened. But one thing I'm pretty sure of; Your mom and my dad carried on an affair while your dad was overseas during the war and it continued long after he came home. Mom remembered that one thing pretty consistently."

Chapter 29

After Catherine left, Mark and Denise embraced inside the front door. The emotion of the past few hours weighing on them, both mentally and physically. Between Joseph Traver's letter and the admission of guilt that it contained, and Catherine's heart-wrenching recollections, they both needed a break from the drama of Mark's father's life. They remained in their tight embrace for several minutes before stepping back from one another, their smiles mixed with fatigue.

They looked around the living room at the decrepit furniture and drab walls. Mark shrugged. "It fits right in with the way I feel; run down, overused and just plain old."

Denise laughed, but her body language conveyed anything but humor. "I'm glad I made the trip up here. I can't imagine you going through this alone." She locked eyes with her husband and said, "Not what you expected?"

"Ha. Not even close. I thought I'd have this wrapped up in a few days and hop a flight home. Now, I don't know." He shook his head, trying to gather his thoughts. "I still have to let Maryanne and Caroline know about their letters from dad. I should just put them in bigger envelopes and send them on. I'd love to be a fly on the wall when they read them."

Denise said, "Maybe you should wait and see what else pops up before sending them. They didn't want anything to do with your father and they don't want anything to do with his estate. Maybe you should just burn them, act as if they never existed. We're the only ones who know."

Mark raised an eyebrow. At first, stunned by her comment, he stared at her, wondering why she would suggest destroying the letters. Then he looked up at the ceiling, gathering his thoughts. He asked, "Why shouldn't I send them?"

"For one, they want nothing to do with your dad, alive or dead. I doubt they would even read them. Second, they've laid all the responsibility and work on you. They've offered no help. On the contrary, they've basically said, you're on your own. I don't think you owe them anything. You're the executor. Technically, the letters might belong to you."

Mark remained silent for a moment then said, "Maybe I should read them and then decide if I should send them on."

"Whatever you decide, you don't have to do anything right now. Put them back in the footlocker for now. Which reminds me, we were going to continue looking through that thing, see what other secrets it holds."

Mark replied, "That's a good idea. Let's get our beers and the letters and head upstairs."

They made it as far as the stairway when the doorbell rang. Mark gave Denise a *What now?* look. He made his way to the door and found Mrs. Holtzmiller looking up at him from the stoop. She smiled and said, "My goodness, I still can't get over how much you look like your daddy."

Mark smiled and said, "Mrs. Holtzmiller, please come in."

As she passed Mark, who still held his beer, and saw Denise standing in the living room, also holding a beer, she asked, "I didn't interrupt a party, did I?"

Mark and Denise laughed. "No. We were just talking."

"I just wanted to come by and see how you two were holding up. It looked like Grand Central Station here for a while."

Mark's smile widened as he motioned towards the dining room entryway. They sat at the dining room table. Denise remarked. "Yes, Ma'am. We've had our share of visitors. Speaking of visitors, what brings you by?"

"A couple things. First, I wanted to see if you needed anything else to eat for the next few days. I can whip up something if you like."

Mark started, "Mrs. Holtzmiller ..."

"Please, enough with this Mrs. stuff. Call me Abbe."

"Alright, Abbe. Danny Balken sent us a bunch of food from his restaurant. Would you like some sandwiches or wings? We have enough for at least four more people."

She waved her hand in a dismissive gesture, then asked, "I thought I smelled wings. Nothing to eat, but have you got another beer? I couldn't share one with you when you were growing up, but I guess you're old enough now."

They laughed at the old woman's joke. Denise left the room to get a round of beers, though she and Mark were still pretty full from lunch. Once everyone took their seats again, Abbe said, "I don't know what you've learned in the time since you arrived back here in town, but I wanted to tell you a few things about your childhood. I hate to gossip, but there are some things I think you deserve to know."

Mark braced himself, wondering if she would drop some new bombshell or if it might be something they already learned. He raised his eyebrows and said, "We have discovered a lot about Mom and Dad, some of it quite surprising."

"What I have to tell you might just be old news then."

Mark wondered what he should tell this woman who lived next door to his parents for as long as his mom and dad lived in the Jay Street house. Maybe she knew everything Mark knew and more. She knew the family through the children's entire youth. It could not hurt to hear her out. He decided to tell her some of what they learned then she could decide if there were gaps that she might be able to fill in.

"Abbe, I'm not sure where to start, so I'll just dive in." He looked to Denise for support. She just nodded slightly. "Mom carried on an affair with my dad's best friend while Dad fought in the war. The affair continued after Dad's return at the end of the war."

Abbe gave Mark a sad smile. She remained silent as if she wanted to hear more before she said her piece.

He continued, "All my life, I was told that Maryanne and I were fraternal twins. We discovered that isn't true. I haven't told Maryanne this yet. She may already know, but I was sure surprised to read about it."

Mark continued with his account of the many things that they discovered in the footlocker, including the letter from his dad to him. He did not mention the other two letters to his sisters.

"So, my entire childhood, what I believed about our family, was all a lie."

While Mark told Abbe Holtzmiller what they discovered, she kept a passive face, her expression changing only slightly. When he finished, she took a deep breath.

"Mark, like I told you before, I hate to speak ill of the dead, but your mother was a real piece of work. When you and Maryanne were quite young, with your dad at work, she would come over and ask if I could watch you two while she shopped. Of course, I said yes, and she would parade you both over. We had a good time while she was gone. You two were good kids, though I never saw any similarities between you. Your mom stayed out for a couple hours. She did this every week for nearly a year.

Over time, I noticed that she never came home with any bags. No groceries, no bags from clothing stores. Nothing. I thought to ask her about that but decided to do a little snooping instead. So, one day I put you kids in the car and followed her … to a hotel. She met a man. Later I learned the man's name …"

Mark interrupted, "Lyle O'Conner."

Abbe looked at Mark, the surprise on her face. "Yes. Lyle O'Conner. After that day, I told her I couldn't watch you kids anymore. Whenever she would ask, I made excuses, like a hair appointment, or housework, or had to get groceries myself. I even asked her if she'd like to join me since we were both shopping. She always declined my offer."

"Did you ever tell Dad about what you learned?"

Abbe briefly remained silent. She finally said, "No. I knew your dad would find out, if he didn't know already. Your mom wasn't a very good liar and, even though she tried to hide her 'shopping trips' I knew he'd figure it out."

The old woman reached into a pocket on her house dress and pulled out an envelope. "Shortly after your sister, Caroline, moved out, she wrote me a letter apologizing for putting me in the middle of her family drama. I read it the day she killed herself."

She handed the envelope to Mark, her face tight with a sad expression. He opened the note. It was a hand-written copy of her obituary; similar to the one his mother had sent to him. She must have been consumed by guilt. Before the obituary she scrawled several lines asking Abbe Holtzmiller for forgiveness, asking that she pray for her soul.

"I didn't know what to do when I read the note. I waited for several hours, wondering if I should call the police, or the fire station. We didn't have 911 back then. Finally, I came over here and rang the doorbell." She paused and took a deep breath. "I heard the shot. It wasn't real loud, because … you know where she did it?"

Mark nodded. "Yeah. In the old coal room."

Abbe's eyes teared up. She cleared her throat then said, "If I'd have come over right away, I might have been able to talk her out of it. Maybe show her that she could make amends, patch things up with your father. But I was too late."

Denise reached out and put her hand over the old woman's hand, trying to offer some comfort.

Mark said in a strong, clear voice, "Abbe, you can't blame yourself for not saving Mom. Father Schultz reached out to Mom, trying to console her, trying to stop her. He invoked the name of God and Jesus, and anything he could think of. Nothing he did could stop her." He paused, then said, "You have nothing to be sorry for. This was all on Mom … and Lyle O'Conner."

Abbe looked at Mark with tears running down her cheeks. Then she turned to Denise and said, "You have a good man here, Denise. Don't let him get away." She smiled.

Denise smiled back. "I'll do my best."

They raised their beers in a toast to each other and took a healthy drink from their beers. When they set their bottles on the table, Abbe said, "One other thing. After I found out that your mom cheated on your dad, I came over here one day when your mom was away and tried to seduce him."

Astonished, Mark and Denise's jaws dropped open. They sat staring at their guest for several seconds, then Abbe Holtzmiller said, "Just kidding. Figured you needed some comic relief."

They exhaled and laughed.

She stood. "I'll show myself out."

Mark and Denise followed her and smiled as she made her way down the steps and headed towards her home next door.

Chapter 30

Still smiling from Abbe's remarks, they headed back to the dining room. Mark looked out the dining room window, noticing the cloud cover breaking up, the late day sun streaking in from the southwest. The combination of Abbe's humor and the prospect of a sunny tomorrow lifted their spirits. For the first time, Mark thought that the earth-shaking surprises might be behind them.

Mark asked, "Where were we before Abbe came over?"

"Up in the attic to look through the footlocker, see if there were more surprises."

"You know, I've been thinking about that broken rifle in dad's gun cabinet. Why would he keep that damn thing? I don't know much about gun repairs, but I don't think it can be fixed. I should probably get rid of it before the auction."

Denise gave her husband an inquisitive look. "Are there any gunsmiths in the area?"

Mark frowned, "I don't know. Maybe if we catch a break in the action tomorrow, I can look around. There's a sporting goods store out towards Milan. I'll call them and see if they know of anyone."

Denise nodded. She asked, "Are you ready to head upstairs?"

Mark nodded, stood, and motioned for her to lead the way. As they climbed the stairs, he smiled and commented, "Nice view from back here."

She stopped suddenly and smiled back at him. "Well, maybe we should call it a day and head back to the hotel."

Mark stopped in his tracks and turned to head back downstairs when the doorbell rang again.

They both looked up, their body language screaming *When will it end?*

They headed back down the steps. Mark answered the door, surprised to find his son, Elliot, smiling up at him from the stoop.

"Hi, Dad. Did I interrupt something?"

"Elliot! Come on in. And, no, we were just heading to the attic. We thought we might look through your grandpa's footlocker again." He turned and said, "Honey, look who's here."

Elliot walked into the house and embraced his mom. She asked, "How was the trip up?"

"For the first hour, it rained. The roads were slick. Then it tapered off, so from Bucyrus to here wasn't too bad. Should be a nice day tomorrow."

Denise said, "Let's sit. You hungry? We have a ton of leftovers; sandwiches, wings, salad; you name it. From Pizza House West."

"Actually, I could use a bite. But no beer. I have to drive back tonight."

"Okay, I'll throw some stuff in the oven. Pop or water?"

"Water's good, Mom."

Mark and Elliot made their way to the dining room and sat as Denise moved around in the kitchen. She brought his water then, with her hands on her hips, asked, "Where are our grandchildren?"

"Marcus is studying for finals, which start a week from Tuesday. He's hoping to finish with a 4.0. He gets pretty intense around this time of year."

Mark said, "He must get his brains from his grandma. He didn't get that from me."

Elliot smiled. "I hope he got some of it from me, but his mom's pretty smart, too. Caitlin isn't worried about anything except boys right now. We'll have to watch that girl. She's at that age where Sandy and I are pretty lame, the worst parents ever, and every one of her friends has so much more freedom than she does, and blah, blah, blah."

Denise laughed and said, "She'll get over that … someday. How are things going for you? Any promotions, opportunities on the horizon?"

Elliot smiled. "I'm pretty happy where I am right now. I've got about ten to twelve years until I can retire with a good pension. I'll still be a relatively young man, then we'll see what happens. Sandy would like to do a little travelling. I would, too. But we'll see what fate has planned."

Denise said, "You could always take a trip to Florida, somewhere like New Smyrna Beach, Daytona, Cocoa Beach. You could spend some time with your sister and her friend in New Smyrna. Your father and I could come over for a short visit. We'd leave you two alone most of the time. You could bring the kids and drop them off at our place."

Elliot's wife, Sandy, had been a stay-at-home wife and mom for over twenty years and wanted to see the world. She had never been to the west coast, Alaska, the Caribbean, or any European countries.

Elliot replied, "I promised to take her on a short trip to Maine this summer, making stops along the way. But we might be able to fit in a week in Florida. I'll run it by her when I get home and let you know."

This made Denise smile. She loved visiting her grandchildren. With Elliot and his sister never meeting their paternal grandfather, she made sure her grandkids did not miss out on that opportunity.

Elliot asked, "So, what interesting things have you found out about grandpa?"

When their eyebrows shot up, he smiled. "From the looks on your faces, something pretty crazy."

Mark spoke, "Where to begin … Maybe, to start, you should read the notes we have for his obituary."

Mark reached across the table to a stack of papers and found Denise's notes. He grabbed the pages off the top and passed them to Elliot who began to read. It took him several minutes to read through the handwritten pages, stopping at certain points, smiling, frowning, shaking his head in wonder.

"Whose obituary is this? I never heard anything good about grandpa from either of you."

Mark shrugged his shoulders. "I can't explain it. I was as surprised as you to hear some of this … praise. I mean, I would run into someone at a store or restaurant and they would say *Hey, aren't you Mark Traver, Joe Traver's son?* Then they'd start telling me about this great guy, Joe Traver. Well, you read the notes. A lot of that came from Danny Balken, who owns the pizza place, and Peggy and Randy Whipple. Peggy used to clean house for Dad."

Elliot looked around, the look on his face all but saying that she didn't do a very good job.

"You can't judge her work by what you see. Your grandpa told her to stop cleaning and just visit with him, which, apparently, she did."

Denise jumped up. "That reminds me. The stuff in the oven is probably ready." She headed into the kitchen and pulled open the oven door.

Mark continued, "He left me a letter, kind of like his dying declaration."

"Wow. Can I read it?"

"I'll have to think about that. It has some pretty … personal things. There are some things that your mom and I need to talk about before you can do that."

"Really? Sounds serious."

Mark nodded. "You'll find out soon enough, but it is."

"What, was he in debt or something?"

Mark slowly shook his head as if he had a lot weighing on his mind. He looked back at Elliot and said, "Nothing like that. On the contrary, he appears to have plenty of money and some investments. We haven't finished that part of the estate yet. Most of what I'm talking about is personal. Honestly, I'm still trying to … umm … sort out my feelings about what we've learned."

Denise walked in with a cookie sheet filled with wings, sandwiches, a chef's salad, plates, and silverware. She placed the food on the table and said, "Dig in."

Elliot still looked at his dad and said, "It can't be that bad." Mark gave his son a look that made Elliot's eyes widen. "Is it really that bad?"

"Let's just say … everything I thought about my life before I moved out of this house," he raised his hand as if modelling a prize in a gameshow, "has changed to some degree. I hope you can let it drop for now.

"Changing the subject, you, Sandy, and the kids will be here for the funeral, right?"

Elliot's brain still churned, trying to figure out just how seismic the information that his parents had discovered could be. He nodded and said, "Sure. Absolutely."

"Great. We'd really appreciate that."

"Are Aunt Maryanne and Aunt Caroline and their families going to be here? You know, I've never met them or my cousins. It would be nice, I think, if we could at least meet them."

Mark cleared his throat, then said, "I wouldn't count on that. Your aunts want nothing to do with any of this, including the funeral."

Elliot just shook his head in disgust. "I think that sucks. Could it really have been that bad living with Grandma and Grandpa Traver back then?"

Denise nodded her head and, in a quiet voice, "Yes. It was that bad. I hated coming here with your dad … so much so that I begged your dad to never bring me here again. It's hard to describe the toxic mood in this house. When we left to get our own place, I made your dad promise that we would never return."

Elliot's head snapped back in surprise. After reading his grandpa's obituary, he found it astonishing that this house could be so unwelcoming. He wanted to ask a few questions, but hesitated. His mother gave him a look that pleaded *Leave it alone for now*. So, he did.

They ate in silence for a time. Mark and Denise only picking at the food, still full from lunch.

Elliot finally asked, "Did you ever figure out who sent that note to grandpa? You know, the one Marcus found on the China cabinet?"

Mark shook his head. "Nope. Just one of several mysteries that we've come across.

Elliot looked from Mark to Denise then said, "I don't mean to be pushy, but would you be totally against me contacting my cousins, you know, to introduce myself?"

Mark and Denise looked at each other, shrugged their shoulders. Mark said, "I don't see what it would hurt." He paused, then asked, "Can I ask why the sudden interest, especially since their mothers want nothing to do with us."

He shrugged his shoulders and said, "Maybe Aunt Maryanne and Caroline want nothing to do with grandpa and this house, even this town, but we'll never know about our cousins unless we reach out and ask. Have you ever asked them if they would mind us visiting them?"

Again, they looked at each other and shook their heads. "We've never even thought to ask. I think we were all in such a hurry to leave that we never considered the future and our relationships." Mark locked eyes with Elliot, "How serious are you about this?"

"I don't know. I've just been wondering what they're like. If we'd have common interests. Stuff like that."

Denise said, "If you decide to reach out to your cousins, you have our blessing." She turned to Mark, "Maybe we should consider doing the same with your sisters."

Mark looked non-committal. He knew he needed to call his sisters soon and give them an update, though they told him that they were not interested except to find out the estate was closed. "We can talk more about it, later."

They talked for about an hour more then Elliot hugged his parents and said goodbye. After he left, Mark and Denise headed to the attic to look through the footlocker. No more calls or doorbells interrupted this time. They looked through medals, uniform hats, and other knick-knacks. When Denise came to the stack of pictures, she came across a black and white photo of a young woman holding an infant child. She smiled, then turned the picture over. She placed a hand on Mark's arm and passed the photo to him.

"What's that?"

When he flipped the photo over, his eyes once again welled. In perfect penmanship, it said, *Me with our precious baby boy, Mark.*

Mark knew the woman was not Ada May Traver. It must be his biological mother, Ingrid.

Chapter 31

Thursday morning came early. Mark had a dream-filled, restless sleep. With the newly discovered picture of Ingrid Engel and her infant son - him - on the nightstand next to his wallet, keys, and cell phone, he tossed and turned until he could no longer stay in bed. He picked up the picture at least half a dozen times, placing his fingers over the image of the young woman, seeing her smile and the look of adoration on her face. He wondered how she could appear so calm and happy, knowing her circumstances at the time the picture was taken. The decision he knew she made, to give her son to another woman, must have been on her mind even as she looked so happy in the grainy, black-and-white image.

At 5:20 a.m., he decided to take a shower without waking Denise. They made love when they arrived back in the hotel room, the act more passionate than their lovemaking for as long as he could remember. He smiled, thinking that he would make the effort to pay closer attention to his wife's needs in the future.

The hot water felt good on his shoulders and back, helping the tightness in his muscles ease. As he reached for the soap, he heard the bathroom door open and the shower curtain slide back.

In a near whisper, Denise said, "Let me help you with that."

"Mmm. Thank you. I was just thinking about you."

Looking down, she said, "I can guess what you were thinking."

They laughed as she turned him so that she could apply soap to his back.

He asked, "Couldn't sleep, either?"

"Maybe a few good hours, but I kept having crazy dreams."

"You, too, huh?"

Denise reached around to his chest and stomach, soaping up everywhere she touched. "I dreamed that our kids had their cousins over to the house for a swim. They were having a great time, laughing, diving for pool toys. Then your sister, Caroline, came out to the lanai and yelled for her kids to get out of the pool, that they shouldn't be swimming with strangers. Then I woke up."

Mark turned to face her, a surprised look on his face. "Was she angry or worried about their safety?"

"I really don't know. The only time I met your sister she was about fourteen. When we were at your folk's house, she would come down from her room long enough to snipe at everyone she saw. She had a smart mouth and your folks … I don't know, but I think they were afraid of her. Tough age in a bad environment."

Mark thought about it for a few seconds then said, "My turn."

He took the soap and turned her around to start on her back. Taking his time while being gentle, he worked his way from the back of her neck, down her arms, then to her back. He watched as she closed her eyes and moaned softly.

They did not speak another word as they made love in the shower. After twenty minutes in the hot spray, they climaxed, gripping each other in a tight embrace.

Once dressed and ready to head back to the house on Jay Street, Mark said, "I have to call that sportsman's store. I would guess that they're open by now."

He looked at the clock; 9:35 a.m. He picked up his phone and searched to find the number. When the Lake Erie Sportsman's Outlet came up on the screen, he hit the phone icon and waited. After two rings, a young woman answered, reciting the store's name, identifying herself as Glenda. Mark asked Glenda if she knew of a gunsmith in the area.

"Why, yes, I do. His name is Herman Lightfoot. He is the best gunsmith around. Well, he's the only gunsmith around that I know of."

Glenda gave Mark the man's number and location on Ohio Route 4. She advised him that the drive would take him about ten minutes. He thanked Glenda and looked at the information he had written on the hotel notepad.

Denise picked up her purse and they moved to the door when Mark's phone sounded. He looked at the number; Allen Westridge. He answered.

"Good morning, Allen."

Allen's voice seemed even more gravelly than the last time they had spoken. "Good morning, Mark." He took a deep, wheezy breath. "I wanted to tell you that your sisters received their copies of the property appraisal." Another breath, then a phlegmy cough. "I asked if they read the will and they both said yes. I'm not sure" … another cough … "I believe them, but, whatever. They again said you'd take care of everything."

The lawyer fell into a coughing spell that lasted over thirty seconds. When he finished, he said, "Sorry about that. Maybe I should quit smoking. That's a joke. Anyway, I have your copy of the appraisal as well. You can stop in anytime and pick it up."

"Thanks, Allen. I'll be in later today, probably before lunch."

"Good, Mark. Don't wait too long. You know what Bob Dylan said about knocking on heaven's door." He chuckled, then coughed as he disconnected the call.

Mark looked at Denise. "My sisters have their copy of the appraisal. They told Allen that I would take care of everything. Remember what you said about their letters from Dad? I'm wondering if we should just shred them."

"It's up to you, Sweety. Do you think they know that your Dad …"

She didn't finish. Mark frowned. "How would they know? I mean, I had no idea."

Denise scrunched up her lips then said, "Caroline lived in the house long after we left. Maybe she found the footlocker and did a little snooping. I don't know. With all this drama, my mind is running in overdrive, thinking of all kinds of crazy thoughts. If she did find out, maybe she spoke with Maryanne and told her what she found out."

Mark shrugged his shoulders. "Who knows? I know Caroline and I have never been close, even when we lived in the same house. Hell, Maryanne and I never spoke much even though we were supposedly twins." He shook his head and motioned for the door. "Let's get going. What do you want for breakfast?"

"How about another shower?"

"We'll starve if we keep that up."

"Cleanliness is next to Godliness."

"Let's go see what surprises God has for us today."

***

They settled on The Better Half, a local favorite on the west end of town on Washington Street. They gave the waitress their order and settled into one of the booths. They ate a couple omelets, hash browns, and wheat toast with coffee. While finishing off the last sip of brew, Mark called Herman Lightfoot, the best and only gunsmith in the area.

Lightfoot answered with a booming "Hello."

"Mr. Lightfoot. My name is Mark Traver."

Lightfoot cut him off and asked, "You Joe Traver's kid?"

"Yes, sir, I am. I was …"

"Sorry about your old man. He was a good fella."

"Thank you, Mr. Lightfoot."

"Call me Herm. Everybody else does. Now what can I do for you?"

"Well, we're going through my dad's belongings and he has a gun that is damaged. I was wondering, could you take a look at it, see if it can be repaired?"

"Why, sure. When can you drop it off? And how soon do you need to know? Depending on the condition, I might be able to tell you right away, or it could take a little time. If you can come by before lunch, I don't have anything pressing right now."

"I should be there in about half an hour."

"Okay. Meet me at the building out front. That's my shop. I'll be in there cleaning up."

When Mark disconnected, he told Denise about the call as he finished his breakfast. When they arrived at the Jay Street house, he hustled out to the garage basement and retrieved the damaged gun from the cabinet. He stopped back in the house, kissed Denise goodbye, and headed for the truck.

***

The drive to Herman Lightfoot's gun shop took twelve minutes. Mark pulled into the gravel parking lot in front of the forty-by-thirty-foot building with tan, metal siding, and a brown shingled roof. When he entered the door with the broken firearm in tow, an old-style bell tinkled above his head. An old man with a short-cropped, gray beard, in blue coveralls and a gray tee shirt approached.

"Herm Lightfoot?"

"That's me." He stopped in his tracks and looked at Mark from head to toe. "You look just like your old man. Spittin' image, I'd say."

He closed the distance between them and extended his hand. As they shook, he said, "Your old man was a real card. He'd a given the shirt off his back if you needed it, then bought you lunch." Herm shook his head. "Damn shame, his passing. He'll be hard to replace in some of the organizations he supported. Enough with that." He looked at the broken rifle in Mark's hand and said, "Let's see what you've got here."

Mark hoisted the rifle to eye level and watched as Herman Lightfoot focused on the weapon. Herm took the rifle in both hands and rotated it horizontally, looking from the tip of the barrel to the bent and broken stock. He closed one eye and looked from the stock down the length of the barrel then flipped it over and examined the bottom.

He said, "Like I told Allen when he brought it in like, fifty years ago, it can be fixed, but it would be an expensive job. It's a cheap gun, so, hardly worth it."

Mark's brow furrowed. "You mean, Joe, my dad."

Herm looked back at Mark and said, "No. This is, or was, Allen Westridge's rifle. He broke it on a hunting trip. Said he tripped on a rock and fell right on top of it. If you ask me, it had to be one hell of a fall down a hill and over a bunch of rocks to do this much damage. You can see where it hit rocks several times."

Herm held the weapon under the barrel so that it remained level from front to back, with the barrel pointing to his left, Mark's right. "Look at the stock. You can see four or five distinct indents in the wood where it struck something solid, like a rock, or a metal post." Herm pointed to the damage as he spoke. "You can see where the stock split and splintered in two spots. On some rifles, the shoulder stock, or some just call it the butt stock, among other things, are completely made of wood. This rifle has a metal inner frame." He pointed to the visible metal under where the wood had split. "That metal frame is bent, as is the block that attaches to the barrel. That took a lot of force. A fall could have done it, but, like I told Allen, it had to be one hell of a fall."

Mark tried to figure out why his dad had Allen Westridge's damaged rifle in his gun cabinet. It did not make sense. He asked Herm, "What did Allen want you to do with it?"

He gave a half smile. "Allen wondered if I could replace the barrel and fix the stock. Funny thing is, he didn't think he damaged the barrel. I told him he'd be better off buying a new rifle and sending this one to the landfill." He smiled then asked, "How'd Joe end up with Allen's damaged gun anyway?"

"Herm, I wish I knew." He stared at the gun in silence for a moment then asked, "Could you dispose of this thing for me?"

"Sure. You got no use for it anyways."

"Herm, thanks. It was a pleasure talking with you."

"Mark, again, I'm sorry about Joe. Good men like him are few and far between. You might be one of 'em."

Mark smiled weakly and said, "I wish that were true." He turned and left the gun shop empty-handed. His next stop; the office of Allen Westridge, Attorney at Law.

Chapter 32

The ten-minute drive north on State Route 4 into the city gave Mark just enough time to call Denise and tell her about his visit with Herman Lightfoot. He told her Lightfoot carefully inspected the rifle and that it was not worth restoring. He also said that he recognized the weapon, having inspected it forty or fifty years ago when Allen Westridge brought it into his gun store.

"Honey, he looked at the gun and swore that Allen Westridge brought the gun to him, asking him if he could repair it and how much it would cost. He swore that Allen claimed he owned the gun."

"So, how did your father end up with it? Did he ask Allen if he would destroy it or somehow get rid of it for him?"

"I don't know, sweetie. I'm on my way to Allen's office now, but Dad explicitly stated in his letter that I not confront Allen about the accident. Maybe there's more to it than what Dad let on." Silence extended for several seconds while they both thought over what Mark just learned. Then Mark said, "I hate to bring it up and stress Allen out. He could die on the spot. He's already got a foot in the grave. I think a few more coughing spells might just do him in."

"That's a horrible thing to say."

"Yeah, but true, I'm afraid. I don't know if I should cancel the meeting or go. He might have a heart attack right in front of me."

'Listen, Mark. Go to the meeting. Get your copy of the appraisal. Don't bring up the gun. If he's really that bad, he doesn't need more stress. You don't want that on your conscience."

Mark turned the corner on Wayne and Monroe Streets. "Okay, honey. I'm a block away so I've got to go. I'll see you in about an hour. Think about what you would like for lunch."

"Abbe Holtzmiller just dropped off another casserole. This one has some kind of German sausage. It smells delicious. We may not need to plan another meal while we're here."

Mark laughed and disconnected the call just as he pulled into the lawyer's driveway.

He walked up the steps to the stately home-office and heard the lawyer coughing loudly as he approached the door. He rang the doorbell then tried the storm door, which was unlocked. When he entered, in a loud voice he said, "Allen, it's Mark."

He followed the coughing to Allen's office door and looked in. The elderly man's face shown bright red as the coughing fit slowed. Without saying a word, he motioned for Mark to take a seat in front of his desk.

Thinking about his wife's advice to not say anything that would upset the frail man, he sat and waited for the coughing fit to subside. When Westridge finally took a ragged breath and did not commence coughing again, he took a drink of water then turned to Mark and choked out, "Sorry about that. I've had a cold since the middle of winter … 2005."

Mark did not laugh but sat stone-faced, his anxiety level pumped up thinking about his and Denise's concern that Westridge could die at any moment. Mark feared that any response to his dark humor might send the lawyer back into another coughing attack. He glanced at the desktop, hoping that his copy of the appraisal would be there so he could take it and head out the door. As his eyes swept over the desk, the lawyer opened one of the drawers and lifted a twelve-by-nine envelope and laid it on the desk in front of him. His pale face assumed a serious tone.

"Mark, as your sisters already made clear, they are leaving everything up to you. They really had no interest in discussing the terms of your father's will. My conversations with them were so short, I didn't have time to ask them any questions." Westridge tried, but could not clear his throat. He tried a second time with some success. "While I agree that you are quite capable of finishing all the steps required to close out the estate, I'm surprised that they turned down the opportunity to learn any details about their potential financial gain from your father's passing."

Mark, hesitant to ask too many questions thus prolonging the meeting, frowned. He wondered what Westridge meant about financial gain. He and Denise had done well financially. He presumed that his sisters and their spouses, though Caroline and her husband had not formally married, also enjoyed a secure financial future, though he lacked specific knowledge of anything about his sisters' lives. The way Westridge said 'potential financial gain' caught Mark's attention.

"What do you mean by that?"

"Well, like I said, your sisters didn't want to talk about estate details."

"No, I mean the term 'potential financial gain.' I know the house is in contract and there's no mortgage. The auction will net some money and I know dad has some gold coins. So all-in-all, there'll be a fairly substantial amount of money left over, unless there is some debt I don't know about."

Westridge locked eyes with Mark, then said, "I'm glad you're sitting down. Your dad … he was a wise man. He saw how things could have been and knew he'd screwed up with his kids. He wanted to make amends somehow. He did it by living a life of service to others." Westridge began to cough. It took nearly a minute to stop and get his breath back, all the while his face turning a deep red from the effort. Once he cleared his throat again and wiped his mouth with a handkerchief, he resumed his explanation. "Your dad invested a large percentage of his income. He had a knack for picking winners. He saw the age of home computers coming and invested early in some companies that have done very well. There are too many to name, but think Apple, Microsoft, Intel, and others, come to mind."

Mark sat slack-jawed, not understanding the gravity of what he just heard. Not a man who needed a lot of material things in his life, Mark cherished his wife, his children, and grandchildren. He loved to travel within the United States, and liked his modest home in Maitland, Florida. He wished to avoid anything that might complicate his life further. His father's death already added far too much drama, which he hoped to escape within the next week or two. But the question hung in the room – *How much wealth are we talking about here?*

Seeing the inquisitive expression written all over his face, Westridge handed him a slip of paper. A dollar figure had been written – $17,000,000.00. *Seventeen million dollars.* Again, Mark's jaw nearly hit the desktop. He looked at Westridge and said, "So, we'd split seventeen million dollars?"

"No, Mark. *Each.* And that's a preliminary figure. And that doesn't include the gold or the house or the auction. That is strictly from stocks and bonds. You'll have to talk with an accountant about the tax consequences, but that's the gross dollar figure." Westridge coughed again, then said, "And your dad already set up annuities for Holy Angels, and several other charitable organizations that he favored, separate from that amount." He paused, then said "He was a good man, Mark. Don't let anyone tell you otherwise."

Mark wondered if Westridge knew of the confession his father had made in his letter and thought, again, about confronting the old man. When Westridge began coughing again, he shook his head, clearing the thought from his mind.

When Westridge stopped coughing, still shocked, Mark asked, "Was there anything else?"

"Just one more thing." He reached into the center desk drawer and pulled out a single business-sized envelope. He handed it to Mark and said, "Please don't open this until you get back home to Florida."

Marked smiled and joked, "Is this your bill?"

The lawyer smiled, but a touch of sadness crept over his face. "No. Like I said before, my work is paid in full. Your dad took very good care of me, financially and otherwise. Just, please, do as I ask and read it later."

Mark took both envelopes, the one with his copy of the appraisal and this new, mystery envelope, and stood. When Allen Westridge started to rise, Mark said, "No need to see me out. Thank you, Allen. I would have been lost in all this without you."

He went around the desk and took the old man's hand in his, noting the pale, multicolored veins bulging tight against the thin skin. They exchanged a final look. Mark turned and left the office, heading back to the house on Jay Street. He heard the lawyer's loud coughing spell as he left the building.

***

Mark pulled into the driveway at Jay Street, his head still spinning with the idea that he and his wife were millionaires. Knowing that his father lived like a pauper while having the means to have any of the material things a person could dream of … simply beyond his comprehension. Allen Westridge's comment that his sisters did not have the time to discuss anything about the estate rattled him. He knew they resented how they were treated so many years ago, but how long can one hold a grudge? The past is just that – the past. Over and done with. In Mark's opinion, they should be mature enough to, at the very least, listen to their father's attorney.

Then Mark thought about what Denise said about Caroline possibly finding out the truth about their father, or more precisely, Mark's father. Had Caroline found the letters in the footlocker and learned about Mark and Maryanne's biological relationship? He wondered if Caroline became so overwhelmed with the gloomy atmosphere that permeated every cubic foot of the house, that she admonished her parents before moving out. *Maybe they know the truth about our family. Or maybe they're just bitter, plain and simple.*

Mark entered the house carrying the two envelopes. He called out, "Hey, Sweetie, I'm back. You won't believe what Allen just told me."

He heard a creaking noise coming from upstairs and headed that way. When he reached the second floor, he called out, "Sweetheart?"

"Up here, Mark."

The call came from the attic. He bounded up the steps. Turning towards the footlocker, Denise sat crossed legged, holding a piece of paper in her right hand and an object in her left.

When Mark walked up behind her, he noticed the object – a large diamond solitaire on a gold band. The paper appeared to be a handwritten note. A small, maroon box sat on top of an envelope on the floor between the footlocker and her. Denise did not turn to face him so he moved around her and looked as tears streamed down her face.

She looked up and handed Mark the note she had been reading. He asked, "Are you okay?"

She nodded and said yes, but a fresh set of tears escaped her eyes. He knelt beside her and hugged her tightly. She began laughing then said, "You're going to think I'm a silly little girl when you read the note and see why I'm crying."

While keeping one arm around his wife, he held up the note and began to read.

Dear Joseph,

First, know that these last few months have been the most wonderful time in my life. You have given me safety in times that I feared nearly everyone with whom I came in contact. You have given me hope, when the world around us seems to have gone crazy. You have given me help when others have abandoned me. And you have given me love – a love the likes I have never felt before and do not expect to experience again.

I tell you this hoping you will understand when I tell you I must return this ring. You can only be devoted to one woman, one family. Ada May needs you. You must devote your life to her and your growing family.

The soldiers and airmen around you need you. I cannot be a distraction. It would be unfair to you and those who rely on you now. Please be safe and do your part to end this terrible war.

Until we meet again, all my love to you,

Ingrid

Mark's eyes welled up. He looked at the ring then back at the note. Ingrid Engel gave up a valuable ring that she rightfully could have kept. It spoke volumes about her integrity - obviously a woman of high moral character.

As he wiped his eyes, he said, "I guess I'm a silly little girl, too."

They laughed, tightening their embrace, lightening the mood.

"But I have even more news from the land of surprises. We're millionaires."

Pushing away from Mark, she frowned and slapped his arm. "Stop kidding around. You're just making fun of my crying."

He shrugged his shoulders. "Sorry, but I'm not kidding."

He sat down beside her and walked through his meeting with Allen Westridge.

The stunning surprises just kept coming.

Chapter 33

Mark and Denise sat at the dining room table eating the wonderful German casserole, compliments of Abbe Holtzmiller, while they discussed the crazy start to their Thursday morning. Still in total disbelief that they stood to inherit a fortune, they alternated between smiling, frowning, and taking deep, cleansing breaths. They hardly knew what to do with the extra income that they currently received each month; Mark's pension and social security, and Denise's social security. With no need to touch their IRAs, they opted to convert them to Roth IRAs to minimize their future tax burden. Very comfortable with their financial situation before Joseph Traver's death, they now faced several major financial decisions. Those decisions were of the good kind, the type of which nearly every working American dreamed. Do they tell their kids and grandkids or do they keep it a secret for as long as possible? Luckily, they could take their time to consider the options. Until the money appeared in their bank account, it was not real.

Three objects had been laid on the end of the table: the envelope with Mark's copy of the appraisal, the mystery letter from Allen Westridge, and the envelope with the cryptic spreadsheet. All through lunch, Mark's attention had been split between his thoughts about millions of dollars, the three envelopes, and his wife.

Out of the blue, Denise asked, "Do you know if Ingrid has any family?"

He shrugged his shoulders, saying no without muttering a word.

She said, "Maybe with all the money we're about to inherit we can track them down."

Mark gave no reply, his mind still spinning, overloaded with everything he encountered during the past week. Allen's revelation about the money energized him, but he quickly lost that emotional spike and came back to the realization that many tasks lay before him to complete before they could close his father's estate.

At 1:50 p.m., they cleared the table of lunch dishes and faced each other in the kitchen. They hardly spoken during lunch, each lost in their own thoughts.

Denise took Mark in a close hug and rested her head on his chest. "Promise me that our lives are not going to change drastically because of this money. Okay?"

Mark took her by the shoulders, held her at arms-length, and said with as much sincerity as he could muster, "I promise."

They both broke down and laughed hysterically. After several seconds, Mark took a deep breath. "How can our lives not change? I mean, we're going to have to talk with a financial advisor, which we don't have … and Ray." Ray Stanley - their accountant. "Maybe he can recommend someone. I sure as hell don't know what to do."

"Mark, we don't need any of this money. Elliot and Eva don't either. They're both in great financial shape. So, what do we do with it"

"I don't know, Hon. I know it's fun to dream, but money like this … it can change a person, not necessarily for the good. We have to be very careful what we do. That's why I think we start with Ray and go from there."

As they stood in the kitchen, they embraced again. Denise said, "In my opinion, we should start thinking of organizations we like where our support might be put to good use. Maybe start a college scholarship or two. There are many charities but I think we need to be careful what we choose to do with it."

"I like how you're thinking. Maybe we can make a list and have it ready when we talk with Ray or whomever he recommends to help us. Is there any area you feel particularly strong about?"

"Cancer research. Veteran support groups. Those are two that come to mind. How about you? Where would you put the money?"

"Your ideas are good. I'd add youth groups. Maybe economic development groups. We can narrow down specific organizations later."

Denise looked up into Marks eyes and smiled, then whispered, "Sounds like the start of a plan," then added, "Do you know how much I love you?"

"I think I do, but show me anyway." He smiled broadly and leaned in for a kiss.

After several long seconds of a tender kiss, Denise backed away. "What else did you have planned for today?"

Mark's face hardened, his eyes drifting into deep thought. "My sisters. I have to call them. I want to talk about the will and ask if they really read it. I think I'm obligated to tell them about the amount of their potential inheritance, but I'm not sure I should, yet." He shrugged his shoulders, hoping Denise would chime in with some brilliant advice. When she mimicked his shrug, he knew he would have to face the calls on his own.

He helped with the dishes and wiped down the kitchen counters until Denise took the dish cloth and ordered him out of the kitchen. "Go make the calls."

Mark sat back down at the dining room table, took out his cell phone, then looked at the envelopes from the safe deposit box. He set the phone on the table, opened the will, and began to read.

Twenty minutes later, Denise walked into the room. With a sly smile and an artificial frown, she asked, "How're those calls going?"

He laid the will down and rubbed his face with both hands. "Busted."

"You can't put them off forever, Dear. Suck it up and make the calls. The sooner you call, the sooner you can put them behind you."

"Okay, okay. You're right."

He picked up his cell phone and did a quick calculation on the time difference. 2:52 p.m. displayed on his phone. That meant 11:52 a.m. in Washington State. He punched in Maryanne's number. She picked up on the third ring.

His sister answered in a voice devoid of emotion, "Hi, Mark."

"Maryanne. How's the weather, is it raining?"

"It doesn't rain every day and night in Washington, contrary to what you hear. But you didn't call about the weather."

He sensed that she had no desire to exchange pleasantries, so he moved right to the point of his call. "Allen said that you received your copy of the will. Did you read it over?"

She sighed, her irritation obvious. "No. I haven't really had the time. Besides, being the executor, you're taking care of everything, right?"

He hoped the conversation would be more cordial, but Maryanne's attitude began to grate on him. He took a deep breath and said, "Yes, but I thought that you and Caroline would want to make sure that ..."

She cut him off, "Mark, we don't really care what you do. We're really not interested in Dad's estate. Just let us know when it's done with and send us the paperwork. We're not expecting much of anything except closure."

"What if there's a significant ..."

She interrupted him again, "Listen, we don't care. Unless you find something earth-shattering, just let us know when you get the paperwork done."

A vision of Catherine O'Conner Sims popped into his head, thinking how much she looked like his sister, Maryanne. He asked, "Did you know a girl from high school named

Catherine O'Conner? She's the daughter of an old friend of Dad's."

The silence on the line dragged for several long seconds, then Maryanne said, "No. Why are you asking?"

"Denise and I met her and her mother the other night. She kind of looks …"

Abruptly, Maryanne said, "Richard is calling. I have to go."

"Maryanne?"

She had disconnected the call. He looked at his phone in disbelief. He heard no clicks or noises that would indicate his sister received an incoming call from her husband or anyone else. Had she made the excuse just so she would not have to answer his question about Catherine O'Conner? The entire call frustrated and angered him. He stood and strode to the kitchen for a beer, hoping to calm down before making the next call to his younger sister, Caroline.

When Denise came back into the kitchen and noticed her husband's face and body language, she knew the call had not gone well. She asked, "I take it Maryanne wasn't in the chatty mood?"

Mark, lost in his confusion at his sister's attitude, did not hear his wife. He honed in on his question about knowing Catherine O'Conner Sims, the woman with the uncanny resemblance to his sister. Why would she become so belligerent about a simple question? Maybe the entire subject of life in Ohio put her over the edge and she just wanted the memories of her youth behind her.

He felt the soft touch of his wife's hand on his shoulder. She said, "You know, you haven't spoken with either of your sisters in ages. So, you're talking to a couple strangers. I wouldn't put much faith in them being friendly, or even civil. Like you, they were estranged from your father since leaving home."

Mark took a healthy drink from his beer then looked around the kitchen, as if seeing the room for the first time. He turned to face Denise, his eyes refocusing after being far away.

He said, "There must be something else, sweetie. Maryanne is angry, bitter. I understand her being mad at Dad and Mom for what they put us through, but we were in it together. We should be on the same team here. Why is she taking out her anger on me?"

She put her arms around his torso, pulled him tight against her, and said, "Maybe you're right. Maybe there's more to it that you don't know. But, like I told you, the sooner you make the calls, the sooner you can put this whole thing behind you. It's been a long time since you've spoken to either of them. You shouldn't expect them to be your friends now."

Mark raised his eyebrows, acknowledging the wisdom in his wife's words. Did he expect too much from two women he had not spoken with in ages? He needed to make one more call. He hoped it would go better, but believed that he should lower the bar on his expectations.

He took his beer and headed back into the dining room. Before he sat, he looked around at the ceiling and walls that needed a coat of paint. Of course, that would be up to the new owners. The closing on the house, the auction, the final goodbyes approached. Finishing his business so he and Denise could get back to their lives in Maitland, Florida should be his top priority. He longed for the ordered, boring life that they worked so hard to achieve. All the drama and surprises from the past week were taking a toll on his physical and mental well-being.

He took a deep breath, sat, picked up his phone, and punched in the number. Caroline picked up the call on the first ring. "Hi Mark. I was expecting your call."

"Hi Caroline. I take it Maryanne warned you?"

"Yeah. She texted me that you called. She's not real happy with you."

Mark wanted to ask why, but figured he did not need to get this call off to a bad start, so he changed the subject. "I'm just calling to ask if you've read the will and if you had any questions."

Caroline did not answer for a few seconds, then said, "I read it. I really don't have any questions. How is the process going? Are you close to closing everything out?"

Caroline's conciliatory tone and lack of animosity surprised him. Even if she held little interest in his answers, she at least sounded cordial. He replied, "It's moving along. We have an offer on the house, the auction is set up, though the auctioneer let me know there won't be a lot of profit from the sale of the household stuff."

Again, a brief silence ensued, then she said, "You should ignore Maryanne's anger. You know what it was like growing up in that house. She seems to not be able to let it go. Dad's death is just another reminder of what they put us through. I know, it wasn't a physical abuse thing, but every day was a real downer. We all hated it. I think Maryanne took it worse than we did, at least from what I can tell." She paused, then continued, "You know, we never really had a brother and sister relationship. Maryanne and I don't stay in touch either. I never gave a thought to contacting you, to learn about your life. Maybe we should change that."

Mark's heart thumped in his chest. He said, "I think I'd like that."

When the call disconnected, Denise peered around the doorway to the living room and smiled. Mark returned her smile with watery eyes.

She said, "You are such a nice guy. That's why I love you."

Chapter 34

Mark looked at the dining room table with papers scattered over one end. His father's will laid open next to the sealed envelope he received from Allen Westridge. Further down near the table's edge, the manilla folder with the estate information sat open with papers haphazardly strewn about; a testament to the chaos he experienced almost from the moment he arrived at the house. Having been pulled in many directions, he decided that he needed to put some priority on what remained to be resolved, to put closure to some items, allowing him to concentrate on others. He briefly thought of Caroline's words that she would like to get to know him and Denise after the estate business wrapped up. He hoped her words were sincere.

He lifted the sealed envelope he received from Allen Westridge. He turned to Denise and said, "I'm so tempted to open this note, but I promised Allen I would wait. But why all the drama?"

Denise asked, "I take it he was serious?"

"Yeah. He made me promise. Since I gave him my word, I figure I better not break it. Which brings me to the letters from Dad to Maryanne and Caroline. I'm thinking about putting them in a larger envelope and sending them on, without opening them."

She smiled, "I sure wish we knew what they said. There were some very personal and frank confessions in yours. I wonder if their letters say basically the same thing."

"Unless they decide to tell us, I guess we'll never know."

Denise looked disappointed. Mark turned to look at her, his hand brushing against a drawer in the China cabinet. He looked at the drawer, remembering the note to his father that his grandson found a few days earlier. He opened the drawer and removed the note, reading it again to himself.

Dear Mr. Traver,

It was a sincere pleasure meeting you and getting to know you in person. Prior to your visits, mother, with a gleam in her eyes, spoke of you often. She had many fond memories of the man who befriended her at a time when most everyone around her treated her as if she might be contagious or a German spy. You helped guide her through a difficult time in her life so many years ago.

She mentioned that you had joined the Army Air Corps in 1943 and she never saw you again. When she off-handedly wondered if you had survived the war, I decided to find out more about you. Imagine my surprise to learn that you lived within twenty minutes of my mother. I was so pleased that you accepted my invitation and took the time to visit mother. Your visits, I believe, extended her life and made these last years her most joyous.

Thank you again, from the bottom of my heart. I hope to one day meet your son. From what you have told me, and knowing that he is in your family tree, he must be a fine man.

I wish I could repay you for the joy you have given our family, but the kindness you showed my mother was beyond measure. The gift of your time, the time that you spent with my mother, was simply priceless.

God bless you, Mr. Traver.

Most Sincerely,

Emma Franks

After reading the note, Mark believed, without a doubt, that Emma Franks must be the daughter of Ingrid Engel, his birth mother. Her note seemed to imply that her mother passed away, but it did not state definitively one way or another. He reread the note, looking for clues as to where she may have lived. He knew it could not be too far away. A twenty-minute radius from Sandusky placed her anywhere from near Vermilion to the east, Norwalk and Bellevue to the south, Fremont and Oak Harbor to the west. He wondered how he would begin to search for her, how difficult it might be.

Denise read his expression and asked, "What are you thinking?"

"I'm going to find out what happened to my mother. I haven't figured out how, but I think her last name may be Franks. No, that wouldn't be right unless her daughter, Emma, never married." He remained silent, thinking of the best way to begin the search.

Denise said, "Maybe you should start with finding Emma Franks. At least you know her name. Ingrid most likely married and changed her last name."

Mark thought for a moment then agreed. The search would have to start with Emma Franks.

Still sitting at the table with the note in his hands, his cell phone chirped. He reached for the phone. The screen said AMVETS Post 17. With his brow furrowed, he answered the call.

"This is Mark."

"Mr. Traver, this is Larry Schupert. I'm the post commander at the local AMVETS. I was talking with Danny Balken last night and he said your dad's funeral is set for a week from today. Is that right?"

Mark thought for a moment, then realized that the funeral was indeed one week from today. He wondered why the AMVETS post commander would be interested in his father's funeral. He said, "Yes, that's right."

"Well, Mr. Traver …"

"Please, call me Mark."

"Okay, Mark. I've talked with the commanders at the American Legion and the VFW and we'd be honored to provide a color guard for your father's funeral. Living veterans of World War II are few. We think it is important to honor those who served so courageously."

Mark did not hesitate. "We'd be honored to have you do that for Dad."

"Mark, your dad was a good man. He did so much for AMVETS, the Legion, and VFW. We're all just so grateful to have known him. He ..." Larry's voice choked up over the phone. He cleared his throat and continued. "He set up an annuity for each of the organizations that will help fund our operations. We can't thank him, and your family, enough."

Mark sat, stunned into silence. He started to respond when Larry said, "I hope this doesn't impact any inheritance to his family. It seemed quite generous."

"Larry, you don't have to worry about that. We're all fine and he must believe in your causes or he wouldn't have done it. Call me early in the week next week and we can make plans for the funeral."

"One last thing, Mark. Danny Balken is the one who suggested that we do it, the color guard, I mean. He deserves any credit for our involvement, all three groups. Danny's a good guy, too."

"Thanks, Larry. I appreciate knowing that. I met Danny earlier this week. I agree, he's a great guy. I learned a lot about Dad just talking with him."

After the call disconnected, Mark told Denise about the call. Bewildered again by the overwhelming community support, they sat and talked about the different people's lives whom Joseph Traver touched. Denise suggested that Mark start the list of charitable organizations that they spoke about earlier. Mark grabbed paper and pen and began writing. After twenty minutes, Denise suggested that they take a ride, just to get away from everything and everyone.

Mark agreed. They left the house at 4:30 p.m., first heading for downtown Sandusky. As they entered town from the west end, Denise remarked about the beauty of Washington Park. The Merry Go Round Museum at the intersection of Washingtons Street, Central Avenue, and Jackson Street, grabbed her attention. With a tan brick façade, tall pillars and rounded front entrance, the historic, grand building had once housed the United States Post Office. Mark drove slowly so Denise could see the large, functioning floral clock with a flower arrangement displaying the date. Several earthen mounds advertised community organizations. The Boy-with-the-Boot statue stood in the middle of a fountain north of the Erie County Courthouse. Further along in the southeast quadrant of the park, a large gazebo drew Mark's eyes.

Mark turned north on Columbus Avenue, passing the little red popcorn wagon. The Erie County Office building and parking garage dominated the western block of Columbus, while numerous empty storefronts stood on the eastern side. Moving into the northernmost block, Mark noted businesses filled many of the storefronts, leaving some empty and in need of revitalization. The next block sported a music store, a coffee shop, a restaurant and wine bar, Daly's Pub, where they ate dinner and met Mildred and Catherine O'Conner, and the State Theater with its early twentieth-century marquee. At the foot of Columbus Avenue, the Schade-Mylander Plaza, with a beautiful fountain, separated the space between Water Street and Shoreline Drive, while maintaining a splendid view of Sandusky Bay.

As they continued their drive, Mark wondered if the city employed an economic development group to assist local businesses. He said, "This is an area where money could go to good use."

Denise raised an eyebrow at Mark. Her look left him wondering if she believed the city needed more than a few million dollars to get many of the old structures up to current standards. It seemed to him that many businesses thrived here, but the significant number of empty storefronts provided opportunity for future growth.

Mark steered the truck back to Route 6 east. They cruised along the southern shore of Lake Erie. They passed open fields, channels where the lake spilled into marshes, small businesses and homes ranging from opulent to mere shacks. When they reached downtown Vermilion, Mark headed south on State Route 60.

Denise asked, "So, where are we headed?"

"I don't know. I thought I'd take a loop drive around Sandusky. When we hit Wakeman, we'll head west to Fremont, then north to Oak Harbor. Then back to the Jay Street."

"Hmm. Sounds like you have something in mind."

"Well, while we're out, riding around the countryside, be on the lookout for nursing homes and assisted living communities."

"I knew it. You're looking for places where Ingrid might have lived."

"Busted. Plus, this is a relaxing drive. I needed to get out of the house, and not just back to the hotel."

Denise placed a hand on his arm. He felt the gentle touch and smiled, relaxing even more.

***

They made it back to Jay Street by 8:30 p.m., having stopped for an exceptional dinner at McCarthy's, an Irish Pub, in Port Clinton. The drive did wonders, helping them both to relax. In the dining room, Mark gathered the loose papers into a neat stack.

Denise asked if he wanted a beer, but he declined the offer saying he had no room after their dinner. As he walked back into the kitchen, the doorbell rang. They both looked up at the ceiling.

Denise asked, "Should we act like no one is here?"

Mark took a deep breath and headed towards the front door. Peggy and Randy Whipple smiled when Mark opened the door.

"Would you like some company?"

Mark opened the door wide and said, "Why not?"

Chapter 35

Mark, Denise, Peggy, and Randy sat at the dining room table after Denise offered drinks. Randy smiled, opened the shopping bag he brought with a variety of drinks and snacks and placed everything in the center of the table. Among the goodies; bags of chips, sliced cheese and crackers and bottles of beer. Mark and Denise, though still full from their dinner, opened a beer. Peggy and Randy did likewise. They offered a toast to Joseph Traver; *A member of the Greatest Generation.* They all clinked bottles and took a drink from their beers.

Mark smiled and said, "Thanks for stopping by. We were going to write up the final draft for dad's obituary. I want to get it to the register tomorrow morning."

Peggy beamed, "We can help with that. Do you have all those notes from the other day?"

Mark pulled the stack of papers from the manilla folder at the end of the table. He leafed through them and counted twelve pages of notes and another page with the opening paragraphs. He read the first two paragraphs out loud while Denise and their guests listened to the standard dates and locations of birth and death. The third paragraph began with Joseph's entry into military service. Mark stopped reading where his father's military training began.

"And this is where I have to enter details of Dad's service information. Any thoughts?"

Randy spoke up. "Yeah. Put in your dad's flight training schools, his class standing, and his being an instructor. Then move on to his deployment to the bomber group in Molesworth. He was the navigator in six successful bombing missions, right?"

Mark nodded. Randy kept going, "Then the war ended. Before you finish with his service information, mention his rank and list the medals he received during his service."

Mark raised his eyebrows, hoping that he could find all that information in his notes. Marcus, his grandson, mentioned that he planned to investigate all of Joe Traver's medals. Since his final exams quickly approached, he had not had the time to complete his research. Randy noticed Mark's bewilderment and asked, "Did he keep his medals?"

"Yeah. There all in a footlocker in the attic."

"Well, let's go take a look … if you don't mind. You know, Max Westridge might do a special segment in the Register on your dad. Memorial Day is coming up. He wasn't killed in combat, but he did his part to stop the war … in a big way. Your dad was a true hero, Mark. He had to be scared shitless to climb into that bomber and fly over Germany with a payload of bombs."

Mark said, "I read the story he wrote about getting hit by shrapnel on his very first mission. I couldn't imagine being in that plane, wondering if every breath I took might be my last."

A shiver rand down Mark's spine. The four remained silent for a minute, each lost in their own thoughts. Then Randy said, "Let's take a look at those medals."

Mark nodded and led the way to the attic.

***

Seated Indian style around the footlocker, Mark opened the lid, pulled out the tray with pictures and other smaller items. He set the tray on the floor next to Randy. He then reached into the lower section and pulled out the boxes of medals and other curiosities. As he moved the boxes onto the floor, Randy noticed the black and white pictures of the men in military uniforms. He picked up several of the photos. He pointed to Mark's dad and said, "I picked your dad out right away. His smile looks the same in this picture as it always did when he was alive."

He handed the first picture to Peggy, who smiled with recognition. "You're right. He's easy to spot."

She looked at the next few pictures and pointed to Mark's dad without hesitation.

Mark's mind wandered as he tried to think of a time that he saw his father smile. He drew a blank.

Randy picked up the black and white photo of bombs exploding, pulverizing large buildings into rubble. His face turned somber. Mark reasoned he must be having the same thoughts as he did, wondering how many people were killed in the bombing raid. Randy shook his head and flipped the picture over. "Munitions factory, Unterluss, Germany, April 4, 1945. My God. Can you imagine …?"

Randy's voice trailed off as his dark thoughts could be read on his face. Mark's eyes turned dark and welled up, threatening to spill down his cheeks, thinking that Ingrid's mother, his maternal grandmother, was killed that day. He tensed, shook his head, and took a deep breath. He said, "Let's take a look at these medals. I think there might be some paperwork in here that identifies each one's purpose."

Before anyone moved, Randy, noticing Mark's reaction to his comment about the munitions factory asked him, "Are you alright? I didn't mean to make light of the bombing picture."

"No. You didn't. I'm sorry. Going through all this stuff of Dad's … it's just a bit overwhelming."

Mark took a deep breath, forced a smile, and reached for the box that measured about six inches square that he pulled out just moments before. Flipping the top open, he reached in and pulled out a single medal, wrapped in plastic. The weight surprised him. He unwrapped the bronze medal and held it close to his eyes. On the circular one-inch disk, the scene depicted a landing craft with soldiers under fire. Mark looked closer and saw an airplane. The words European-African-Middle Eastern Campaign were above the landing craft. He flipped the medal over. An American bald eagle graced the reverse side with the dates 1941 and 1945 to the left of the eagle and the words United States of America to the right.

The multicolored ribbon included brown, green, white, red, and blue vertical stripes. Mark believed that the colored stripes and their arrangement on the banner held some significance, but he could not even venture a guess as to what they represented.

He showed Denise the ribbon first, then passed it on to Randy and Peggy. The medal appeared to be in mint condition. Randy handed it back to Mark, saying, "I don't want to handle it. Knowing my luck, I'd rip the ribbon or some other clumsy thing."

Mark rewrapped the medal and placed it on the floor next to the box. He reached in the box and pulled out a second medal, this one slightly heavier than the first. A woman holding a broken sword in her hands displayed on the front of the one-and-a-quarter-inch disc. On either side of the woman, the words World War II were displayed. On the reverse side of the disc the inscriptions "FREEDOM FROM FEAR AND WANT" and "FREEDOM OF SPEECH AND RELIGION" displayed above and below a palm branch. The words "UNITED STATES OF AMERICA 1941 1945 encircled the text. The predominantly red ribbon was flanked by rainbow colors along its vertical edges.

Mark passed the ribbon around again then asked, "Is anyone taking notes?"

They laughed. Randy suggested that they take the box of ribbons downstairs and copy the information right from the ribbons. Everyone nodded approval.

Mark reached into the box once more, finding a third ribbon. When he unwrapped the medal, he noted the sixteen-point bronze piece with a diving American bald eagle holding a lightning bolt in each talon. The blue ribbon had two vertical orange-gold stripes. He passed the medal to Denise.

He reached into the box and pulled out the last ribbon. He immediately knew this ribbon without looking for an inscription – A Purple Heart. He took a deep breath and held it up for everyone to see.

Mark held it for a moment then said, "I know Dad's thigh was burned from a piece of shrapnel. In the letter he wrote about the incident, he characterized it as a minor burn. I wonder if he suffered any other injuries or if he downplayed the severity of the burn."

Peggy said, "He never said anything to us about his injury or anything else about the war for that matter. He always wanted to talk about us, how we were getting along, what we liked to do."

Randy nodded. "He never said anything about getting injured."

Mark looked into the footlocker, wondering if any supporting documentation existed. He noticed an old thirteen by nine, white envelope, yellowed with age. He pulled the envelope from along the back side of the trunk. Except for the color, the envelope looked untouched. He pulled back the flap, looked inside and pulled several documents out. He briefly looked at each document and smiled.

"It's the paperwork that goes along with the medals. Let's take this stuff downstairs. We need to finish that obit tonight."

Once again, sitting around the dining room table, Mark took a pen and began to write about Joe Tarver's training, then his assignment to the 303rd Bomber Group at Molesworth Air Base in England. He added that his father participated in six missions near the end of the war and that he received an honorable discharge in June, a month after his arrival home in Sandusky, Ohio.

Mark took the pages of notes and reviewed the organizations, both religious and civic, in which his father actively participated. He wrote nearly eight pages when he finally completed that portion of the article.

Mark moved on to the most difficult part of the obituary: those preceding his father in death and those who survived. The anguish on his face showed, but he charged ahead, knowing he would write half-truths.

Mark wrote that his father's parents predeceased him, as did his loving wife, Ada May Lapoint Traver, one brother, and a sister.

He is survived by one son, Mark Traver ...

Then he arrived at the part that gave him pause. Knowing he must acknowledge his sisters, that what he wrote down would forever be perceived as truth, when he knew with certainty, that it was a lie.

... and two daughters, Maryanne Traver Campbell, and Caroline Traver Eastman.

He looked up at his wife, then he continued listing Joseph Traver's grandchildren. With the survivors listed, Mark wrote down the date, time, and location of the funeral.

Nearing the last paragraphs, Mark looked to the Whipples for a little help. "The last part is about charitable contributions. Any suggestions?"

Randy looked thoughtfully at the light fixture, then said, "Why don't you leave it broad, suggesting that they should contribute to the charity of their choosing. Just say that organizations favored by Joe include veteran support organizations, churches, and medical research organizations, particularly those designed for care of childhood illnesses."

Mark and Denise both smiled. Mark said, "I love it."

Denise chimed in, "Perfect."

When finished, Mark sighed and put the pen down. He lifted the sheets – all twelve pages – and nodded to their guests.

Randy looked at the clock, 10:40 p.m., then said, "I know it's getting late, but how about one more beer."

Everyone agreed and twisted the cap off the late night round. Randy lifted his bottle and said, "To Joe!" They clinked bottle necks and took a long drink from their beers.

Peggy smiled and said, "We didn't tell you before, but we named our son Joseph after your dad."

Mark nearly spit his mouthful of beer out, but managed to keep from spraying their guests. "I'm sorry, but after the week we've had, that just hit me as funny."

Everyone laughed, finished their beer with some light conversation, then said good night.

Chapter 36

After the filling dinner the night before, they stopped at The House of Doughnuts for breakfast, then headed downtown to the Sandusky Resister building to submit Joseph Traver's obituary. They walked in the door of the historic building, immediately awed by the high ceilings and massive windows, all products of centuries-old architecture and workmanship. Even the ceilings sported what appeared to be the original metal tiles, painted black. They stepped up to the counter where they were immediately greeted by a representative of the paper.

The young, black woman in her mid-twenties and a head shorter than Mark said, "Hello, Mr. Traver. We've been expecting you."

Mark's mouth opened, but his words were lost in his surprise. Denise reached her hand across the counter and said, "I'm Mark's wife, Denise. We'd like to place Joseph Traver's obituary in the paper's next available edition."

"Certainly, Mrs. Traver. My name is Charlotte. Mr. Westridge would like to meet with you if you have a few minutes."

Mark cleared his throat and looked at Denise, then turned to Charlotte and said, "Sure, we can do that."

Charlotte came around the counter and said, "Follow me, please." She turned and said, "You know this better than we do here at the Register, but your dad was a real charmer."

Mark nearly tripped upon hearing another stranger sing his father's praises. They made their way down the hall into the news room where a dozen desks sat in groups of two, facing each other, mostly unoccupied. Much of a reporter's work happened in the field, so the absence of a crowded room did not surprise him. Charlotte directed them to an office in the back of the newsroom where a tall, slender man with salt and pepper hair stood in the open doorway. He walked towards them and raised his hand to shake Mark's first, then Denise's. "Hello. I'm Maxwell Westridge, but call me Max, please. I understand you've met my father, Allen."

Mark replied, "I have. Denise has not."

He smiled at Charlotte and thanked her for guiding the Travers back. Charlotte returned the smile and nodded towards Mark and Denise, saying as she departed, "It was a pleasure meeting you."

As Charlotte turned and walked back through the newsroom, Max said, "Well, Dad's seen better days, health-wise. I'm surprised he's made it this long, with his lung cancer, and other ailments over the years, but he's a tough old cuss. Anyway, I wanted to let you know that there is an ad – a tribute, really - in today's paper for your dad. Several community organizations got together and purchased the full-page ad. They each provided remarks about what your dad did for their respective groups."

"That's very generous and thoughtful of them. Can we see the ad?"

Max walked behind his desk and lifted what appeared to be a picture frame covered in a thin cloth. He set the bottom edge of the frame on his desk and prepared to lift the cloth, then said, "I hope you don't mind. I took the liberty of framing the ad, as a gift to you."

He uncovered the frame displaying the full-page tribute.

The entire background featured a watermark of an American Flag waiving in the breeze, the pale red, white and blue so subtle that it did not distract from the printed content of the ad. A five-inch by seven-inch picture of Joseph Traver in his Army Air Corps dress uniform drew their attention to the center of the ad. Under the picture a caption read *Joseph Traver - A Member of the Greatest Generation.*

As Mark and Denise read the notes of appreciation embedded within the ad, Mark noted that they were similar in tone to what would appear later in the week in his father's obituary. The many thanks listed by the organizations included salutes for acts of kindness, appreciation for his sizable donations and ongoing bequeaths for the future, and his countless volunteer hours.

In the center of the page, a resolution passed by the Sandusky City Commission honoring Joseph Traver, described a selfless man who would do anything for anyone in need; a man, Mark thought, who must be headed for sainthood.

Mark's inner turmoil began to rise. The man he knew growing up in the house on Jay Street, the man who confessed in a letter to killing a former friend, justified or not, bore no resemblance to the man described in the obituary he just submitted, nor the framed one-page tribute from many local organizations and their leaders. His stomach began to churn as his mind tried to reconcile the disparity of the two very vivid, but contrasting mental pictures of his father.

Denise, applying a slight tug on his arm, brought him out of his funk and back to the moment. He forced a smile and hoped it did not appear too plastic, too contrived, as he looked at Max.

"This is quite amazing. Thank you. Thank you, very much."

"The obituary will appear in Monday's paper. That should give anyone planning to attend the services time to prepare. I think the whole town knows about it. I've heard a lot of folks downtown talking about it. I'd plan to shake a lot of hands this Thursday, but you never know how many will actually attend at the church, make the trip to the cemetery, then back to the church for the dinner."

Mark extended his hand to Max and they shook. Denise did the same. Max covered the framed tribute with the cloth again and then placed it in a cardboard box that had been behind his desk. He handed the box to Mark and escorted them to the front door of the building. As Mark and Denise exited, several staff members hollered, "Goodbye Mr. and Mrs. Traver."

Then they were outside in the crisp air and the bright morning sun. They climbed into the truck and headed west towards Jay Street.

As they made their way down Washington Street, Mark remained silent. Denise looked at him, a concerned look on her face. He briefly turned to her and said, "Wow. Just … wow."

"I think I feel the same way you do. It's like they're talking about a stranger. I don't know what to think."

Mark shook his head slowly, trying to keep his eyes on the road while his mind sped way beyond the posted limit. "I guess we have to assume that Dad had a life changing experience at some point. But when? After he plugged his best friend, the cheater, or when mom killed herself? Was there something else that changed his heart, his mind? And when he changed, why didn't he share this wonderful epiphany with me and you and our family? Or with his other children, even though he knew they weren't actually his children?"

Mark turned onto Madison Street heading west, then drove the two blocks to Jay Street. He hoped Denise did not see the tears welling in his eyes, but he knew that she did, because she put one hand on his leg and another on his shoulder.

She said, "We're almost done here, Sweetheart. When we're finished, we're going to go home … to Florida. Thank God you only have to do this once."

As Mark pulled into the driveway, the bottled-up emotion exploded. He pounded on the steering wheel in anger. "Why didn't he call me, or write, or whatever, anything to get in touch with me? Why didn't I call him? Oh, jeezus, Denise. I feel … I don't know what I feel." He covered his face, then said with a shaky voice, "All these people, they loved Dad. All these years, they were a part of his life, and he a big part of theirs. I'm his flesh and blood and I feel like I failed him. I missed out on the best years of my father's life. How does that happen? Why?"

Still in the truck, they leaned together and embraced, Marks tears flowing freely, Denise's eyes tearing as she tried to console her husband. They sat there in the truck in front of the Jay Street house where Mark, his sisters, the only mother he knew, and his father lived like strangers; his entire childhood, nothing but a bad memory. He wanted answers to why that happened. Some of the clues were revealed in the letters between his mother and father. Allen Westridge revealed other clues. But was that it? Would there be no more explanation?

Through a runny nose and a chuckle, Mark said, "I feel so damn silly. I'm so sorry."

Denise tightened her embrace on her husband. He appreciated her more than ever, and needed her more than that. He hugged her back, fiercely.

"You are my rock, you know that?"

She replied, "That's us. A couple of rocks hanging out together."

That broke the spell and they both laughed and headed inside, both rubbing the moisture from their eyes.

Once seated at the table again, Mark looked at his phone for the time. 10:50 a.m. Still too early for a beer. *I guess, in my condition, I shouldn't even think about a beer.*

Denise again broke into his thoughts and asked, "What else is on the agenda for today?"

"Not much, really. Maybe we could start the search for Emma Franks."

"We could do that. Where do we start?"

Mark remained silent, deep in thought. He really did not have a clue where to start.

Mark's cell phone rang. He looked at the screen and saw Peggy Whipple's number. He swiped across the screen.

"Hi, Peggy. How are you and Randy doing this morning?"

"We got off to a slow start, but we're on the move now. The reason I called, I remember you saying that Abbe Holtzmiller said something about a woman who came to visit your dad in his later years and took him out for a ride. They'd be gone for hours. I remembered her name."

Mark said, "Emma Franks."

Shocked, she said, "Yeah. Emma Franks. How did you know?"

"We found a note from her to Dad, thanking him for visiting her mother. It said it may have added years to her mother's life. Do you know anything more about Emma Franks?"

"Not much, except that there is a family with the last name of Franks who lives in Vermilion."

Mark looked over at Denise who seemed to sense something positive about the phone call. He asked Peggy, "How do you know about the Franks family?"

"One of my friends dated one of the Franks boys. You might be able to find their name on the internet white pages. That would be a good place to start."

"Peggy, you are wonderful. Thank you, so much."

"Hey, Mark. It might be nothing."

"It's a start."

Chapter 37

As lunchtime approached, Mark and Denise discussed where they wanted to eat. Denise reminded him that they had another casserole from Abbe Holtzmiller and Mark agreed they should try it. As Denise preheated the oven, Mark's cell phone rang. He rolled his eyes as if annoyed by the call, but he reached for the phone and looked at the number. He did not recognize it and after thinking about it for a moment, swiped the red handset and ended the call before it connected. He noted the area code and did a search to find out from where the call had originated – 212 – New York City.

"Hey, honey, do you know anyone from New York City?"

Denise peeked around the doorway from the kitchen, a frown on her face. "No, do you?"

"I don't think so. Probably spam. I didn't answer it."

As the words left his lips, the phone rang again, the same New York City number displayed. This time, he swiped the green handset and answered, "Hello."

A gravelly woman's voice said, "I'm trying to locate Mark Traver, son of Joseph Traver."

"This is Mark Traver."

"Mr. Traver, thank you for taking my call. My name is Ginny Manetti. I am so sorry to hear of your father's passing."

Mark paused briefly then answered, "Thank you. You said your name is Ginny Manetti?"

"Yes, that's right. I am … or was your dad's publicist. He was my client for about thirty years, maybe a little longer."

Mark thought, *Why did Dad need a publicist?* He asked, "What exactly does that mean?"

"My company did all the promotions and marketing for your dad's books."

Mark tensed and rolled his head around, hearing the pops in his neck at the base of his skull. He thought, *Is this woman pulling my leg?* He asked, "When you say, 'Dad's books,' what exactly do you mean?"

This time, Ginny was quiet. After a moment she said, "You don't know about your dad's books?"

Mark wondered again if this woman might be looking for a gullible target for a scam. He said, "What is this about?"

"Have you ever heard of J. T. Skipjack?"

Mark thought for a moment, then replied, "Yes. He writes historical fiction about World War II, right?"

Ginny sighed, then said, "Mark, your dad was J. T. Skipjack. He penned sixteen bestselling novels. He had a manuscript that he said was about ninety percent complete but he stopped working on it about two years ago. He said he had something more important to tend to."

"Ginny, are you serious? Is this true?"

"Yes, Mr. Traver. Your dad was the best-selling author J. T. Skipjack. He was an amazing writer and my top client … my favorite client."

Again, caught off-guard, Mark collapsed into the closest dining room chair, stunned by his father's life, and the fact that he knew nothing about it. At some point during the call, Denise stepped into the dining room and sat next to him. She could only hear half the conversation, but Mark looked at her and realized she could sense that another big mystery emerged.

Mark remained silent when Ginny asked, "Mr. Traver, are you still there?"

"Yes, Ginny. And please call me Mark. Um, what is it that you need?"

"Okay, Mark. I need to let you know that your father's books are still in print and are sold in many book store chains and on-line outlets. They still sell, not as if they were new mind you, but he still receives royalty checks every month. I need to make sure that we should continue to have the checks sent to the same account or if there will be a new account set up to receive the checks."

"Ginny, I really don't know what to tell you right this minute. This is a new wrinkle so I'll have to talk with Allen Westridge, his attorney. Can you tell me where the checks go now?"

Ginny passed the information to Mark then told him to let her know as soon as possible if there will be a change to the "target account."

"And Mark, please accept my sincere condolences. Your dad ... he was a peach. When I say he was my favorite client, I mean that sincerely. If I had a rough day, I'd call him to chat and he had a way to boost my spirits. He always beat his deadlines, always said kind words about me and the service I provided. He was very generous. He always sent me flowers, champagne, gift cards, and, sometimes, jewelry after a big book launch. God broke the mold after your dad was born. They don't make 'em like him anymore."

"Thank you for that, Ginny, and thank you for calling. I'll get in touch with Allen today and get back with you on that account matter. I have your number in my cell. Let me send you my home address in Florida so we don't lose touch after we leave Sandusky."

"Mark, when and where is the funeral?"

"Holy Angels Catholic Church here in Sandusky. I'll send you the particulars."

"I'll be there, Mark, unless the sky falls. Looking forward to meeting you. I wish the circumstances were different, but I will be there. Count on it."

After the call disconnected, Mark turned to Denise and said, "You know how a fairy tale starts out, 'Once upon a time ...?' Well, you're not going to believe this shit."

After Mark explained the purpose of the call, Denise said, "He has a bookshelf in the other room that is overflowing with books. I thought I saw a couple J. T. Skipjack books in there."

Mark stood and said, "Let's take a look."

They walked out of the dining room, through the living room, then into what could best be described as a family room. A short, metal filing cabinet sat in the corner next to a table with an old Compaq computer and HP laser-jet printer. The plastic cases for both pieces of electronic equipment had yellowed with age. To the right of the table, a four-foot tall by three-foot wide bookcase stood against the wall. They squatted down on their knees in front of the bookcase, sitting back on their haunches.

The bookcase held about seventy books or more. Most of the books were placed on the shelves with the spines facing out, showing a vertical view of the titles and authors. Mark observed that most were by popular mystery or suspense authors. A few of the titles were how-to books on the stock market, investing in general, and business. Mark noticed a book on writing and another on self-editing.

An entire shelf had been dedicated to J. T. Skipjack novels, either in hard-cover or paperback. Mark noticed that several of those titles had a gray band down the spine. He pulled one of the books from the shelf and saw the word 'Proof' across the cover page. He opened the book to the first page and again noticed the word 'Proof.' As he leafed through the book, handwritten notes had been marked in the margins. He recognized his father's handwriting from the many letters that he read from his father to his mother, Ada May Traver.

Mark placed the book back on the shelf and turned to Denise who had one of J. T. Skipjack's books in her hand, engrossed in the words on the second page of chapter one. He waited for her to reach a breaking point, but it took several minutes. So taken by the writing, she did not notice him watching her.

When she finally turned to him, her cheeks reddened, embarrassed that she had been so engaged in the story. She said, "Wow, your dad really knew how to write. I'd like to take this one back to the room tonight, if you don't mind."

Mark smiled, then began to laugh. He said, "You can take them all if you want. They're ours."

He rolled onto his behind with his knees spread so that his elbows could rest on them. He put his face in his hands and took a deep breath. "I have to call Allen. I hate to, but I need to know where the royalty checks from the publisher should be deposited. I think the current accounts are frozen. I don't know what to tell Ginny."

Once again, Denise moved closer to Mark and took him in a comforting hug. They stayed that way for nearly five minutes, then she kissed him on the lips and said, "I'll warm up the oven. You better make that call."

They stood, hugged again, then Denise headed for the kitchen. Mark sat at the dining room table, cell phone in hand. He looked at the screen – 12:22 p.m.

Moments ago, his stomach growled, the hunger catching up to him. Now, with this latest revelation, he lost his appetite, his attention drawn to another in a series of unbelievable discoveries about his father. How had his father accomplished so much in his life while remaining an enigma to his own family? Why didn't he seek out Mark and his sisters, hoping to make amends for their deficient upbringing. No physical abuse took place, but even the local, elderly priest, Father Schultz, said, by today's standards, the atmosphere in the home bordered on child abuse. While Mark doubted the reality of that observation, he knew that the conditions in the home were horrid, so terrible that all three children fled with their significant others and never returned to the Jay Street house.

Mark's phone rang in his hand. He snapped out of his deep thoughts and looked at the screen – Allen Westridge.

"Allen. I was just going to call you."

In a strained, gravelly voice, Allen said, "Hello, Mark. What were you going to call about?"

Mark explained the call from Ginny Manetti and asked if a new checking account should be established for the royalty checks. Allen began coughing. Mark waited a full minute before Allen cleared his throat. Mark cringed as the attorney sounded as if he spit out phlegm.

"Sorry about that. You should wait until we have approval from the court to establish the new account. I expect we'll have that in a few days. This is moving rather quickly, the probate process, I mean. I'll give you the go-ahead to establish the new account. Now, you might have to set up three …" he began coughing again, then stopped. "Forget I said that last part. When the time comes, we'll deal with it. For now, tell Ms. Manetti to keep depositing the checks in the same account."

"Okay, Allen." He paused then said, "You called me, so is there something else?"

"Yes, there is. If you want, you can go ahead and read that letter I gave you." He coughed hard again. When he stopped, he said, "I don't expect to live much longer so it doesn't much matter whether you read it now or later." Another coughing spell. "I promised your dad that I would take it to my grave. He said no one was to know." A long silence, then Allen Westridge said, "Your dad didn't kill Lyle O'Conner. I did."

Mark nearly fell off his chair.

Chapter 38

While Mark stared off into nothingness, not moving a muscle, his cell phone still in hand, Denise walked into the dining room, and sat down beside him. With his mind numb to the latest news, Mark felt her presence and slowly turned towards her. Was it good news to hear that his father had not killed Lyle O'Conner, though the elder Traver certainly had good reason? And what would motivate Allen Westridge to kill their one-time friend? Did he kill O'Conner because of his betrayal of Joe? Maybe the lawyer's letter held the answers.

Denise placed one arm around his back, her hand resting on his shoulder. She leaned her head on his other shoulder. The soft touch and warmth of her arms, her body against his, shrouded him in the warmth and comfort that he needed. Denise did not know the details of his call with Westridge. She must have sensed that the news brought to light another mental shock. This past week put her husband on such an emotional roller coaster. How much more would he discover? It seemed logical that they would run out of surprises, though the stream of shocking revelations just kept coming.

Denise lightly ran her fingers through his hair. At her touch, he felt the tension melt from his neck and shoulders, down his back. He leaned his head so that his cheek rested on the top of her head. They both took a deep breath.

Denise asked, "So what new bombshell did Allen drop on you?"

Mark remained silent for several seconds, then said, "I'm not sure what to make of it, but Allen said Dad didn't kill O'Conner … that he did - Allen. Maybe he said that just to cover Dad's good name. Maybe they conspired to do it and this was part of a scheme to protect each other from prosecution? I don't know.

"He suggested that I go ahead and read the letter, that he won't live much longer, so there's no reason to wait."

Denise asked, "What are you going to do?"

Mark raised his head, looked over the papers on the table, and found the envelope with Allen's letterhead. He reached across the table and grabbed the envelope, holding it in front of his eyes, staring at it as if it might reveal the answers without opening it.

Denise grabbed the envelope and ripped the seal with her fingernail and pulled out the two-page letter, unfolded it and handed it to him. In a stern voice, she said, "Read it, out loud."

Mark looked at her, surprised by her order. "Yes, ma'am."

He read the typed letter:

Mark,

If you are reading this letter, you are probably back at home in Florida, thinking the worst about your father. I am probably dead, or knocking on death's door. I know he intended to write you and your sisters, confessing to a heinous crime. I suspect he told you in that letter that he killed Lyle O'Conner in a jealous rage because Lyle took advantage of your mother. While I would have applauded him for killing that bastard, he did not do it. In fact, all he did was help a friend cover up the murder, much to his peril.

Lyle O'Conner (it puts a bad taste in my mouth just saying his name) raped my wife while I was stationed overseas with the same bomber group as your father. We were in England, fighting the war, and that son of a bitch stayed here, safe in America, and seduced all his friend's wives.

But my wife wouldn't give in to his charms and told him to leave her alone. He didn't get what he wanted, so he took her. I didn't find out about it until that fateful hunting trip.

We were drinking a bit too much, and Lyle's bragging got the best of him. At first, your dad confronted him about his affair with your mom. He had known about the affair for some time, your mom having confessed to him at some point. Then the son-of-a-bitch bragged about taking what he wanted from my dear Teresa. She never admitted it to me, even after I told her I killed the bastard. She was so ashamed. I told her it wasn't her fault, but our marriage was never the same after that. She died from ovarian cancer in 1961.

You must forgive your dad. He had nothing to do with Lyle's death. I hope O'Conner rots in hell.

Mark, your father was a good man - a great man. He would do anything for anyone in need. I hope you can forgive him for the terrible childhood you and your sisters suffered because of the deeds of that sorry bastard, O'Conner.

And don't blame your mother. She fell prey to a sly, charming predator at a time when she was most vulnerable. That damned war had more victims than just the soldiers and civilians stuck in its path. No one completely escaped unscathed.

God bless you and your family, Mark. I know you're getting more money from this estate than you could imagine. Based on what your father told me and having met you, I know you will do good things with it ... just like your father did.

At your service,

Allen Westridge

When Mark finished, he turned to Denise and embraced her as tears spilled onto her cheeks. Neither said a word for a long time, until the oven timer buzzed.

Denise shook her head and body, wiped the tears from her eyes and said, "Abbe's casserole is going to burn up."

She stood and headed for the kitchen. Mark took a deep, cleansing breath and reread the letter, hoping to glean some new insight into his father, his relationship with Allen Westridge, and the incident that ended Lyle O'Conner's life. The news that his father had not murdered another man remained unclear in his mind. But the fact that Allen took the rifle used to kill O'Conner to Herman Lightfoot, the gunsmith, seemed to fit that part of the puzzle. Allen, Mark surmised, took his gun to the gunsmith hoping to repair the weapon and alter its ballistics signature on any rounds fired from the weapon.

Denise came back into the dining room with two beers, two plates, napkins, and silverware. She placed everything on the table. She stepped back into the kitchen, returning with pads and a piping-hot casserole dish.

"That smells delicious. What is it?"

Denise shrugged her shoulders and said, "Something German, I think. I can smell some kind of sausage. Let's dig in and see if we can figure it out."

As they ate, Denise remarked, "You know, we've gone this far, reading Allen's letter. What do you say we read the ones to your sisters?"

He took several gulps from his bottle, rolled his head on his shoulders – he seemed to be doing that a lot in the past week – and said, "Maybe we should. If Dad confesses to the murder in those letters, and he really didn't do it, then maybe we shouldn't send them. It might do more harm than good."

"We can always put them in new envelopes and send them if there's nothing to be concerned about."

They finished eating in silence, Abbe Holtzmiller's casserole hitting the spot. After cleaning his plate and pushing it aside, Mark leaned back and took the last sip of beer. He stared at the ceiling for a moment, then without looking at Denise, leaned across the table and picked up the two letters from his father to his sisters.

He opened the letter to Maryanne and unfolded the four-page letter. He turned in his seat to face Denise. She looked back at him, a look of anticipation on her face.

Mark cleared his throat and began to read out loud:

Dear Maryanne,

If you are reading this letter, I am likely dead and your brother has forwarded this letter to you. I expect that you did not participate in the probate process. If you did, kudos to you for putting your hatred of me behind you. If not, that is on me. You, your brother, and your sister suffered in a home devoid of love and affection – hell, of any positive emotion at all.

I could blame many things for the dysfunction in our house. The war played a big part. It put your mother's and my relationship on a difficult path before it even started. Your mother and I had broken off our engagement until she learned she was pregnant. I had already committed to join the military and left for duty the day after we were married. But those are excuses. Simply put, I had a responsibility to my family and I blew it.

Your mother despised me. I blamed her for trapping me into marriage. The reasons behind all that animosity are irrelevant at this point.

Despite your mother's and my feelings for each other, we had no right to put you children through hell during a very impressionable time in your young lives. We should have put aside our hatred and concentrated on the three of you. Maybe in doing so, we could have found common ground and rebuilt a relationship that fostered some harmony in our household. There is no way to go back in time and repair the damage done.

I have followed you and your family through different channels. I am so proud to know that you took the example that your mother and I set for you kids and used it as a model of what to not do when raising a family. I know your marriage is strong and loving, your children are smart and have accomplished much in their short lives. You picked a good man to share your life with. By all indications, you are happy - financially and emotionally on solid ground.

I knew when you left Sandusky that you would never come back. If I were in your shoes, I would have done the same thing. But please do not blame your mother for your misfortune of living in a loveless household. If you want to place blame, place it squarely on my shoulders. I take, and deserve, full responsibility for the atmosphere in our household. Had I done things differently ... well, just realize that your mother loved you with all her heart, but she didn't know how to express that love in front of me. If you feel inclined to visit your mother's final resting place, I scattered her ashes at Oakland Cemetery here in Sandusky along Pipe Creek. There is no marker.

You were always the quiet one, keeping your emotions bottled up, not lashing out like your younger sister. As I'm sure you remember, Caroline had no filter when it came to expressing herself. Though I never said anything when you were a little girl, I worried that you would keep your emotions inside until you would someday explode – not literally, of course. But I knew it couldn't be good for you to take all the misery from our household and keep it bottled up like that. You must have found an outlet for that dark pressure, or you've allowed it to bleed off over time.

I want to end by telling you how deeply and truly sorry I am for what I put you through. I do not seek forgiveness or pity or *anything else from you. I just wanted you to know that I am proud of you and hope that, with my death, you can put those hateful feelings behind you. Bury them with my ashes.*

I am in no position to give family or relationship advice, but do not do what I did. Love your husband with all your heart. Love your children with all your being. Love your grandchildren, love them as the most precious gifts that they are.

I hope God forgives me for what I have done. But that is not your concern.

God bless you and your beautiful family, Maryanne.

Though I have never expressed it to you, I love you.

Joe

Mark set the letter on the table, realizing that Denise had put her arm around his back and placed her head on his shoulder again. He said, "He never mentions her biological father. Not once."

Chapter 39

Still seated at the dining room table at 3:45 p.m., Mark and Denise prepared to read Joseph Traver's letter to Mark's sister, Caroline. Still pondering the letter to Maryanne, Mark wondered why his father did not come out and say he blamed Ada May for her infidelity, or that Lyle O'Conner was her biological father. When he wrote the letters to his children, he must have been aware that he had precious little time left. As with his friend, Allen Westridge, he wanted to put things right, but he left details out that some might find important. If his sisters decided to have an ancestry test performed, they might be surprised.

Mark took the envelope from his wife, pulled the multiple pages out, unfolded them, and prepared to read when his cell phone rang. He shook his head slowly and smiled at Denise as if saying *What now?*

"Mr. Traver, this is Max Westridge. I wanted to tell you before you heard it elsewhere - Dad died. I found him about an hour ago at his desk; the emergency room doctor said most likely a heart attack."

"Oh, Max. I'm so sorry."

"I thought you should know that he made arrangements to pass on your father's probate to another local attorney in the event of his death. So that process shouldn't be interrupted; maybe a day or two, at most."

"I just spoke with him this morning."

"Well, it's not a big surprise. His damn smoking had been killing him for years."

There was a silence on the line, then Max said, "I'll let you know about funeral arrangements. If you're still in town, I would be honored if you and your wife would attend."

"Let us know. I think we'll be here a little longer than we planned. I appreciate your calling, Max. Again, we're sorry for your loss."

After the call disconnected, Mark told Denise about the call. They hugged, remained silent in their own thoughts for a bit, then turned their attention back to the letter to Caroline.

Mark Read out loud:

Dear Caroline,

If you are reading this letter, I am likely dead and your brother has forwarded this letter to you. I expect that you did not participate in the probate process. Of my three children, you were the one who did not hold their tongue. You let us know exactly what was on your mind. You and your sister and brother suffered because of your mother's and my hatred for each other. At the time, we did not consider the toll it would take on the three of you.

I could blame the war or any number of factors, none of which has to do with you or your siblings. Though the war played a big part in the scheme of things, it was over when I arrived back home. Somehow, your mother and I should have been able to put that behind us. Prior to my leaving for the war, your mother and I broke off our engagement. Then she learned she was pregnant. I already committed to join the military and left for duty the day after we were married. But enough excuses. Simply put, I had a responsibility to my family and I blew it.

Your mother despised me. I blamed her for trapping me into marriage. Despite your mother's and my feelings for each other, we had no right to subject you children to the hell we put you through during a very impressionable time in your young lives. We should have concentrated on the three of you. Maybe in doing so, we could have found common ground and rebuilt a relationship that fostered some harmony, some feeling of love in our household. That opportunity is long gone.

I have followed you and your family through different channels. I remember you yelling at the two of us that you would never marry, because you thought it made us miserable. I'm telling you now, it wasn't marriage that made us miserable. But I won't try to justify my actions, because there is no justification. I know your family is strong and loving, even without being married in the church or by the government. Your marriage is in your heart and mind. As I've come to know, Stephen is a good man. He must be to live with a headstrong woman like you. I mean that in a good way. Your children are smart and have accomplished much in their short lives.

I knew when you left Sandusky that you would never come back. You stated as much when you left and I believed you. If I were in your shoes, I would have done the same thing. I know you blame your mother for your misfortune of living in a loveless household. If you want to place blame, place it squarely on my shoulders. I take, and deserve, full responsibility for the atmosphere in our household. Had I done things differently ... well, just realize that your mother loved you with all her heart, but she didn't know how to express that love in front of me.

As I said, you were always the outspoken one, wearing your emotions on your sleeve. You accused your mother of destroying your life. She had help — me. I never said anything when you were a little girl, but I worried that you would carry your animosity into your relationships. I can see that you rose above that. You may think that you were the reason for your mother taking her own life because of your outbursts at the two of us. If you harbor feelings of guilt, you should not. I was the problem. I made her feel worthless. That is all on me. All of it. If you feel inclined to visit your mother's final resting place, I scattered her ashes at Oakland Cemetery here in Sandusky along Pipe Creek. There is no marker.

I want to end by telling you how deeply and truly sorry I am for what I put you through. I do not seek forgiveness or pity or anything else from you. I just wanted you to know that I am proud of you and hope that, with my death, you can put any hateful feelings behind you. Bury them with my ashes.

I am in no position to give family or relationship advice, but do not do what I did. Love your family with all your heart. Love your children with all your being. Love your grandchildren, love them as the most precious gifts that they are.

I hope God forgives me for what I have done. But that is not your concern.

*God bless you and your beautiful family,
Caroline·*

*I know this is probably too little, too late,
but I love you·*

Joe

Mark took a deep breath, fighting off the tears, but he already shed too many since arriving in Ohio. He hoped to finish the probate process within the week, but with the death of Allen Westridge, it might be longer.

As he turned to Denise, noticing that her eyes appeared red and puffy, he smiled and asked, "Were you crying?"

In a mousey voice she replied, "No."

They laughed and hugged. Then Mark's cell phone rang.

They both rolled their eyes as Mark looked at the phone's screen. He answered, "Hi, Caroline."

Denise's eyebrows shot up.

"Hi, Mark. I wanted to tell you that I haven't been totally honest with you about something."

Mark frowned, bracing for some new shocking revelation, then asked, "About what?"

After a brief pause, Caroline asked, "Have you read the letters?"

Mark rolled his head around on his shoulders, wondering which letters Caroline meant. He hoped she wasn't referring to those that he and Denise just read, then realized that it would not have been possible for her to have seen the one in his hand. Their father had just written them in the last year or so. Caroline moved away from Sandusky decades ago.

"Are you talking about the letters in Dad's footlocker?"

"Yeah. The ones between Mom and Dad."

Mark let out a silent sigh of relief. "When did you read them? You haven't been in Sandusky in ages, right?"

"Yeah. Since I left with Stephen … long ago. I read them after Maryanne left. I was alone in that hell-hole for years. I used to explore the basement and attic for something to do so I wouldn't lose my mind. I found the footlocker in the attic and started going through the pictures and letters. The pictures didn't really interest me, but those letters between Mom and Dad? Wow."

"To answer your question, yes. Yes, I did. Denise read them, too."

"Then you know, Dad wasn't really my dad. He wasn't Maryanne's dad either. Some guy named Lyle O'Conner was. And you know about your real mom."

Mark admitted, "Yes, I know. And they explain a lot. Why they hated each other. Why Maryanne and I don't look or act anything like brother and sister, especially twins."

"Yeah. There's a lot there." She paused, then said, "I told Maryanne about the letters. At first, she didn't believe me. She's still mad about her childhood. She hates Ohio. She hates … I mean, hated Dad. She calls him 'my fake dad.' I tried to reason with her, but she won't let it go. She is bitter about her entire childhood. She hates all of us, like we had anything to do with it."

"I can't say I blame her, but it isn't hurting anyone but her." After a pause, Mark said, "Let me ask you something, Caroline. Are you happy with your life?"

"Yeah. Our family has a few problems, like every family, but we're good. When we talked before, I was thinking back on our childhood and how much it sucked and how much I never wanted to think about it again. I kind of lashed out at you, but after I hung up, Stephen and I talked. He made me realize what I just said, we didn't have anything to do with it. We were the victims of Mom and Dad's bad choices. But you know what? I just decided long ago that I'm not a victim. I can't do anything about the past and I'm not going to let that happen to my family." She paused. "You've been married to Denise all this time, right? No separations, no divorce. So, you must have figured it out."

"It isn't because of me, believe me. Denise is sitting right here, so I can't say too much good about her. It'll go to her head." Denise smacked him on the arm. "We've had a few differences of opinion and some shouting matches, but we're very happy. We have great kids and grandkids. Life is good."

"That's exactly how I feel. Since leaving that house, I wouldn't change a thing."

Mark thought about the money they stood to inherit, but decided to wait so he could get a clearer picture of the total probate package. He did not know either sister's financial situation, but millions of dollars could change a person's life, sometimes not in a good way.

"Caroline, I know you don't plan to come to Dad's funeral, but please reconsider. Denise and I would love to meet Stephen and your kids. I know Elliot and Eva would like to meet their Aunt Caroline and Uncle Stephen and their cousins."

The silence on the line broke when Caroline took a deep breath. "Mark, I'll talk with Stephen about it, but please don't count on it. I will say this, maybe it's time we buried the past, right along with Dad."

"That's all I ask. We'll talk soon. Believe me, we have a lot to talk about. Oh, I just found out that Allen Westridge, Dad's lawyer, died this morning. I'm sure the new attorney will call with his contact information soon."

With the call disconnected, Denise said, "That seemed to go well. What did she say?"

Mark paraphrased the conversation to Denise and expressed hope that his youngest sister would make the trip to Sandusky for the funeral. Caroline sounded genuinely interested in having her family meet theirs.

"And we're repackaging these letters and sending them on to my sisters. They deserve to hear Dad's feelings directly from him."

Chapter 40

Mark sat at the dining room table with his head in his hands, thinking about his conversation with his sister, Caroline. She seemed genuinely interested in having their families meet. It surprised him to learn that, even though they lived out west in relatively close proximity to each other, she and Maryanne seldom spoke prior to their father's death. The two sisters' personalities differed significantly. They likely lived different lifestyles, though they resided in states with liberal leaning populations and state governments. Mark knew that Maryanne's husband held an upper-management position for a large technology firm. Caroline's husband worked for an environmental remediation company, one of the most profitable in the country. So, neither family should be having financial difficulties.

Something about Maryanne's attitude bothered him. Always one to keep her feelings and emotions bottled up inside, she never engaged anyone when confronted. The topic did not matter. She backed away and clammed up. Her defense always reverted to statements like *I don't want to talk about it* or *We're not having this conversation.* When younger, she would simply say *Leave me alone,* and walk away. As a child, she would cry if pressured too much.

Mark decided to call Maryanne and not allow her to cut him off. That might be difficult since she could simply hang up on him, but he believed he must try to get her to let go of her anger. Somehow, he needed to convince her that she and her family were the only ones hurt by her hanging on to angst from the past.

Mark lifted his head and noticed Denise staring at him with an inquisitive look. With his hands raised, he said, "What? I'm just thinking."

"I can see that. It's what you're thinking that worries me."

He smiled. "You can always read me like a book."

She raised her eyebrows, the smile remaining on her face, prodding him to explain. "Well?"

"I'm thinking about calling Maryanne back. I have to try and get her to stop living in the past. She always bottled up her feelings. What we went through in this house is going to bug her until the day she dies. It might just shorten her life with all that pent-up anger."

"Don't you think you're overstepping a bit? Your sister is your age; a grown woman."

He raised his shoulders. "Maybe, but I feel like I have to try."

"She might take your call as an intrusion and tell you to go to hell. You could make her situation worse."

He raised his shoulders again. "If I don't try to get through to her, I'll always feel like I should have done more. We'll see."

He stood, leaving his phone on the table. He said, "I have to pee and I need a beer."

"You know, it's getting close to dinner time. Why don't you put off that call until we finish eating, then if you still feel like calling her, you can. That'll give me time to talk you out of it. Plus, Washington is three hours behind us. You can wait until later tonight to call."

"Hmm. Okay. What would you like for dinner?"

"We haven't had a hamburger since I've been here. Are there any good American restaurants close by?"

"Yes, there are many, but the one I'm thinking about isn't real close. It's on East Perkins Avenue, not too far from the mall. According to Peggy, the Old Dutch has the best burgers within a hundred miles."

"The Old Dutch it is." Denise paused, then said, "How about we head back to the hotel and relax tonight instead of coming back here. I think we need a break from this house. Maybe we could do a few laps in the pool or spend some time in the hot tub."

Mark smiled. "You're trying to seduce me."

Denise winked then asked, "Is it working?"

***

Back at the hotel room after a remarkable burger and an hour in the hot tub, Mark and Denise relaxed on the king-sized bed, holding each other, comfortable in the quiet surrounding them. Still early in the tourist season, just a handful of patrons besides the two of them occupied rooms. They made love, slow and easy, setting an intimate, sensual mood for the rest of the evening. Mark believed that they were on the downslope of the crazy week that revealed so many surprises, twisting his mind and muscles into a series of high-tension, emotional ups and downs.

Denise stroked Marks chest as they laid together, the accumulated stress now exorcised from their bodies. Mark's eyes remained closed, a smile on his face, feeling so relaxed that he nearly fell asleep. He had not felt this content in months.

He turned his head and looked at the room clock – 9:56 p.m. With a deep breath and a sigh, he said, "I guess I should make that phone call."

Denise grabbed a handful of chest hair. "Stop right there, mister. I'm not through with you."

She let go of the hair and rubbed his chest. She moved on top of him, pinning him to the mattress. He gave her a big smile and said, "I surrender."

After making love a second time, a feat they rarely performed, Denise decided to take a shower before retiring for the evening. Mark thought it might be a test to see if he followed through on a call to Maryanne. When he heard the shower water flowing, he put on his pajamas and reached for his cell phone. He found the call history and scrolled to his sister's number. He rolled his head around, realizing that his neck did not make any popping sounds, a sign that they expelled his tension. He smiled and hit the dial icon.

He looked at the clock – 11:22 p.m. - 8:22 p.m. in Washington.

"Hello, Mark."

She did not sound thrilled to take his call, but at least she answered. "Hi, Maryanne. Did Caroline tell you that I'd be calling?"

"No, but I figured you'd call back. You just can't leave it alone, can you?"

Mark let the comment roll off his back and jumped right in. "Maryanne, I know you don't want to talk about Mom and Dad, about our childhood, about how angry you are, but I think we have to talk about it. I know how you feel …"

Maryanne cut him off and replied with a terse, sharp rebuke, "Mark, you have no idea how I feel, how I've felt for years, every single day for as long as I can remember! I never learned how to relate to people, how to talk, to laugh, how to have a relationship. You and Caroline were outgoing. It was easy for you both to make friends. It wasn't like that for me."

Mark let her vent. He hoped that she kept talking, letting her frustrations out. He lived in the same house with her until he moved out at twenty-two. She moved out soon after. Throughout their youth, he never heard her express her opinion, cry out for help, or say a coarse word to anyone. He did not realize at the time that her silence was a cry for help. By the time she met her husband, Richard, Mark and Denise left Sandusky and moved to central Florida.

"I'm so sorry, Maryanne. I didn't realize you felt this way. We all went through the same, horrible upbringing, but I didn't know how much harder it was on you. I think we all just wanted to get the hell out of the house and away from Mom and Dad. If I'd have known, I …"

"You wouldn't have done a damn thing. You were too busy with your friends." She paused, but before Mark could reply, she continued, "You know, Caroline called me shortly after she moved out, right before Mom killed herself. She told me that Dad wasn't our real dad. He was yours, but not ours. Did you know that?"

"I just found that out this past week. She read the letters while she still lived there. I just discovered them in Dad's footlocker while going through his stuff."

"My real dad … I never got to know him. My fake dad, I never really knew him either. It was like living in a tomb, a fricking tomb." Maryanne began to cry. Mark remained silent, hoping that she would get everything out of her system. She blew her nose loud enough that Mark held the phone away from his ear. When she came back on, she said, "You know, I thought about killing myself more than once. I was so depressed, but I was afraid to say anything to Mom. She was a waste. Did you know that she took valium? She wanted to escape that house so bad that she did drugs."

"I didn't know that …"

"I wish I was more like you … no, that's not true … I wish I had been more like you back then. Maybe I could have let all the pain roll off my back like you did."

Mark thought it unfair for her to assume that about him, but he let her continue. This was the most she ever said to him in their entire lives. He didn't want to interrupt her thoughts.

She continued, "I envied you and Caroline. Caroline especially. I remember her yelling at Mom, telling her to snap out of it, to get her shit together … she said that, I swear. She said, 'Mom, get your shit together and move the hell away from Dad. You're killing each other. You might as well be dead.' The last time I spoke with Caroline, before this, I mean, was right after Mom killed herself. She told me she thought it was her fault, that she drove Mom to pull the trigger. I hated Caroline so much. You know what I said? I told her, 'You're right. It was your fault. Yours and Dad's. You both might as well have pulled the trigger.' I never apologized for saying that. I cried myself to sleep for weeks, I felt so guilty for saying that. But knowing Caroline, she probably forgot about it right after I said it."

The line became silent except for deep sucking breaths from Maryanne as she tried to regain her composure. Mark took a deep breath himself then said, "Maryanne, are you happy? I mean, before Dad's death brought all this back to the surface, were you happy? Is your family life good? Is Richard a good husband? Are your kids and grandkids doing well?

Mark heard his sister sniff back tears. She said, "Yes to all of that. I have a great life. I made sure that my family life looks nothing like the life I went through. When I met Richard, he helped me be more outgoing. He helped me become more social. After a while, I came out of my shell. I started having friends, going out for dinner and drinks with my new friends. It was like an epiphany."

"Well, I have another epiphany for you. None of this was your fault. It wasn't Caroline's fault. It wasn't my fault. All this pain, all this hurt, it all started before any of us was born. Mom and Dad, their marriage was doomed from the start. The war played a part. Other problems plagued them, too. But there never was any excuse for what they put us through." Mark paused, thinking about his next words. "Our parents are dead. I think we all need to bury the pain and hatred with them. I'm begging you … please let it go."

The silence lasted nearly a full minute, then Maryanne said, "I'll try, Mark. I really will."

When the call disconnected, Mark took a deep breath, his eyes welling, but no tears spilled onto his cheeks. Then Denise stepped out of the bathroom, her hair still wet, wearing a white, fluffy robe. She walked to him as he stood. They embraced in a tight hug. He smiled as the tears rolled down his cheeks.

Chapter 41

Mark and Denise stopped for breakfast at a restaurant on Tiffin Avenue next door to Dick's Carryout. The small diner on the west end of Sandusky had been recommended by Peggy and Randy Whipple, telling Mark they had great omelets and other breakfast choices with good prices. They sat at a table eating their breakfast as patrons came and went. Based on the handful of tables and booths, Mark reasoned that carry-out orders constituted a large part of the restaurant's business. Several customers looked their way and smiled, but no one interrupted them while they ate. The server did mention that Mark looked like his father and that they always enjoyed having Joe Traver dine in with them. When they finished, Mark left a generous tip and they headed for the house on Jay Street, just two blocks away.

Denise remarked, "That was quite good." Then she asked, "What's on the agenda for today?"

"I'm not sure. I should probably look through the basement below the garage one more time. There may be a couple things that I'd like to keep from Dad's tool collection."

"Don't you have most every tool known to mankind in your garage?"

"Honey, a man can never have too many tools. If you do, you build a bigger garage."

Denise smiled and shook her head.

The doorbell rang. Together, they walked through the living room and opened the door, surprised to see their son, Elliot standing on the stoop.

Denise opened the door, then her arms. As he walked into her hug, he said, "Hi, Mom."

She tightened her arms around him then ushered him into the living room, and asked, "Where are my grandchildren?"

He laughed. "Back home. Marcus is still studying. Caitlin is probably texting with her friends or talking with her boyfriend." He rolled his eyes as he said 'boyfriend.'

"Well, as I remember, you and Sandra were inseparable at that age. We practically had to use a crowbar to pry you two apart. That seemed to work out. How is Sandra, by the way?"

"She's good. She's already dreading the kids growing up and leaving home. But we're starting to look at RVs and travel destinations. We really want to spend some time seeing the country."

"Well, you should follow through on that." She turned her head towards Mark and said, "Maybe we could help with those plans. What do you think, Dear?"

Mark shrugged. "Maybe. You never know." He stood back, allowing the two to catch up a bit. He held out his hand, motioning for his son to follow them into the dining room. He asked, "Anything to drink? I can make coffee."

"Not me. I just ate about an hour ago: a little place in Bucyrus that I like when I make the trip up this way."

Mark asked, "So, what brings you to Sandusky?"

"Just wanted to see if you needed any help, and catch up on where everything stands."

Mark and Denise looked at each other, eyebrows raised, not sure where to start. Mark asked, "Should we tell him about the letters? Wait, before we talk about that, Allen Westridge, Dad's lawyer, died yesterday. The doctors said probably a heart attack."

Elliot's shocked expression appeared almost comical, but he quickly asked, "Are you kidding? Will that slow anything down?"

"No joke. But it shouldn't delay anything. He put a plan in place in case he died. He had stage four lung cancer and he coughed constantly. Really bad. His son is the local paper's editor. He told us that his dad was living on borrowed time, so it wasn't completely unexpected. I haven't met the lawyer who'll be taking over but I should hear from him on Monday."

"Wow. That's crazy."

Denise laughed then said, "Sorry about that. It isn't funny. But if you think that's crazy, wait until you hear about the rest of your dad's week."

Elliot looked towards his father, turning his hands towards the ceiling in a gesture that said *I'm all ears.*

"Well, son, it turns out that your aunts and I are not brother and sisters. We're not blood related, anyway."

Elliot's jaw nearly hit the table, his eyes wide, and his body appearing to go numb. When he recovered enough to speak, he said, "Now you're pulling my leg, right?"

They both shook their heads, then Mark began to explain what they learned in the letters found in the footlocker. Elliot sat, stunned, listening to the tale of his family's twisted history.

After half an hour, Denise said, "Now you know why your father appeared stressed when you visited last week. When you called me, concerned about your dad's mental state, he was finding out some of this stuff about your grandparents' history."

The doorbell rang. Mark took a deep breath and headed to the front door. When he opened it, he found a woman about his age standing there with a plastic grocery bag in her hands. She gave Mark a tentative smile and said, "You must be Mark Traver."

A flash of recognition passed through his mind. Her silvery-gray hair hung to near her square shoulders. Something about her face and stature ... he must know her from somewhere. But how could that be?

"Yes. I am. And you are?"

The woman held out her hand, "I'm Emma Franks. I knew your dad."

He recognized the name as the woman who wrote the note on the China cabinet. The look on his face must have surprised the woman because she smiled at his reaction, showing near perfect teeth.

Mark smiled and said, "Excuse my lack of manners. Please come in."

As Emma Franks passed into the living room, she looked around, taking in a deep breath, recognition on her face. She had been here before. Elliot and Denise stepped from the dining room and greeted the woman. Mark introduced the two to their guest. When Mark saw Elliot and Emma Franks together, he noticed facial features that appeared similar. Their thin noses and narrow faces seemed to be formed from the same mold.

Denise spoke up and said, "Please come have a seat in the dining room. Would you like something to drink? We have a variety of soda … I mean pop. I can make some coffee."

As she placed the plastic bag on the table, she said, "Don't go to any trouble, thank you. A glass of water would be fine."

"Coming right up."

When Denise returned with Emma's water, everyone took a seat at the table. Mark smiled, then said, "You wrote this note to Dad." He turned towards the China cabinet, grabbed the note, and handed it to Emma.

She smiled. Her eyes seemed to drift away, looking at nothing. She said, "Yes, I did." She took a deep breath and said, "Your father … I don't know where to start."

Mark smiled. "Well, you thanked him for visiting your mother."

"Yes. Your father visited my mother at the Erie County Nursing Home at Osborne Park. She'd fallen and couldn't walk. Broke both her hips; bedridden. She was in her late eighties at that time and so depressed. She nearly died. She wouldn't eat for several days, refused to take her medication. They repaired her hips with surgery, but she lost her will to live. The only thing that kept her going was telling me stories about her trip from Germany to America as the war in Europe intensified. A young American man befriended her. They fell in love. She would tell me stories about how they would meet after classes and just talk. Just as his company carried her through her difficult times so long ago, those memories carried her through her surgery and recovery while in the nursing home."

Mark's eyes remained glued to Emma Franks' face as she recounted the stories of her mother and his father's visits. He knew where the story would lead, but he let Emma continue.

"When Mom would tell her tales of this dashing young man, I wondered what became of him after he joined the American Army to fight the war. So, I asked her what she knew about the man. She said he lived in Sandusky, that he attended college near Cleveland, but, at that time, he had dropped out and joined the military to fight the Germans in the war. Before he left for his first assignment, his ex-girlfriend came to him and told him she was pregnant, that the child was his. He told my mom that he was sorry, that he had to marry the woman, that it wouldn't be right to leave her stranded with his child. Mom said that she understood, that she agreed with him. But she was heartbroken. He did not know that mother was also pregnant ... with you."

Elliot sucked in a deep, loud breath, surprised by the revelation. She stopped and shivered, apparently chilled by her retelling of her mother's story. She took a deep breath.

Mark's eyes teared up as he recalled the letters between his mother and father, and the letters from Ingrid Engel, noting how Emma's story matched what he and Denise had read in the letters.

"With what Mom told me, I began to search for your father, thinking that he may have been killed in the war, or moved his family to a different part of the country. I did a few internet searches. When I read all these stories about Joseph Traver and his work with local charities and veterans' groups, not to mention Holy Angels Church and small businesses, I was shocked. Even more amazing, he lived here, in this house, less than twenty minutes from the nursing home. I wanted to run and tell Mom about it right away, but I didn't want to give her false hope that the man that she described in her stories was the man I found. So, I knocked on that door and introduced myself. Your dad dropped everything at that very moment and followed me to Mom's room."

Mark looked at Denise. Her cheeks were soaked with tears. She smiled, even as more tears poured from her eyes, and moved closer to Mark, putting her arms around his shoulders.

Elliot sat stunned, engrossed in Emma Franks' telling of her mother's life, astonished that his grandfather held such secrets.

Mark looked at the plastic bag on the table. Emma noticed his curiosity and said, "My mother kept this box by her bedside."

She pulled a wooden box, approximately eight inches by five inches, and four inches deep. The hardwood box had intricate carvings on all sides and small claw feet. She opened the box and pulled out a stack of black-and-white pictures. She smiled and handed them to Mark.

There were eleven pictures in all. Each picture showed an infant child and a beautiful young woman. The innocence of the child was matched by the adoration on the face of the woman.

Mark flipped the picture over and read the names and dates on the back, but he already knew … the pictures were of him being held by his mother – Ingrid Engel.

Chapter 42

After looking through the pictures of his mother holding him as an infant, Mark hardly knew what to say next. Emma Franks, the daughter of Ingrid Engel must be his half-sister. Did she have other siblings? Did his mother marry after giving birth to him? Where had they lived? The questions flooded his mind, coming so fast he could barely keep his thoughts straight.

Finally able to gather his thoughts, Mark said, "So, I hardly know where to start. We're brother and sister?"

"Well, yes, half-brother and half-sister anyway. Mom married my dad about two years after you were born. Alfred Langdon; a kind man. He ran a strict household but the rules were centered around swearing, being home and to appointments on time, no dating until sixteen. Things like that. Other than that, he let us be kids, made sure we wanted for nothing. He and Mom wanted us to have a happy childhood. As long as we didn't break the rules, we did. And we knew he loved Mom with all his heart. He passed away in 1969."

"Your last name, Franks, is from your marriage?"

"Yes. Cameron Franks. He passed about a year ago. He was about ten years older than I. He died suddenly from a brain aneurism. He and some friends were out on a fishing charter on Lake Erie when they noticed him slump over in the boat. He immediately became unresponsive, so they think he didn't suffer. He didn't cry out in pain or anything like that. They called out a mayday on their radio, but he was gone. The doctor told me that he had no chance of surviving."

"I'm so sorry for your loss. That must have been difficult, I mean, with no apparent illness, then the suddenness of it. Are you doing okay?"

"Yes. It took a while, but I don't cry myself to sleep anymore. He left me in good financial shape. He worked out at the power plant by Camp Perry."

The room remained silent for a moment. Then Elliot said, "So you're my Aunt Emma. Do I have any other aunts and uncles?"

Emma chuckled. "Yes. Yes you do. You have an Uncle Gerrard. When you meet him, call him Uncle Gerry. He hates when people call him Gerrard. And you have a few cousins."

Emma became serious and said, "After your dad began to visit Mom at the nursing home, you could tell they were still deeply in love. Your dad would sit at her bedside for weeks. Over time she could get up and ride around in a wheel chair. He took her out onto a patio on the grounds. After a few weeks, Mom got up and walked with a walker. They would take short strolls, visiting other residents, going outside when the weather improved. They reminisced about how they met, their friendship, then their courtship. They talked about the war and how the only good thing that came out of it was that they met." Her eyes teared up. "They talked like a couple of teenagers; the most precious thing that I've ever witnessed.

"This went on for over a year. I would pick your dad up here and take him to see Mom. He would spend the day, then I'd bring him home. Then Mom got sick. They transported her to the Cleveland Clinic; some kind of viral infection. She was in the ICU for over a month. During that time, your dad started to get depressed again. He was near ninety years old and fearful that Mother wouldn't make it. I visited him several times, but I spent most days in Cleveland, tending to Mom. I wish I could have done more, but he just seemed to give up without Mom here to visit."

The doorbell rang. Denise stood and went to answer it. When she returned, Abbe Holtzmiller walked into the dining room, a smile on her face.

She took one look at Emma Franks and said, "That's her, alright. She's the woman who came to visit your dad."

Emma smiled. "You're the neighbor-lady whom Joseph spoke about."

"He probably called me the nosey neighbor. I'm Abbe."

They all laughed at her 'nosey neighbor' comment.

With a bright smile still on her face, she introduced herself, "Emma Franks. Joseph spoke highly of you. He said you took care of him after … his wife's death."

Abbe's face turned grim. "That was a bad time for him, but he snapped out of it. I've never seen anyone so focused as old Joe Traver. I remember it like yesterday. He came home from church. I came over to visit with him and he looked me in the eyes and said, 'I'm not spending another minute wallowing in my own pity. If you see me moping around here, you come and yell at me to stop.' After that day, he was like a machine, busy doing something. Either working on that car, doing some kind of woodworking project, volunteering for the AMVETS, American Legion, VFW, or something for the church. That's after a full day of work."

Abbe stopped talking and stared off into nothingness. Her eyes teared up as her fond memories of her neighbor flooded in.

Emma put a hand on the old woman's shoulder. She said, "Thank you for looking after Mr. Traver. He told me that you were the first person to offer support after his wife's death. Whatever you said to him, he took it to heart and rededicated his life to do as much good as his time left would allow."

Mark asked, "So, Abbe, what did you say to him that lit a fire under him?"

Abbe rubbed her eyes with her pale hands. She said, "You have to remember, Joe had been through a lot. He risked his life in that bomber. He had two children before he turned twenty-three, from two different women. I learned more details about his wife's …"

She glanced at Elliot whose eyes were glued to her as she spoke.

"We'll just leave that right there. Both conceived out of wedlock, mind you. Back then, that was a serious sin. Then, he married a woman who didn't love him." She turned to Mark and said, "Sorry, Mark, that's just the simple facts.

"I didn't really say anything in particular, just that he had two choices – he could either waste the rest of his life, like the last twenty-five years, or he could get off his ass and make something of himself. He looked at me, hugged me and kissed me … on the cheek, of course. I saw the light come on in his eyes. And the rest is history."

Mark got up from his chair and got on his knees next to Abbe. He wrapped his arms around the old woman and held her tight.

Emma joined him in hugging Abbe and said, "By saving Joe, you made my mother very happy. By jolting Mr. Traver out of his depression, he lived an amazing life. Then he helped my mother break out of her depression."

Denise watched as the three hugged, rubbing the tears from her eyes. Elliot looked on, still trying to process all that he heard this morning.

After a minute, Mark and Emma returned to their seats. Abbe smiled through her own tears. "I really didn't do anything that any other human being would have done."

As he looked at his half-sister, Mark's memory flashed. While in Margaritaville looking through the window towards the waterfall, he noticed a woman looking his way. He remembered the long, gray hair, her smile, and that she sat in a booth across from a man near her age. Then he turned his attention to Jody, the barmaid, and talked a bit about his dad. When he turned back, the woman and the man were gone. But he now knew the woman's identity – Emma Franks.

"That was you at Margaritaville last week."

Emma smiled and nodded. "I saw you at the bar and knew immediately who you were. I thought about approaching you, but I wasn't sure how you would react. I didn't know if you had any idea about our parents' relationship. So, Gerry and I – that was my brother with me – just left. We finished our dinner and were just watching the trout jump into the waterfall. I told him that we should leave. I was getting a little uncomfortable knowing what I knew and not sure what you knew. He didn't know anything about all this until I told him a few days ago. He convinced me to come here today."

Mark replied, "Well, I think I speak for everyone. We're all very glad that you did. I just wish we could have met your … our mother. When did she pass?"

Emma's face took on a look of surprise. She shook her head, smiled and said, "Mother hasn't passed away. She's still very much alive. She recovered from that infection. It took her several months to fully recover but she's back at the nursing home. That's one of the reasons for my visit. She would love to meet you. All of you."

They all sat, staring in stunned silence, until Emma said, "I take it you'd like that."

They all stood, except for Abbe Holtzmiller. She looked at Mark and said, "This is a moment for family. I don't want to intrude."

Emma said, "Abbe, Mother would love to meet the woman who pushed her Joseph, and got him living life again. He spoke often about you and how you saved him from continuing to waste his life away. Please come with us. You can ride with me, if you like."

Again, tears filled Abbe's eyes as Emma helped her to her feet. Mark asked about the best way to get across town to Osborne Park, to which Emma replied, "The easiest way is to just drive down Perkins Avenue east. Just before you come to Cleveland Road, you'll see sports fields on your right. There's a sign near the entrance. Turn right and you'll see the signs for the nursing home. Park in the visitor's lot. We'll gather there and go in together." Emma's smile lit up the room. "Mother will be thrilled to meet all of you."

Mark took a deep breath, reached for Denise, and gave her a tight hug. He pulled Elliot into the hug.

Mark said, "You guys head out front. I have to grab a couple things."

Everyone left the living room and made their way to the front door. After a few minutes, he bounded down the front steps, smiling. He held the wooden box Emma had brought with her.

He said, "I'm ready."

They made their way out into the warmth and bright sun, the nicest day of spring to date.

Chapter 43

Mark looked at the clock on the wall as he, Denise, Elliot, Abbe, and Emma stood in front of the counter just inside the entrance to the Nursing Home; 11:20 a.m. The attendant politely directed them to sign his/her name and contact information on the check-in sheet. Her name, Jillian, displayed in large letters on a blue plastic tag on her collar. She did not ask whom they planned to visit. She smiled with recognition as she spoke with Emma, addressing her by first name. She mentioned that Ingrid appeared to be having a very good day. She pointed to the fireplace along a wall in a commons area where several comfortable looking chairs and a couch sat. The room looked empty, but Mark could see the gray hair of someone sitting in a chair facing away from them and towards the fireplace. The air smelled faintly of industrial cleaner mixed with a fresh flower scent. Emma thanked Jillian and led the group into the sitting room. When they formed a loose semi-circle in front of the chair, the woman opened her eyes as if sensing their presence. She smiled, her body seeming to swell with newfound energy.

Emma spoke. "Mother, you have visitors."

The old woman's gaze turned to Mark, her eyes glistening, tears threatening to spill on to her cheeks. With a barely discernable German accent she said, "Mark. Let me look at you. You have grown to be as handsome as your father. I thought I would never live to see this day, to lay eyes on you again."

Mark stepped closer to her and knelt on one knee in front of her. He opened his arms. She did the same and cautiously leaned forward. They embraced. Mark's arms encircled her, afraid to hold her too tightly, thinking he might snap her bones. He could feel her thin, frail body through the sweater and blouse. But she tightened her arms around his neck and kissed his cheek repeatedly. He felt her tears, wet on his cheek.

He whispered, "Mother."

The old woman laughed, hearing those words. "I was afraid that you would hate me for what I had done so long ago. I abandoned you."

"No, no, you didn't abandon me. You made sure I was in good hands. You were so young, alone, and faced with a crushing decision. I could never hate you for that."

"My sweet child, I have much to tell you, but we should go somewhere more private." She turned to her daughter. "Emma, dear, let's go outside to one of the tables."

When Mark released her, Ingrid pulled a walker closer to her and stood with little effort. The new-looking walker sported hand-breaks and wheels on all four contact points with the floor. It also had a built-in seat which could be lifted, exposing a basket where personal items could be stored.

During their trek outside, Ingrid looked over her group of visitors. "This must be your dear wife, Denise."

Denise said, "Yes, ma'am. And this is our son Elliot."

Ingrid stopped walking, looked at Denise, and said, "My dear, let's dispense with the manners. Please, just call me Mom. Elliot, you can call me Grams or whatever you wish." She looked at the older woman with them and said, "And you are Abbe Holtzmiller. A good German name. Joseph said that you saved his life. Thank you."

Abbe blushed, "That's a bit of an exaggeration. I just did what any neighbor would do. He needed a friend to talk with, and I did, that's all."

"From what Joseph told me you did far more than that. He needed a good kick in the pants, so to speak. He said you gave him a reason to live again. That is true friendship."

Abbe just nodded and smiled as they continued to walk in the bright sun. The heat of the day promised to rise into the mid-seventies as they took seats around a table away from any crowds. Ingrid sat without assistance and seemed comfortable, very spry for someone nearing ninety years old.

Mark said, "You're moving around well. Are you completely recovered from your hip surgery?"

Ingrid looked at Emma. "I see my daughter has told you about my ills. She must have told you about my most recent health scare. I'm afraid that one took a toll on me. My recovery in Cleveland lasted much longer than I hoped. I don't need a walker, but my daughter and my doctor insist that I use it. And I do when they're looking." She smiled and winked at Mark.

He asked, "Can you tell me about how you and Dad met?"

Her smile grew and she looked over Mark's head at the trees as the slight breeze caused the leaves to flutter. Her mind appeared to drift to another time. Then she spoke. "Back in Germany, in a small town south of Hamburg, as a young woman, I enjoyed a good life. My friends and I grew up together throughout my childhood. Then one day, Papa and Mama came to me and said I must go to the United States to further my education. I was shocked. This came out of the blue and I argued with them. I had no desire to leave my home. I was distraught for weeks. Finally, they told me the real reason. Hitler's army was losing men faster than they could recruit and train them. My father received notice to report for military training within a month. My father was nearly forty years old at that time. Mother received a letter ordering her to work at the Unterluss Munitions Factory over half an hour from our home. She had no idea how she would get there. But others in our neighborhood received similar letters.

"A friend of theirs planned to send their son to America on a merchant vessel. He planned to accompany me on the trip, but when the day came for me to leave, the authorities showed up at his house and took him away, drafting him into the German Army on the spot. My parents took me to the port and made sure I boarded the ship. They gave me some food and a change of clothes. We said goodbye … and I never saw them again. Father left for training within a few weeks and mother started working at the factory the following month. My mother wrote to me with updates, mostly on the war, and news of friends from our neighborhood. Then the updates stopped altogether."

Mark thought about the picture from the footlocker of bombs exploding and the description on the back. *Unterluss Munitions Plant, April 4, 1945*. He hesitated, not wanting to mention the tragic coincidence. But Ingrid said, "I can see it in your eyes, Mark. You saw the photo from your father's footlocker. When he realized that his bomber group dropped the bombs on the factory the same day as Mama was killed, it nearly broke his heart. He was so distraught. There's no getting around the tragedy, the heartbreak. But it wasn't his fault. It certainly is not your fault. Only one man can be blamed for all the death and destruction, the ruination of lives, of family, of so many Jews, of the German legacy - Adolf Hitler! It leaves a bitter taste in my mouth just saying his name. But we must move on. We cannot place false blame for the war on others. Your father was a hero, as were all his fellow soldiers. They stopped that madman and saved millions more lives in the process.

"Always remember, if not for the war, I would not have made the trip to America, and met your father. And you would not be here."

Mark smiled, but his eyes held a touch of sadness. He asked, "How did you wind up in Ohio?"

Her gaze again drifted and she began to recollect her journey. "After the ship docked in New York, a large group of us was told that no work existed in the city, that we should head west and south to Pennsylvania, Ohio, Michigan, Kentucky, and further. Everywhere I traveled, I asked if schools accepted foreigners, and women. Everyone said no. Men were expected to work. Women were expected to marry and support their families. But when I arrived in Cleveland, I met a woman who took me under her wing. She got me enrolled in college and helped me buy new clothes. I took some tests and passed them all easily. I started classes the next day. That's when the hostility began.

"The war in Europe intensified. The allied forces began to strike back at Germany. Bombing raids began. Then the factories and train stations were bombed. My classes were over ninety percent male. They called me vile names and did everything they could to get me to drop out." Then she smiled and said, "That's when I met your father. He defended and befriended me. My knight."

Ingrid coughed. Then she looked at Emma and asked if she would get her some water. Denise looked at everyone else and asked if they would also like water. When everyone agreed that they would appreciate that, Emma and Denise headed back to the main building.

Mark looked back at his mother and asked, "Did you and Dad fall in love right away?"

Ingrid cleared her throat and said, "I did. He was very kind, so helpful, and protective. He wouldn't let our classmates bully me. Whenever we were together, the men would leave me alone. I would get dirty looks, but no one said anything bad, not like they did before your dad intervened.

"Now, I can't say that about your father. He still loved Ada May. I warned him that he should not spend so much time with me, that their relationship would suffer. And sure enough, he introduced me to Ada May and her friend, Mildred. The jealousy burned from their eyes. Both women hated me before I said hello. Within a week, your mother broke off their engagement. From then on, your father spent all his free time with me."

"When did you know that Dad had fallen in love with you?"

Her smile widened. "Right after the breakup, with us spending so much time together, I could tell that we had fallen for each other. Within a month, he hinted that he wanted to ask for my hand. But he never got to ask the question. He even gave me a ring, but I returned it."

Elliot frowned, "Grandma, why did you return the ring?"

Emma and Denise returned with plastic bottles of water. Emma opened one for her mother and handed her the bottle. After everyone took a drink, they turned their attention back to Ingrid.

"I gave the ring back because your father had to marry Ada May. She told your father about her pregnancy, that his child grew inside of her, and that he must marry her." She paused and took another drink. When she finished, her eyes welled with tears and she said, "He came to me with the news and said he was sorry, that he must do the honorable thing and marry her … and I agreed with him. I could not trap him into a marriage and make him feel guilty for the rest of his life, thinking that he abandoned Ada May and their child. As it turned out, that is exactly what Ada May did. The child was not his, and he let the bitterness in his heart destroy his family. Only after Ada May … well, you all know."

Mark took a deep breath and said, "I think it's time we repaired the damage."

He reached into his pocket and pulled out an envelope. He opened the envelope and pulled out a picture and a ring. He held out the picture; the black and white photo of her holding him as an infant. "I found this in the footlocker. You sent it to dad in one of your letters to him. And I believe this is yours."

Mark held the ring that he found in the bottom of the footlocker. He asked for her left hand. As she extended her hand, it began to shake. He held the hand still and slipped the ring on. He said, "Now it is where it belongs."

There was a moment of silence until Ingrid motioned for Mark to give her another hug. He said, "We found all of the letters that you sent to Dad while he was in the military, but there were no letters to you."

Ingrid told Mark to bring her walker closer. When he did, she lifted the walker's seat and reached into the storage compartment underneath. She pulled out a bundle of envelopes, bound with an old, faded, pink ribbon. The envelopes were yellowed and torn, as if they had been handled often.

Ingrid said, "That's because I have them. I read them often. They keep your father's love alive, burning in my heart, in my mind, and in my soul."

Chapter 44

The framed painting of Joseph Traver in his military uniform sat on a tripod to the left of the center aisle at the front of the sanctuary. A friend of Joe's from the AMVETS in Sandusky created the beautiful rendering of Mark's father. The amateur artist used a picture that Mark found in the footlocker. It looked like a professional job, capturing the deceased Traver's image perfectly. The wooden box that once stored the black and white pictures of Ingrid holding her infant son, Mark, now contained Joeseph's cremains. Mark placed the box on a table below his father's painting.

Mark and Denise greeted mourners as they made their way into the entrance from the parking lot and the streets surrounding Holy Angels Catholic Church. With twenty minutes remaining before the start of the funeral service, the church neared capacity. The parish staff set up an overflow room in the gathering space between the church and school.

It appeared that Joe Traver was a very popular, and giving, member of the local community. Many attendees commented on the positive work that he performed and the good he did for the city, the church, and veteran's organizations in town. They commented at how amazed they were that Joe remained so active, even as he approached his ninetieth birthday. Mark maintained his composure, but not without difficulty as many of those he greeted broke down in tears as they spoke of his father and his many deeds.

As the time for the service neared, Mildred O'Conner approached, assisted by her daughter, Catherine Sims. When Mark held out his hand, she lightly brushed it aside and gave him a light hug. In a quiet, shaky voice, she said, "I am sorry. I said some things the other day that I should not have said. Your father was a good and honorable man."

"Thank you, Mildred."

Catherine smiled at Mark and Denise, then she led her mother into the sanctuary.

Moments later, Ingrid Langdon walked in using her walker, her daughter, Emma Franks, and her son, Gerrard Langdon, at her side. Ingrid set the walker to the side and embraced Mark, reaching up to kiss his cheek. She said in a quiet, shaky voice, "I'm so happy that you came out to visit me these past few days. I loved sharing your father's letters with you. I have them all but memorized. I could recite each one, his words are imprinted in my heart."

Mark smiled, his eyes clouding with tears as they maintained their embrace. "It gave me chills to see how much he loved you – how you loved each other. We reread your letters to him when we returned to the house. You should have been together through life. I'm so sorry you never had that chance."

"Oh, Mark, don't be sorry. We had our time together. You are proof of that. But life got in the way, and eventually, we made our way back to each other. I cherish every minute, every second that we were together, even if those times were only through our letters. We have to make the best with what time the good Lord gives us." She looked at Denise and smiled, then turned back to Mark, "You treasure this woman and every moment that you spend together. There is no telling what fate has in store for you both."

She extended her arms to bring Denise into a hug among the three of them. They stayed that way until they heard an usher mention that just five minutes remained until the start of the ceremony. The usher escorted Ingrid and Emma to the front pew reserved for family members.

Mark and Denise greeted the remaining mourners, then walked into the church, up the main aisle, and sat with Ingrid and Emma on one side, Elliot and his wife and children on the other side, then Eva Traver and her live-in friend. Moments later, the organ began playing the entrance song and Father Nicholas Schultz walked into the church behind a procession of altar boys and a Eucharistic Minister.

The memorial service of Joseph Traver had begun.

***

At the niche in the southeast corner of Calvary Cemetery, Father Schultz led a series of prayers as Joseph Traver's ashes were secured in place. The line of cars filled nearly every paved inch at the cemetery grounds and extended out onto the edge of Sandford Avenue, curving around the edge of the golf course. Mark sat with Denise, Ingrid, Emma, Gerrard, Elliot, and Eva until the crowd dispersed, most heading back to the church where the Bereavement Committee prepared tables furnished with drinks, silverware, and plates. The food and drinks were supplied by Pizza House West, Amvets, and Dick's Carryout. The family remained at the cemetery sitting together for a time, just relaxing and talking with each other when a middle-aged woman approached.

"Mr. Traver?"

Marked looked up. "Yes?"

The woman extended her hand. "Ginny Manetti. We spoke on the phone."

Mark stood and took the woman's hand and shook. "Yes. I'm so glad you could make it."

"Well, sorry to say I missed the service at the church, but I made it here to the graveside service. I wanted to pay my respects. And I have a note from your dad's publisher."

She handed Mark the envelope. He accepted it and thanked her.

"After this is over and you're rested, I would like to talk with you about your dad's book rights. Some interesting developments have come to light. It can wait though. There is no rush."

Mark's interest piqued, but he decided that this was not the proper time or place to discuss business of any kind. He said, "Call me this evening. Are you staying in town, at least overnight?"

"Yes. I don't fly out until Saturday, so I have all day tomorrow. Maybe we could meet for breakfast."

Mark nodded and said, "That will work. Call me later."

They shook hands and the woman headed back to wherever she parked. Mark watched her go, wondering about the developments to which she alluded.

He turned to his family and asked, "Ready to head back to the church?"

Ingrid replied, "My dear, I'm a bit tired. I think Emma and I will head back home. Please come visit whenever you wish." She stood and looked him in the eyes and said, "You've made me so very happy. To see you again … to see how happy you are … to meet your wife, my daughter-in-law, and your children" – she looked at Elliot and Eva and smiled brightly – "my grandchildren. It fills my heart with joy. If time permits, I would love to meet the rest of the family."

"I will make sure that happens. I will see you soon – Mom."

They hugged and kissed. Mark hugged Emma and thanked her for coming to the house, making sure that he had the opportunity to meet his mother. He shook hands with his half-brother, Gerrard. After reluctant good-byes, Mark, walked Ingrid, Emma, and Gerrard to their car. They all waved and blew kisses as Emma pulled the car away and onto Sandford Street, turning left towards the nursing home.

Mark sat on the bench by his father's niche, feeling drained, wishing that he did not have to go back to the church. Denise sat next to him and placed her arm around his shoulders.

Denise said, "It's almost over, Dear. We'll go back to the church and sit and talk and thank everyone, hug our children and grand-children. By the time it's over, we'll be ready for bed and we'll sleep like babies."

He looked at Denise, leaned over and kissed her lightly on the lips. He sighed, then looked at his father's niche. "I wish I had known Dad like all the folks in church today did."

Denise replied, "You got to know him through all those people; the changed man, not the man that you knew growing up. Whatever happened completely changed his outlook on life."

"Yeah. I just wish he'd have reached out to me. I would have loved to know that father." He put his face in his hands and cried.

***

Back at the church, Mark could not find a parking place near the church, so he parked a full block away on Pearl Street. He and Denise entered the gym where the crowd gathered, already indulged in eating and trading stories about life, family, community, living, and dying. As they looked around at the mass of people sitting at tables and congregating in groups, Denise said, "Oh, my. Look."

She turned Mark's shoulders towards the front of the hall. Mark's sister Maryanne and her family stood with Caroline and her family. They were in conversation with Danny Balken and Peggy and Randy Whipple.

Mark said, "Wow. Just … wow."

They made a bee-line for the group. Maryanne saw them approach and gave Mark a nervous smile. As they hugged, Mark could feel his sister's tension as her body shook.

He said, "This is a nice surprise."

Maryanne's husband walked up and shook Mark's hand. "Richard, thank you for coming."

"We're happy to be here." He whispered, "I think your phone call put things into perspective for Maryanne. She and I had a great talk afterwards. I think she's finally going to let the past go. It's time. Thank you."

Mark smiled and nodded. "I agree. Thank you for convincing her to come today."

Maryanne gave Denise a hug and they started to chat, both women smiling.

Caroline moved towards Mark with a man in tow when Richard backed away. "Mark, I'd like you to meet my husband, Steve."

The men smiled and shook hands. "Steve, it's nice to finally meet you."

The families took a table and talked for nearly an hour as the crowd thinned. At intervals, they refilled drinks and plates of food, conversing easily, getting to know each other again and for the first time without anxiety. They spoke of their lives and family, work and play, hobbies, sports teams, love, politics, and religion, or lack there-of. Their children and grandchildren talked with each other as well.

Elliot walked over to Mark, Maryanne, Caroline, and their spouses and said, "Marcus thinks that we should have a family reunion. We've never really had family before, so he thinks it would be a great idea to spend a week together at some resort. He's been talking about it with his cousins and everyone likes the idea. He said that he and a couple of his cousins could plan the whole trip. What do you think?"

Mark nodded his head thinking that it would be great getting the family together in a relaxed setting. He looked around the table. Everyone nodded their heads and smiled at the beginning of the plan.

Elliot said, "Yes!" and headed back to the table where the younger family members waited for a response.

Mark turned to his sisters and asked, "Where are you staying while in town?"

Caroline replied, "We're out at the Comfort Suites on US 250, just off of Route 2. We're booked for five days. We thought we'd take a day and go to the amusement park and maybe the waterpark. Maryanne and Rich are there, too."

Mark said, "Would you mind coming to the Jay Street house tomorrow night? I'd like to tell you a few things about the estate and distribution of assets."

Maryanne tensed a bit. She said, "I think we're still of the mind that we don't want anything to do with Dad's estate."

"Would it be better if we met somewhere else? I think you're going to be surprised."

They agreed to meet at a conference room at the Comfort Suites Hotel Friday night at 7:30 p.m. When they looked around, their families were the only people left in the gym. Mark looked at his phone. 4:46 p.m. He said, "I think we should clear out and let these folks get the hall cleaned out."

They nodded, stood, hugged, and headed back to their hotel rooms.

***

The next morning at 7:30 a.m. sharp, the children and grand-children of Joe Traver met in a conference room at the Comfort Suites Hotel. Marcus and his cousins were up late the previous night making plans for the first Traver Family Reunion, to occur in June, 2010. The specific dates needed to be determined as school schedules would impact the available dates. But the plan proposed that the families meet in Ohio, near Sandusky so that the cousins could take advantage of the local amusement park and waterpark. The reunion would be six days long allowing for travel time on both ends of the trip.

The official meeting didn't last long. The adults agreed to the proposal put forth by the kids. The families asked what their plans were for the day. Mark told his sisters that he and Denise would meet them anywhere they liked – after 6:30 p.m. He and Denise planned to spend the day with his mother at the nursing home. By 9:00 a.m. they said their goodbyes and left the conference room.

Mark and Denise pulled out of the parking lot and were seated with Ingrid Engel Langdon ten minutes later, continuing the reunion of mother and son.

Epilogue

Thursday, June 4, 2009

In the week following Joseph Traver's funeral, the families of the children of Joseph Traver met daily to talk, laugh, cry, hug, and learn. Mark, Maryanne, and Caroline spent hours talking about their horrid childhood, but they spent more time talking about their present lives and the future. All their conversations included their spouses and, in some cases, their grown children. They took a page from the lessons learned by Peggy and Randy Whipple; be totally honest without being malicious. Find the good in each person. Everyone is flawed, there are no exceptions. But with love and care, the flaws can be overshadowed and the good in each person can be brought to the forefront to shine.

On Friday evening following Joseph Traver's funeral, the three siblings, with their spouses, sat down and discussed the estate. Shocked that they stood to inherit a fortune, Maryanne, Caroline, and their husbands acted much the same as Mark and Denise had. They confirmed that they had no need for the money and wondered what to do with their newfound wealth. Mark mentioned the ideas that he and Denise earlier batted around. Caroline suggested that they should talk about the possibility of pooling the majority of the money and set up a charitable foundation. Her experience with a group in Oregon gave her knowledge of how a foundation functioned. She warned that the rules from state to state may differ, but they all agreed to explore the idea further.

With that in mind, they settled on putting aside fifteen million dollars each from their inheritance and getting professional advice on how to organize such an endeavor. They sealed the initial agreement with a hug.

Before the siblings departed, Mark handed Maryanne and Caroline sealed envelopes with their names on them. He said they were from their father, the one they lived with for all their young lives. He said that he received one, as well. They both took their envelope, a shocked look on their faces. When Caroline asked about what each letter said, he showed her the note instructing him to deliver the letters unopened. Thankfully, they did not ask any further questions and Mark did not elaborate on the content of each letter.

The grand success of the auction of Joseph Traver's worldly goods the previous Saturday surprised Mark. Almost every item in the household sold. Some of the furniture did end up in the landfill, but all tools, cabinets, lawn equipment, guns, ammunition, gun cabinets, and anything else of value sold to anxious buyers. The Mustang sold to a classic car enthusiast from Sandusky. A local coin dealer brokered the sale of the gold coins. The auctioneer made a good profit on the sale with the balance distributed to Mark and his sisters.

Late in the afternoon on Friday, May 22, Ginny Manetti, Joseph Traver's publicist, called Mark and asked if they could meet. Mark agreed. Ginny, Denise, and Mark met at an Italian restaurant for dinner on Route 250 just south of their hotel. Ginny still felt guilty about missing the funeral, but Mark assured her that she should not feel bad. His father would have been pleased knowing that she made the trip to Sandusky to show her respects.

Ginny told Mark that several agents approached her and asked if the family of Joseph Traver, *aka* J. T. Skipjack, would be interested in having them take over the series and continue writing under his pen name. After very little discussion, Mark agreed to the deal. The series would continue, the family would receive royalties from the sale of the novels, at a reduced rate, but the tales and legacy of J. T. Skipjack would continue. Ginny left after dinner, thrilled that her favorite author's work gained new life. Before she left the restaurant, Mark handed her a flash drive that contained the last, but unfinished, manuscript of J. T. Skipjack. He mentioned that Denise looked forward to reading the new novel.

With the closing documents signed and the deal complete, work on the Jay Street house began in earnest. A large dumpster sat in the cracked, uneven driveway. Mark and Denise drove by on Tuesday morning, June 1, and noted that the bin neared capacity with plaster and lathe debris, old doors, ancient kitchen cabinets, and flooring. Mark took a deep breath, but smiled.

***

Nearly two weeks after the funeral of Joseph Traver, Ingrid Engel Langdon died in her sleep. The attendants at the nursing home said, even in death, her smile was much like the one she wore ever since her son's and family's first visit. Emma called Mark and let him know of her passing so he would not make the trip across town. He made the trip anyway to help plan his mother's funeral and burial. She would be laid to rest at Meadowlawn Gardens in the Langdon family plot next to her husband, Alfred.

Mark had known that his mother did not have much longer to live, but her energy and mobility made him believe that the end would be a year or more into the future, not mere weeks. Her passing left a big, sorrowful hole in his heart. Denise comforted him as much as possible. It would take time for this wound to heal. She knew he would come out of his funk when he thought back on the time they spent together talking about his father and the love they shared. Ingrid made it clear to Mark how happy his presence made her feel.

***

Mark, Denise, and Emma Franks stood in the entryway to Holy Angels Church, greeting the few mourners as they made their way into the sanctuary. Mark found it difficult not to draw comparisons between his father's funeral and the current ceremony.

Danny Balken walked into the entryway, looking at the three standing there to greet him. He gave all three a tight hug, smiling as he did. He said, "This is tough having three funerals in just a few weeks. How are you holding up?"

Mark gave a weak smile and shrugged his shoulders, thinking about his father's funeral and the massive crowd in attendance. Then, last week came the funeral of his father's lifetime friend, lawyer, and co-conspirator, Allen Westridge – well attended, but not nearly the spectacle of his father's.

Now, attending his mother's funeral with the sparse crowd - a fraction of those who attended the funeral of the man she loved – he wondered why he held higher expectations for the current turnout of mourners. Regardless, Mark knew his mother died with some regrets, but with joy much greater than those regrets. She did not allow the many challenges she faced defeat her. Even when she could not be with the man she loved, she loved the family she made, remaining content with what the Lord provided to her. In the end, she persevered over the odds and died with joy in her heart.

Mark said to Danny, "I'll snap out of it. I have this lady to help with that." He looked at Denise, his smile widening. Then he said, "I'm more worried about Emma. She won't have a shoulder to cry on once we leave."

Danny looked at Emma and asked, "Is that true? You're single?"

"Widowed. But it is true."

'We can't have that. I know this isn't the proper place to ask a woman out for a date, but how about joining me for dinner sometime? I can call you if you give me your number."

Emma closed one eye as if suspicious of his motives, then said, "Sure. Let's meet after the service in the gym."

Danny nodded. "It's a date."

He shook hands with all three then walked into the sanctuary.

As soon as he rounded the corner out of sight, Peggy and Randy Whipple walked up. After everyone exchanged hugs and greetings, Peggy looked from Mark to Emma and back and said, "Your mom was such a sweet woman. I can see why your dad fell hard for her. She must have been beautiful when she was in her twenties."

Mark reached into his pocket and pulled out the black and white photo of Ingrid holding him as an infant. He showed Peggy and Randy the picture, the love apparent in his mother's gaze.

Peggy said, "Awe, that is so precious." She looked at Emma. "And she is beautiful. You look a lot like her."

Emma blushed. "Thank you. She was the best mom in the world."

One of the ushers peaked around the corner of the passageway to the sanctuary and said, "Five minutes, Mr. Traver."

Mark waved. "Thank you."

Peggy and Randy hugged Mark, Denise, and Emma then made their way into church just as Abbe Holtzmiller walked in from the parking lot. She walked straight up to Mark, Denise, and Emma and gave them each a hug. She already held a tissue in her right hand, ready in case she needed it. Addressing Emma and Mark, she said, "Your mother was such a darling woman. It is wonderful that she and Joseph were able to reconnect after all these years. It boosted his spirits." To Emma she said, "I saw it in him from the day you arrived at his front door. When she left for the Cleveland Clinic with her infection, it took the wind out of his sails, sure that Ingrid wouldn't return. His health suffered terribly and he lost his will to live. He never said as much, but I don't think he could've lived without her again. The thought of such a fate sent him into depression. For him, it was the beginning of the end."

Emma's eyes glistened with tears. She lowered her head, then said, "My heart exploded with joy when I learned that Joseph survived the war. At first, I was reluctant to contact him. I wasn't sure if he would be willing to see Mother again. But I thought I should leave that decision up to him. That's when I decided to ask him if he would mind coming to visit her. I've never seen a grown man cry with tears of joy like he did. When he entered Mom's room at the nursing home, I've never seen such love between two people in my life." She looked at Abbe. "We owe that to you."

They all hugged, shedding tears as they did.

Mark said, "We should head inside." They pulled away from each other, walked into the sanctuary, and headed towards the front pew. Less than fifty people sat in the mostly empty church. His sisters and their families sat in the pews behind Mark and his family. Several staff members from the nursing home sat together near the center of the church. Catherine Sims caught Mark's eyes as he and Denise strode to the front of the church. She and Mildred O'Conner sat to the right of the main aisle, a few pews from the back of the church. He smiled and nodded to Catherine. Her face formed into a nervous smile while she held her mother's hand. Mildred wore the same stone-face expression she had worn when they met at Daly's. She did not turn his way.

A painting of the love of Joseph Traver's life, Ingrid Engel Langdon, sat on a tripod at the front of the church. An urn holding her cremains sat on the same table where, two weeks earlier, his father's cremains had been. Mark turned and scanned the scant crowd. The eerie likeness of the scene in front of the altar like déjà vu until one looked at the small gathering in the church; a drastic contrast from the hoards that packed the church just two weeks earlier.

Mark turned back towards the altar. *Mom deserves better.*

She had upended her life to flee the whims of a madman who turned the world on its axis, only to find a hostile atmosphere where she landed in the *Home of the Free*. One man helped turn her life around and gave her hope, a hope crushed by the lies of a desperate woman.

Ingrid had been so honor-bound that she walked away from the man she loved so he could do what he thought was right, moral, honorable, and his duty. She deserved better in life and in death. But she felt complete and fulfilled by simply reuniting with the man who loved her with all his heart.

Mark relaxed when Denise placed her hand over his and leaned into his shoulder. He promised himself right then that he would devote his life to making sure this woman, their children, and their grand-children never experienced the pain he felt as a young man, living in a home devoid of love.

***

Mark and Denise decided to drive back to Maitland and take the scenic route through the mountains in North Carolina, then take backroads through Georgia and northern Florida. They rented a Chevy Tahoe with plenty of room for suitcases and any items they might purchase along the way. After all, their grandchildren must be spoiled.

They also needed plenty of room for the one item that changed the course of many lives. Still not sure that he uncovered all the secrets it held, he planned to comb every square inch of Joseph Traver's footlocker.

###

Aurthor's Notes

The Footlocker is a work of fiction based on my recollection of my father's footlocker in the attic of our house on Jay Street in Sandusky, Ohio. At five years old, I came across that footlocker and began to explore the contents. I found photos of Dad in his military uniform. I remember finding his hat with the lieutenant's bar and a number of black and white pictures of bombs exploding, destroying buildings and anything else on the ground. I used these recollections to form the basis for the fictional story *The Footlocker*.

During my research of Dad's military history, I found his DD-214 (his discharge form) and learned of his participation in six bombing missions near the end of the war. He was a Mickey Navigator assigned to the 303rd Bomber Group, 359th Squadron. I used some of this factual information in a fictional manner in *The Footlocker*. The bombing of the Unterluss Munitions Factory was a real event, but I have no knowledge of any persons killed or injured in that bombing mission. For anyone wishing to learn more about the men assigned to the 303rd Bomber Group, the website www.303rdbg.com contains a wealth of information.

The fictional Traver family in *The Footlocker* bears no similarities to the real-life Nicholas A. Grondin family. You should draw no inferences regarding the real Grondin family from this story.

I would like to thank local businesses in Sandusky, Ohio and other area businesses for allowing me to use their names in this story. I encourage readers to patronize these businesses when you visit this amazing, robust city and the surrounding area. It is a beautiful, vibrant, welcoming region with a wide variety of activities for people of all ages. The businesses are, in no particular order, Pizza House West, El Grand Patron, Berardi's Family Kitchen, The Original Margaritaville, Dick's Carry-Out, The Better Half, Daly's Pub, The Old Dutch, The House of Doughnuts, and McCarthy's Restaurant and Pub in Port Clinton, Ohio.

Nicholas A. Grondin
(September 10, 1919 – June 13, 1994)

Dad never spoke of his time in service during World War II, but he wrote the below account of his training and his assignment to a bomber group. An incident from his first mission is briefly described below.

TERRIFYING EXPERIENCE
by Nicholas A. Grondin
Written November, 1990

In looking back on my Airforce career, I see now that I was very fortunate. I reposted to Fort Hayes, Columbus, Ohio October 15, 1942, and within a day or two was sent to the army air force classification center in Nashville, Tennessee. The battery of tests to be taken were designed to select the people who were most qualified to be pilots, navigators, or bombardiers. I qualified for the first two and had a choice which was to be a navigator. I was moved again, this time to Monroe, Louisiana, pronounced "<u>Mon</u>'roe", for preflight school, followed by advanced navigation school, on the other side of the same base, Selman Field.

My fiancée, Paddy Canning, and I were married in the chapel at Selman Field, Monroe, Louisiana, and I graduated and received my wings one week later, June 12, 1942. In checking the assignment sheet, I found that I was picked to be an instructor, which I was at Selman Field until November, 1944. We really enjoyed life in Monroe, even though every other weekend I had to fly with a pick-up crew of two pilots and three navigators. We took "Proficiency Flights", which were designed to prepare us for combat when our time came.

In November, 1944 I was sent to Langley Field, Virginia to pursue a course in radar in order to qualify as a Navigator/Radar Observer, which I successfully passed.

Tearfully, my wife headed for Sandusky, Ohio pregnant with our first child. I was assigned to a plane leaving from Mitchell Field, New York to England via Gander, Newfoundland, Iceland, and Shannon, Ireland. (We landed on St. Patrick's Day).

I was assigned to an Eighth Air Force Group called Hells Angels. The Navigator/Radar Observers, nicknamed Mickey Men, flew in the lead ship of a formation, and at that time in the war directed the other planes to the assigned target and when the weather was clouded over, even dropped bombs using the radar. When the lead plane dropped its bombs the rest of the planes in the group also dropped theirs. It was called saturation bombing.

On my first mission I was to watch and learn from the assigned Mickey Man. I was seated on a box beside the Mickey in the nose section of our B-17. As we neared our target, the flack became thicker and one burst sent a lot of shrapnel through the nose section where we were seated. A piece came up between my legs, cut my flying suit, and bounced off the frame of the airplane over my head. My leg was burned but it was not serious, and I did find and keep the piece of shrapnel. Obviously, I was terrified. I flew five additional missions over Germany, and then the war in Europe was over, thanks be to God.

PS. After being moved from my base and awaiting a plane home, I arrived in Sandusky one and a half hours before my daughter, Valerie was born. Thanks again.

Other PJ Grondin Suspense Novels

All titles are available in trade paperback and various eBook formats.

A Lifetime of Vengeance
McKinney Brothers Book 1

A Lifetime of Deception
McKinney Brothers Book 2

A Lifetime of Exposure
McKinney Brothers Book 3

A Lifetime of Terror
McKinney Brothers Book 4

A Lifetime of Betrayal
McKinney Brothers Book 5

Drug Wars
Peden Savage Book 1

Flash Drive
Peden Savage Book 2

Past Sins
Peden Savage Book 3

Under the Blood Tree

Visit www.pjgrondin.com
pjgron@pjgrondin.com

Author Information

Pete 'P.J.' Grondin, born the seventh of twelve children, moved around a number of times when he was young; from Sandusky, Ohio to Bay City, Michigan, then to Maitland and Zellwood, Florida before returning to Sandusky, Ohio, where he married the love of his life, Debbie Fleming.

After his service in the US Navy, in the Nuclear Power Program, serving on the ballistic missile submarine U.S.S. *John Adams*, Pete returned to his hometown of Sandusky, OH where he was elected to the Sandusky City Commission, serving a single term. He retired from a major, regional, electric utility after twenty-six years of service.

The Footlocker is his tenth novel. His other works are *Under the Blood Tree*, a non-series novel. *A Lifetime of Vengeance, A Lifetime of Deception, A Lifetime of Exposure, A Lifetime of Terror,* and *A Lifetime of Betrayal* in the McKinney Brothers suspense series. *Drug Wars, Flash Drive, and Past Sins* are the first three novels in the Peden Savage suspense series.